W9-AAA-568

Now You See It

Carol J. Perry

Kensington Publishing Corp.
www.kensingtonbooks.com

KENSINGTON BOOKS are published by

Kensington Publishing Corp.
119 West 40th Street
New York, NY 10018

Copyright © 2023 by Carol J. Perry

All rights reserved. No part of this book may be reproduced in any form or by any means without the prior written consent of the Publisher, excepting brief quotes used in reviews.

To the extent that the image or images on the cover of this book depict a person or persons, such person or persons are merely models, and are not intended to portray any character or characters featured in the book.

This book is a work of fiction. Names, characters, businesses, organizations, places, events, and incidents either are the product of the author's imagination or are used fictitiously. Any resemblance to actual persons, living or dead, events, or locales is entirely coincidental.

If you purchased this book without a cover you should be aware that this book is stolen property. It was reported as "unsold and destroyed" to the Publisher and neither the Author nor the Publisher has received any payment for this "stripped book."

All Kensington titles, imprints, and distributed lines are available at special quantity discounts for bulk purchases for sales promotion, premiums, fund-raising, educational, or institutional use.

Special book excerpts or customized printings can also be created to fit specific needs. For details, write or phone the office of the Kensington Sales Manager: Attn.: Sales Department. Kensington Publishing Corp., 119 West 40th Street, New York, NY 10018. Phone: 1-800-221-2647.

The K and Teapot logo is a trademark of Kensington Publishing Corp.

First Printing: October 2023
ISBN: 978-1-4967-4364-0

ISBN: 978-1-4967- 4365-7 (ebook)

10 9 8 7 6 5 4 3 2 1

Printed in the United States of America

For Dan, my husband and best friend.

"It's not what you look at that matters, it's what you see."
—*Henry David Thoreau*

CHAPTER 1

Labor Day in Salem means a day off from work, maybe an end-of-summer cookout, and the annual putting-away of all the white jeans, jackets, dresses, and shoes. Nobody knows who made up that "no white after Labor Day" rule, but my Aunt Ibby raised me to take it as gospel.

I'm a thirty-five-year-old redhead, born in Salem. My parents, Jack and Carrie Kowalski, named me Maralee. Orphaned when I was five, I came to live with my research librarian aunt, Isobel "Ibby" Russell, and grew up in the old family home on Salem's Winter Street. I'd known from the time I got a part in my seventh-grade school play that I wanted a career in television, and thanks to an Emerson College education, a lot of persistence, and some dumb luck, that dream came true. Maralee Kowalski became Lee Barrett when I married NASCAR driver Johnny Barrett, but sadly, I became a young widow when Johnny died in an auto crash. As Lee Barrett, I've been a weather girl, a home-shopping show host, and I even did a brief and unmemorable stint as a call-in psychic. I'm currently the program director and occasional field reporter at Salem's WICH-TV. But much more important than that, I'm now Lee Mondello, newlywed. My husband, Salem police detective Pete Mondello, and I now have our own home on Winter Street, and it was there, on the Wednesday evening before the Labor Day long weekend, that I washed, ironed, folded, and neatly packed that summer wardrobe into a large, covered blue plastic container.

My aunt and I had shared our home with a big, beautiful yellow gentleman cat named O'Ryan, and now, since we both lived on Winter Street, we had a kind of "shared custody" arrangement. With cat door entrances to both homes, O'Ryan came and went as he pleased, so I wasn't surprised when he strolled into the bedroom, hopped up onto the top of the plastic box, lay down, and closed his eyes.

Aunt Ibby's house is a lot bigger than ours, with plenty of spaces—cellar and attic, closets and cupboards—for storing off-season clothing, sports equipment, and things "too good to throw away" or "might come in handy someday." I stood in the center of the master bedroom and turned in a slow circle, wondering where I could stash the now-full blue plastic box. I could, of course, take it to Aunt Ibby's.

"No," I told myself. "You're a grown, married

woman with a home of your own. You've been depending on your aunt for far too long. Figure this out for yourself."

O'Ryan opened golden eyes. "Mmmrupp," he said, as though echoing my thought.

"There's the den, and the second bedroom and bath," I said aloud to the cat. "There's space in each of those that'll do for now." I picked up the box, carried it down a short hall to what we called the "guest room," and shoved it into the bottom of an empty closet. "It's a good thing we haven't invited any guests," I told O'Ryan. "If things go the way Mr. Doan plans, this room might have to become my home office."

Bruce Doan is the station manager at WICH-TV. He's well-known for expecting *all* his employees to "wear more than one hat," as he playfully describes it, and he'd offered me a brand-new hat that very morning. I already wore two—one as program director, the other as an occasional field reporter. Since neither job was what one might consider "full-time," he apparently felt justified in offering me yet another title.

"Lee, how would you like to be my historical documentary executive director?" he'd asked. "Sound good?"

"It sounds pretty highfalutin," I'd acknowledged. "Exactly what does it mean?"

"You know Rupert Pennington, of course," he began. He knew perfectly well that I did know Mr. Pennington, the director of Salem's prestigious Tabitha Trumbull Academy of the Arts. I had, in fact, worked as a television production instructor there a few years earlier—to say nothing of the fact that Mr. Pennington is one of Aunt Ibby's favorite gentleman friends. I waited for him to continue.

"You've heard about the Salem International Museum project, of course?" he asked.

"Of course," I agreed.

I knew that the new museum was to be located in a sturdy, old brick building that once had housed an A&P grocery store. Fortuitously saved from the wrecking ball of Salem's infamous "urban renewal" phase, the place had housed a series of retail stores, a couple of restaurants, and most recently, a fitness center. Unlike the justly famous Peabody Essex Museum and the much younger Witch Museum, the International Museum was not intended to house a permanent placement, but rather to be a location for traveling blockbuster exhibits from around the world.

"There are already floor plans for exactly how much space each display will take," Doan explained. "They've brought in some big-shot art directors and history experts who'll figure out where everything is supposed to go—you know, paintings on the walls, expensive stuff in locked glass cases. You just follow them around and get them to talk to you. Piece of cake."

I was pretty confident it wasn't going to be all that easy, but it was an interesting challenge. I'd heard my aunt discussing the museum with her girlfriends, but my knowledge of what it was all about was pretty sketchy. It was time for me to do some serious homework if I was going to don the hat of "historical documentary executive director."

"When would you want me to get started on this?" I asked. "I'll have to figure out how to fit it in with my program director duties." I'd been "promoted" to program director when Buffy Doan, the station manager's wife, had insisted that a job as field reporter be handed over to her straight-out-of-broadcasting-school nephew Howie—that's Howard Templeton. That moved Scott Palmer—not my favorite person—into the lead reporting position I'd held. Don't get me wrong—I love being program director. The hours are way better for married me, and it came with a little pay raise. But sometimes I miss the edge-of-your-seat, race-out-the-door, day-or-night excitement of being in the middle of the news action—and every time I see Scott Palmer doing a report on something I'd have loved to cover, I feel a little pang of jealousy.

"You can get started right away—" Mr. Doan paused, giving me a kind of up-and-down look. I realized I looked awfully casual for a highfalutin job in my faded jeans and loose T-shirt. "You might want to update your wardrobe a little. I'll tell you what. I'll get you started with one of our new green WICH-TV jackets." Big smile. "Enjoy your weekend and Labor Day Monday off. Let's see. Today is Wednesday. You might as well take tomorrow and Friday off, too, and get yourself organized. Maybe do some shopping. They'll be starting to get stuff shipped in to the museum pretty soon. The designers might already be working in there. Your press credentials will get you in so you can get some 'before' footage of the place while it's empty. Get with Francine Hunter. She'll be your videographer for this. Just get your programs lined up first, then get right on it. If you start on Tuesday, that'll give you and Francine a good three weeks to get it all filmed and edited—from the empty rooms right up until the mayor cuts the ribbon for the October opening."

"Start Tuesday," the man says! "Get your programs lined up first," the man says! Does he think it's easy making sure all the shows under my direction are properly staffed every day with sets and props in place, scripts up-to-date, talent prepared, wardrobe clean and pressed, lights and sound and cameras tested, and everything ready on time? I was in charge of the morning kiddie show, *Ranger Rob's Rodeo*, the daily *Shopping Salem*, and *The Saturday Business Hour*. I also did some of the set décor for *Tarot Time with River North* and *Cooking with Wanda the Weather Girl*. None of it was a piece of cake or even easy as pie. Fortunately, plans for the following week's shows were already firmly in place. Ranger Rob and his co-host, Katie the Clown, would feature fun indoor and outdoor games and some interviews with local high school football players. *Shopping Salem* had a lineup of the newest back-to-school fashions. The man who did the Business Hour was always prepared; all I had to do for him was keep his set neat and clean and make sure he had plenty of yellow legal pads. I knew I was going to take the new challenge. At least I'd be in front of the camera again, talking to an audience, introducing them to something new and hopefully exciting in my city. I told the boss I'd do my best.

"Good," he said, as though he'd never had any doubts about it. "Stop and see Rhonda and she'll fix up your new schedule."

Rhonda manned the station's reception desk

and kept careful track of everyone's schedule and did myriad other things. I told her I'd see her on Tuesday and asked her to alert Francine about what was going on. "Wow," she said. "This must be important. He gave you two extra days off? With pay?" She was still marveling at such a miracle when I left the office and took the aged elevator—we call it "Old Clunky"—down to the first-floor lobby, climbed into my almost-new Jeep, and went home to prepare for my new journey into New England history.

Over dinner that night of baked chicken breasts, mashed potatoes, and canned peas—I'm not much of a cook yet, but I'm learning—I told Pete about my new assignment. The only thing I knew for sure about the show was its name—*Seafaring New England*—and the fact that Salem was to be the show's first stop. Mr. Doan had assured me that my documentary would be of "major importance" because "the first time is when they get all the bugs out, and the TV audience loves being in on all the screwups."

Pete, as always, greeted the news with loving enthusiasm and cautious optimism. "This sounds like it's right up your alley, babe, with your love of history, and with a research librarian for an aunt. It's all on top of your regular job, though. Are you sure you can handle both?"

I wasn't sure, and I told him so. "I promised Mr. Doan I'd do my best. If it's not going to work out, I guess I'll know it before long. I've already started a file."

He grinned. He knows my penchant for creating

files, filling out index cards, and posting sticky notes. "Of course, you have. What are they calling it?"

"Nothing fancy. Just *Seafaring New England*. The whole thing is centered around New England's maritime and seafaring history from the arrival of the Pilgrims in Plymouth in 1620 up to the present," I explained. "The exhibit starts off right here at the new Salem International Museum. After us, it goes to Mystic Seaport in Connecticut and after that to Newport, Rhode Island. Each city hosts the exhibition for six months."

"The department is already gearing up for extra security," Pete said. "They've got their own people, but there'll be a lot of really expensive stuff in there. Chief Whaley doesn't want anything bad to happen on our watch."

"That's good," I said. "I hadn't even started to think about that part of it."

"Oh yeah. The whole building will be rigged up with cameras and alarms everywhere. Naturally it's all insured to the hilt. For millions, I'd guess." He smiled. "It should draw some good crowds."

I agreed. From what little I'd learned so far, the show would cover a lot of territory. Maritime history and industry from every New England state would be displayed, including commerce, fishing, whaling, and ship building. I figured a pretty good-sized chunk of it would come from the days when Salem ships were legendary—the vessels that historians claim traded with more different peoples in Asia, India, Africa, South America, and China than all the ships of other American ports put together. The more I learned about it, the more my interest in the project grew.

I cleared away the dinner plates and took a couple of Fiesta ware bowls from the cupboard. I hadn't attempted anything in the way of real homemade desserts yet, so I depended pretty much on a variety of ice-cream treats. This evening's offering was Little Debbie brownies topped with vanilla ice cream and sprinkled with crunched-up Oreos. Worked for me, and Pete didn't complain. "Has O'Ryan been by to visit today?" he asked, adding some more Oreo crumbs to his bowl.

"He helped me put the summer clothes away," I told him. "It was just one big plastic box full, but I didn't know exactly where to put it, so for now, it's in the guest room closet."

"Maybe we should start using our side of the attic," he said. "There's plenty of room up there." Our house was built like a "row house," with a wall separating our half from the mirror image other half. But the top floor—the attic—was one long, unfinished room, which the two sections of the building shared.

"I suppose we could," I said, without enthusiasm. In the first place, I don't like attics. I had a really bad experience in one once. Now all attics creep me out, and it didn't help that our next-door neighbor whom we shared one with was a convicted wife killer. Oh, Dr. Michael Martell had served his twenty years and was totally rehabilitated, according to the authorities. He'd even become a close friend of my Aunt Ibby's and was a respected creative writing instructor at Salem's Tabitha Trumbull Academy of the Arts, where Mr. Pennington was the executive director. Besides that, while Dr. Martell was "doing time," he'd become a mystery writer and—as Fenton Bishop—had authored a series of best selling "Antique Alley" murder mysteries.

"It's not as though a box of old summer clothes is of very much value," Pete pointed out. "I doubt that our attic-sharing neighbor would covet any of them.

I had to laugh at that idea. "I wasn't worried about Dr. Martell showing up in my white jeans, silly. I just don't want to go up there."

Pete understood about my fear of attics. Aunt Ibby and I had once been trapped in one by a killer. O'Ryan had saved our lives, and Pete also had begun to understand that the big yellow cat had some special skills that regular, everyday housecats don't have. When Pete and I were in the "getting-to-know-you stage" of our relationship, there was another thing I'd had to share with him that up until then, only Aunt Ibby and my best friend, River North, knew about me. I am what's known as a *scryer*. That's a person who sees things in reflective surfaces—things other people cannot see. River calls me a "gazer," and says that the ability is a special gift. I don't think of it as a gift. Almost all the visions I've seen—in mirrors, windows, silverware, hubcaps, anything reflective—have had something to do with death. I dislike my "special gift" even more than I dislike attics. Pete tries to understand that secret scryer part of me, but he doesn't like to talk about it.

"It's good to have the extra space, though," Pete continued on the subject of the attic. "Maybe someday we'll put up a wall, put in some dormers, finish it off for an extra bedroom."

"That would be okay. Then I wouldn't mind it at all."

"When do you get a look inside the museum building?"

"We start filming officially on Tuesday morning," I said. "But Mr. Doan says all I need to do is show my press pass, and I can get in before then."

"I hope you won't be too disappointed with what you see. They've got the place clean, and the floors look good. They haven't painted all of the walls yet, though and some of it looks like—well, one big, old attic."

An attic? I took a deep breath. "You've been inside?"

"Sure. Security survey." He used his cop voice. "We've been climbing all over the place, checking on where alarms should be, camera placements, where guards need to be stationed. All that."

"I'm glad you told me. I've been picturing glass cases, overhead lights, you know. Like the Peabody Essex Museum, only empty."

"Don't worry. It'll get there. They're doing a really careful job." Big, encouraging smile. "It'll be good for your documentary—showing the audience everything from the beginnings right up to the opening day of the show."

"I guess you're right," I agreed. We picked up our dishes and loaded the dishwasher.

"Shall we watch some TV, Mrs. Mondello?" Pete gets a kick out of using my new name—and I get a kick out of hearing it.

"Good plan, Mr. Mondello." We settled down together on the living room couch. Pete had just turned on the wall-hung TV when O'Ryan strolled in and hopped up onto the couch, wedging himself between us.

"Speak of the devil," Pete said. "I was just asking about you, big boy." O'Ryan responded by giving Pete a pink-tongued lick on the nose, then tapping the remote control with a fuzzy yellow paw.

"It looks as if O'Ryan wants to choose the channel," I observed, not at all surprised by the cat's deliberate motion. I reached for the *TV Guide* on the coffee table and flipped through the pages. "Yep, there it is. *Wicked Tuna* is on tonight. That's one of his favorites."

Pete is still fairly skeptical about O'Ryan's unusual talents, even though he's witnessed enough of the big cat's remarkable feats to become a bit of a believer. O'Ryan, after all, once belonged to a real Salem witch. She'd called herself Ariel Constellation, and before her unexpected demise in the cold waters of Salem Harbor, she'd hosted the late-night movies on WICH-TV. She'd named the cat Orion, for the constellation, and claimed that he was her "familiar." When he came to live with Aunt Ibby and me, we decided that the Irish name O'Ryan suited him better—always bearing in mind the fact that in Salem, a witch's familiar is to be respected, and sometimes feared.

"It's not on until eight," Pete said, adding with just a tiny hint of sarcasm. "I hope he doesn't mind if we watch the early news first."

"Mrruptt," O'Ryan purred, which I took to mean it was all right with him. "No problem," I said. "Anything special we're looking for on the news?"

"Kind of," he said. "And maybe it has something to do with your museum. We're not sure about that at all."

"What are you talking about? *My* museum?" Pete isn't exactly in the habit of discussing his job with me. We'd had an agreement about that back when I was a field reporter. Combining his confidential police work with my on-air investigative reporting didn't mix well. But these days, since I'd become program director, the old conflict of interest just didn't exist. "Can you tell me about it?"

"It seems one of the Public Works guys found a body this morning. It was under a pile of leaves where some of the early arriving artifacts for your *Seafaring New England* show are being stored—in the vault of a small branch bank that's been closed for a while," he said. "The dead man was a bonded driver for an armored truck company. His truck was empty. The items had been unloaded, counted, numbered, and examined before they were locked in the underground vault. Nothing was missing."

"Since the body was under a pile of leaves, I'm guessing someone hid it? That this wasn't an accidental death?"

"Suspicious circumstances." Cop voice. "He'd been shot. Let's see if any new details have been released yet." The WICH-TV logo appeared on the screen with a "Breaking News" banner. Phil Archer, the early news anchor, did the voice-over while a video showed a fenced-in area where gold and brown fall leaves covered the ground. Yellow crime-scene tape surrounded the area, and the camera zoomed in on a disturbed area, where leaves were in a mound-shaped heap and spots of bare ground showed nearby. "Early this morning, the body of an armored car driver was discovered beneath a pile of these colorful leaves, in the vicinity of a secure facility in downtown Salem," Phil intoned. "The driver's name has not been released, pending notification of family, but authorities say that the cargo he carried in the vehicle was intact. Police have disclosed that the man had been shot at close range. An investigation is underway. Here's Scott Palmer with details."

Wouldn't you just know it? This one should have—could have—been all mine, and there's Scott Palmer, all smirky and full of himself—with the details of what had to be a murder.

CHAPTER 2

It turned out that Scott didn't have much more to share with the viewers of WICH-TV than what I'd already learned from Pete and Phil Archer. He mentioned that the contents of the armored car had contained artifacts destined for the upcoming *Seafaring New England* show at the new Salem International Museum, which he described as "a facility designed to show a variety of traveling blockbuster exhibits from around the world." A file shot of the old A&P building was followed by a picture of a ship model. "The show will display articles from all around New England, including this model of George Crowninshield's great ship *America*, on loan from the Peabody Essex Museum in Salem. There'll also be a large model of an elephant, because in 1796, the same ship brought the first elephant to arrive in America to Salem. There'll be a giant model of another Salem ship, the *Naiad*, too." Scott used his breathless, network-announcer voice. "Preliminary investigation indicates that the shipment within the armored vehicle was undisturbed, and that even the dead man's wallet and personal belongings were found intact."

I was glad that none of the truck's cargo had been stolen. Items to be displayed in the museum were irreplaceable. I'd heard there'd be items from important venues, even the Smithsonian—as well as artifacts from private collections from some of the oldest Salem families—things that had never been on public display before.

"I'll bet my aunt has more information than Scott has about it," I suggested to Pete. "What do you say we let O'Ryan watch his show here while we go over to her house so I can ask for some research librarian help?" I added a little incentive. "She told me she made one of her famous lemon-bar pies this morning."

"Sounds like a good deal to me," he said. "The cat can catch up with the *Wicked Tuna* crews, you can do some homework, and I can enjoy Ibby's homemade pie and coffee. Let's do it. Should we call first?"

I'd already reached for my phone. Her answer to my text was swift. **Please do come over. Is O'Ryan with you?**

I assured her that our shared feline was safe and happy, and Pete and I stepped out into the pleasant evening coolness onto Winter Street. Our street is one of Salem's old ones, complete with redbrick sidewalks and lots of old-growth trees, oak and chestnut and maple. This cooler-than-usual September had presented one of Salem's most glorious early "leaf-peeping" seasons, and tour buses throughout the city had brought a rush of camera-toting visitors.

"Between the opening of the museum, the fall foliage fans, and next month's Halloween craziness, Salem should be pretty darned active for a while," I said, my boots crunching through newly fallen red and yellow leaves. As I looked down, though, the colorful sight reminded me of Scott's video of the forlorn pile of vegetation that had covered the body of the so-far-nameless murdered truck driver.

"Phil Archer said the driver had been shot," I said, kicking a spiny green horse chestnut capsule onto the curb.

"Yep. Close range. Not pretty. And sadly, off the record, there's a possibility that he may have been killed with his own gun."

"He was armed?"

"He was licensed by the state to carry a weapon. We're checking his home to see if it's missing from there." Pete shook his head. "Funny, though, about nothing being missing."

"Was it one of the shipments from the other museums?"

"No. Actually, it was a private collection put together from a couple of families with connections to those old Salem sailing fleets—like sea captain's special souvenirs they must have liked well enough to use in their own homes."

We'd reached Aunt Ibby's front steps. "Did you get to see any of it?" I wanted to know.

"Nope. Everything was wrapped up in Bubble Wrap and taped into packages," he said.

"Then how do you know nothing is missing?" I rang the doorbell, even though I had my own key.

I heard the chime ring out the first few bars of "The Impossible Dream," and my aunt appeared at the door.

"Original seals intact. The number of boxes and packages matches the invoice sheet. The contents of each one was marked on the outside," Pete said, as the front door opened and we stepped into the foyer of Aunt Ibby's wonderful-smelling house. There were hugs and "good-to-see-yous" all around. We followed my aunt through the living room and into the kitchen. "I've invited Rupert to join us," she said. "He's on the committee that brought the *Seafaring New England* show to Salem in the first place. I'm sure he can be helpful to you." "Rupert" is Mr. Pennington, the director of the Tabitha Trumbull Academy of the Arts. She couldn't have invited a better person for my purposes.

"Wonderful." I gave her an extra hug. "Is he here yet?"

"On his way." She opened the refrigerator, proudly carried the confectioner's sugar–topped pie across the room, and placed it in the center of the table, then added plates, forks, and four coffee mugs. "He says he has a copy of the floor plans to share with you, Maralee. Pete, I imagine you've already seen them because of the security concerns."

"I have," Pete said, "but I don't have permission to show them to anybody, not even my wife. I guess it helps to have friends in high places!" He grinned, and we three sat in the captain's chairs surrounding the round oak table. Once again, the chimes rang out "The Impossible Dream." My aunt stood quickly, patted her still-red hair, smoothed the skirt of her dark-green shirt dress, and hurried back to the foyer to greet her long-time friend.

Mr. Pennington was once an actor, and he still carried himself in the way one could imagine that a Shakespearian actor might. He dressed the part, too—all tweedy and leather-patchy and occasionally he sports an ascot tie. He made what might be considered "an entrance," giving my aunt a perfunctory peck on the cheek, then joined us at the table. "A pleasure to see you, my dear Maralee, and you, Detective Mondello." He had a wonderful speaking voice. Maybe he'd agree to narrating part of the documentary. He shook his head in a mournful way. "Terrible news about that poor fellow, buried—as it were—beneath fall leaves." He looked at my aunt. "The horror, the horror." He rolled his eyes.

Aunt Ibby cocked her head to one side. "Marlon Brando," she said. "*Apocalypse Now.* Nineteen seventy-nine." I should point out that my aunt and Mr. Pennington have a long-standing competition, trying to trip each other up with famous movie quotes. Sometimes, if you're not in on the game, it can be quite disconcerting—like the abrupt subject switch from a dead truck driver to an old Marlon Brando movie.

Mr. Pennington acknowledged my aunt's quick response, and Pete put us back on track. "We were discussing the floor plans for the new museum. I understand that you've seen them, Mr. Pennington."

"Yes, indeed." He produced a long cardboard tube. "As a member of the East India Marine

Society, I'm entitled to have them. Ibby seemed to think it would be helpful for Maralee to take a peek at them. To help get her oriented, so to speak."

"I do appreciate your sharing them, Mr. Pennington," I said. "I have no idea what the inside of the place looks like."

"These are just floor plans, my dear. They're marked, though, with where most of the various proposed exhibits will be when the installations are complete." He slipped two rolled sheets of paper from the tube, laying them on the nearby kitchen counter. I looked over his shoulder at the neatly drawn schematics.

I studied the first sheet. It appeared there would be ship models and figureheads in the large entrance hall, as well as a special display of treasures from India on a raised circular platform in the center of the room. Other pages were marked with the names of continents and countries—Asia, India, Africa, China, and others. The show would apparently cover both stories of the old building. Much of the second-story plan was blank. The first story was divided into alcoves surrounding the main hall, a few of them marked with names familiar to me—old Salem family names, like Ropes and Orne and Pickering.

"May I keep these for a little while, Mr. Pennington? So I can study them and maybe get myself oriented before I tour the building?"

"Of course you may, my dear," he said. "That's why I brought them."

We four sat at the round table, and my aunt poured the coffee. "Do you know when the walls will be painted? The light fixtures installed? The glass display cases put in place?" I wanted to know.

"I understand there's some painting going on as we speak. There's plenty of time for the other things. The event doesn't start for several weeks. The city plans to have everything ready for a grand opening in October."

"Just in time for Halloween," I put in.

"We hope to show our visitors that there is much, much more to Salem than witch shops and that statue," Mr. Pennington said with a bit of a sniff.

The statue he referred to was the one of Samantha—she of *Bewitched* fame—just down the street from City Hall. Half of Salem loves her, and the other half does not. I think there's plenty of room for statues of famous folks in Salem, and let's face it, Samantha made witchcraft cool. There's room, too, to celebrate those brave voyagers who brought fame and fortune to our city beside the sea. "Salem is the perfect place to begin the tour," I said. "It'll be good to let people get a firsthand look at the treasures those old seamen brought home with them."

"I'm especially excited to see the things that Salem folks have loaned to the project. A surprising number of the descendants of those old sea captains and sailors still live in the area," my aunt said.

"I understand the armored truck that poor man was driving carried articles from the homes of some of those old families," I said.

"Oh, dear. Is that right, Pete?" Aunt Ibby had just begun to slice the pie, and she paused mid-slice.

"Yes. But as far as we can tell, nothing is missing," he assured her.

"Strange, isn't it?" Mr. Pennington asked. "Why would someone go to the trouble of diverting an armored truck and then not steal anything? And then to murder the driver! It doesn't make sense."

"It doesn't," Pete agreed. "It looked at first like a typical hijacking gone wrong."

"Maybe someone came along and interrupted the thief before he could get what he—or she—was after," Aunt Ibby suggested.

"A possibility," Pete said. He'd begun to use his cop voice, so I was pretty sure there wouldn't be much more information coming from him.

"Scott said that even the driver's wallet wasn't stolen," I said. "What could the killer—or killers—have been after?"

Mr. Pennington frowned. "Whatever it was, it looks as though they didn't get it. Am I correct, detective?"

"A possibility," Pete said again. He lifted his plate. "That pie looks wonderful, Ibby."

My aunt smiled her most heartwarming smile. "Never judge things by their appearance," she said.

It was an odd statement. Did she mean the pie? Or the undisturbed armored truck? Pete looked confused too.

Mr. Pennington snapped his fingers. "Good one, Ibby! Julie Andrews in *Mary Poppins*. Nineteen sixty-four."

CHAPTER 3

Again, we were diverted by an old movie quote. But still, Aunt Ibby's remark—or Julie Andrews's uttering, as the case may be—had some relevance to the hijacked truck and the murder of the as-yet-nameless driver.

"*Never judge things by their appearance.*"

The words rattled around in my brain while my aunt resumed slicing the pie—which did look wonderful—and placing identically sized slices onto our upheld plates. The truck's cargo *appeared* to be intact. The driver's personal belongings *appeared* to be untouched. Even Pete had said it *appeared* to be a hijacking gone wrong.

"Pete," I said. "There must be operating security cameras on the bank, even though it's been closed for a while."

In an uncommon burst of straight cop talk, he admitted, "It's an old bank. There are two cameras in front of the place and one in the back. There's no sound. We have clear video of the truck pulling in behind the bank and a bank employee helping the driver unload the cargo. It's not a big load—a few good-sized crates filled with smaller, wrapped packages."

"But you can't see anybody shooting the driver, burying him under the leaves?"

"No. As soon as the bank's doors were closed, we see the driver walking back toward the truck. The driver's side of the vehicle is facing away from the camera. So is the pile of leaves where he was found. The man was shot at close range. The shooter must have been hiding nearby while he was inside."

"Scott didn't report any of that. Why not?" I wondered aloud. I sure would have if the information had been available. "Didn't anyone hear the shot?"

"It's possible," he repeated. "I guess Scott didn't know. The video hadn't been released yet. Anyway, I'm sure it'll be on the late news, along with a plea from the chief for information from the public."

"Maybe nobody heard the shot. The mall is closed, and there aren't many houses nearby." I thought about what Pete had told me off the record about the driver having a gun permit. Did the security footage indicate in any way that he'd been armed when he moved the boxes from the truck to the bank? I planned to ask him as soon as we were alone.

Shoot. If I still had my field reporter's job at the station, I'd have known about this as soon as the bank footage had been discovered. Instead, I'd been sent home early and all anyone had talked to me about was an old, closed-up A&P store instead of an old, closed-up branch bank with a vault full of treasures and a dead body out back. I almost pouted. Instead, I returned to the safe subject of pie.

"I'm starting to think about making real desserts, Aunt Ibby," I said. "Would you make up a file card for this pie? For when I get a little more advanced? I did the Betty Crocker version of baked chicken tonight, and it turned out pretty well."

Pete nodded, smiling his agreement. "It was darned good, babe."

Mr. Pennington returned us to the more important subject at hand. "You say, Detective Mondello, it's a 'possibility' that the person or persons who committed these crimes did not get what they were after." He paused, with a forkful of pie halfway to his mouth. "May I interpret that to mean that it's also a possibility that they *did* indeed get away with something?"

Pete nodded thoughtfully. "I try to keep an open mind about these things. At the beginning of an investigation, just about anything is possible. Then, if all goes well, one at a time, the possibilities are eliminated."

"Until only one possibility remains," my aunt offered, "and the crime is solved."

Pete grinned again. "That is a distinct possibility."

Talk of hijacking and murder was replaced by lighter topics, some about the museum opening, some about food, some about the elegant homes still owned by some of Salem's oldest families—a few of which were open to the public for guided tours—while we finished off every last crumb of the pie and each drop of the coffee.

O'Ryan appeared in the kitchen just as Pete and I were saying our "good-byes" and preparing to walk home, me with the precious cardboard tube of floor plans under my arm.

"I guess *Wicked Tuna* must be over," Pete said, bending to pat the cat, who responded with a cat approximation of a fist-bump to Pete's hand.

"That's cute," I said, leaning forward, offering my hand. Ignoring my outstretched palm, O'Ryan used both paws to dislodge the tube from my clutching elbow, watching it tumble to the kitchen floor. It rolled a bit, and the cat stopped it, once again gripping it with both paws.

"That's *not* cute," Aunt Ibby scolded. "Naughty boy!"

My aunt and I both know for sure that O'Ryan rarely does anything out of the ordinary just to be naughty. Pete has come to some sort of understanding—if not belief—that the handsome gentleman cat is far from an ordinary housecat. Mr. Pennington had, as far as I knew, never been informed of O'Ryan's special talents, and his expression revealed stern disapproval of such disrespect for his carefully packaged floor plans.

I knew immediately that the cat wanted to see the plans. That would be hard to explain to Rupert Pennington. I was positive that none of his many academic degrees included any kind of cat psychology—or that he'd ever studied the mystic connection between witches and their cats. O'Ryan had once been, after all, a witch's "familiar."

I was wrong. The very proper Mr. Pennington

got down on his knees, then leaned forward so that he was face-to-face with the tube-grabbing feline. "Interesting," he said. "Fascinating. The animal has deliberately taken possession of something he cannot eat. Why did he do that?" He moved even closer, O'Ryan's luxurious whiskers almost brushing his face. "I once spent several semesters studying Egyptology at the American University in Cairo," he murmured, still watching, but not touching the cat. "Of all the ancient civilizations that revered cats, Egypt is the most well-known for it. Felines were held in great esteem, believed to enter the same afterlife as human souls." He looked up at me. "Didn't you say this one once belonged to a person who fancied herself to be some sort of witch?"

"I did," I admitted. "Ariel Constellation. She used to have a late-night show on WICH-TV. She did psychic readings for people over the telephone."

Mr. Pennington's voice took on the professorial tones of one of his classroom lectures. "Ah, yes. I remember that. In Egypt, cats were considered dual-natured—connected with the gods, as well as being domestic companions that protected the home, but capable of being lethal predators when provoked."

The analogy about the cat's dual nature suited O'Ryan. He could be a kittenish playmate, an aloof and snooty ignorer of humans, or a fiercely protective companion. The attic incident wasn't the only time O'Ryan had bravely defended me from harm. He'd done the same for others I knew of too. I wasn't about to share any of that history with Mr. Pennington. I also knew that as soon as I got a chance, I was going to share the floor plans of the Salem International Museum with our dual-natured cat.

"Interesting. Fascinating," Mr. Pennington repeated, standing and stretching his shoulders and back. "Cats are worthy of study, indeed. Well, thank you, Ibby, for inviting me to share a splendid evening of conversation and delicious repast. I'll call you soon. Perhaps you'd accompany me for a performance of the Boston Pops. I have season tickets, you know."

My aunt colored slightly as she walked with us to the foyer. "I'd be delighted, Rupert," she said. She kissed me on the cheek, hugged Pete, and wished us a good night. O'Ryan jumped up onto the seat of a tall, mirrored hall tree beside the front door, stretching a paw high enough to tap the rolled-up tube I carried under my arm. "Yes, I've got it," I told him. "I'll show it to you later." I tried to look away. I don't like that mirror. Too late. The flashing lights and whirling colors that always accompany a vision appeared on the mirror's surface. It was a quick picture, flashing into my mind, then disappearing. It was a picture of that pile of disturbed fall leaves I'd seen on the news. But nearby the colorful pile of leaves, I saw a pair of legs with black-booted feet.

I have reason to dislike black. Especially black shoes. The damn visions began with shiny black patent-leather Mary Janes when I was little. A black automobile had caused the death of my late husband, Johnny. A black obsidian ball on Ariel's set at WICH-TV brought all the horrors back. I never wear black, never drive a black car. The color symbolizes bad things to me.

O'Ryan stepped down from the seat of the hall tree and started up the curving front staircase, apparently assured that I understood about sharing the floor plans and opting to spend the night at Aunt Ibby's house. I grasped Pete's hand, and we hurried outside together into the cool, good-smelling fall evening. Pete has always been perceptive, good cop that he is, and as time has passed in our relationship, he's become more and more attuned to my reactions to the visions. He calls it "seeing things." As brief a glimpse into that sad scene as it was, he caught the slight shift in my attitude. As soon as the door closed behind us and Mr. Pennington had driven away in his elderly Porsche, Pete put a supporting arm around my waist. "Seeing things?" he asked softly.

"I was," I admitted. "In the hall tree mirror."

"Not the first time." His jaw tightened. "I wish Ibby would get rid of that thing."

I shrugged. "It wouldn't matter. I'd see the same thing in a silver teapot or a store window or a puddle in the street. It would find me."

"Want to tell me about it?"

"Yes." I don't always share the visions with Pete right away. Sometimes they just don't make any sense at all. "This one might mean something. I saw the pile of leaves where they found the body. It was exactly like the picture on the news—except someone was standing beside it."

"Someone you recognized?"

"Not at all. It was just the feet. In black boots." I stopped walking and closed my eyes for a moment, seeing the picture again, leaning against Pete. "Short boots, you know, not the tall kind."

"Was it a man or a woman? Could you tell?"

"No. I mean, men and women both wear those short ankle boots. Even kids wear them." I thought about it some more. "It looked like the person wore jeans. Flared out a little over the boots."

We'd reached our own front door. Pete pulled out his key and unlocked it. "I'm sorry you have to see the things," he said, "but sometimes they can be helpful."

"I know. Speaking of seeing things," I said, "when you saw the surveillance film of the armored truck driver, could you tell if he was armed?"

"No. We couldn't tell. If he was, the gun was concealed." Serious cop voice. I wasn't going to get any more information on the subject.

We stepped into our front hall. "What's that on the floor?"

He picked up a folded sheet of paper. "It's probably just an ad somebody slipped under the door." He clicked on the overhead light and unfolded the paper. "Huh. It's a note from our new next-door neighbor. An invitation to his housewarming." He handed the note to me.

I read aloud. "Hello, neighbors," it began. "I know this is short notice, but Friday evening I'm hosting a little housewarming event. Rupert Pennington told me of Mrs. Mondello's new venture into Salem history, and I think you might be interested in meeting some of the other invited guests. Dr. Sant Bidani is a professor of Indian culture and has knowledge of commerce between our countries during the seventeenth and eighteenth centuries. Ms. Kitsue Sullivan is a direct descendant of a man who made several trips between China and Salem and has some interesting primary-source written material, as well as a fine collection of items brought to Salem from the Orient. I hope you can join us at around eight o'clock on Friday. I plan to invite Ms. Isobel Russell and Mr. Rupert Pennington as well. Sincerely, Michael Martell." His email address followed.

"What do you think? Want to go?" Pete asked.

"Why not? The guest list is intriguing," I said. "Besides, if it gets dull, we don't have to travel far to get home." I followed Pete into the living room, where, I noticed immediately, the TV set had been turned off. O'Ryan had long ago learned to tap the red *off* key when he got sleepy or bored with the subject matter. It was one of those things about him we'd all come to take for granted. I pointed to the remote on the couch. "Smart cat," I said.

"He kind of showed you the boots and the leaves thing, didn't he, when he jumped up onto the hall tree seat?" Pete remarked.

"He did," I agreed. "Not the first time he's done something like that, either." I thought about other visions, other images, I'd seen in that same mirror—more than a couple of them had been prompted by the cat. "O'Ryan tapped the tube with the floor plans with his paw too," I told Pete as I placed the tube on the coffee table. "I guess he really wants to look at them."

"I guess you'll have to share them, then." He smiled, humoring me as he often did when I talked about O'Ryan's special talents, then changed the subject. "Do you want to catch the late news? I'd like to see how the chief did with his presser about the bank security-camera video." He chuckled. "Boy, he hates doing those things."

"I'd like to see it too," I said, thinking about how if I still had my field reporter's job, I'd have been at the presser myself. I'd already have seen the video, and *I'd* have a spot on the late news. I wouldn't have to watch it on TV with everybody else in the city. Even Pete had already seen it. This time, I actually pouted for real.

"Aw, babe, you miss being on TV all the time, don't you?" He gave me a warm kiss, making the silly pout face go away. "Don't worry, when you get going on the documentary, you'll be on camera for so many hours you'll get tired of it." He stood back a bit and looked at me—up and down. "I guess you'll need some new clothes. Why don't you plan a little shopping trip. Get a few things a 'historical documentary executive director' might need."

What a guy! He knew exactly how to cheer me up. "Mr. Doan suggested the very same thing," I told him. "I might as well pick up something to wear to our neighbor's housewarming, too," I said. We sat together on the couch, and Pete retrieved the recently cat-controlled remote and selected the WICH-TV channel.

Scott was on camera, but he simply introduced the Salem police chief. Pete was right about the chief being nervous when he had to do these things. Funny, how such a take-charge person, actually more than once decorated for bravery, could be so intimidated by some bright lights, a few cameras, and some curious press people. But it was true. Chief Whaley approached the lectern as usual, tall, handsome in his uniform, with a chest full of medals and the official blue-and-gold cap. His hand shook ever so slightly when he picked up the small stack of papers in front of him.

The poor guy is never going to like this part of his job,

I thought, *and I loved that part of mine.* I settled back on the couch, Pete's arm around my shoulders, just like back when we were dating. I loved this part of my life too.

"There was a shooting in Salem this morning, which is currently under investigation," Chief Whaley said, looking down at his script, avoiding facing the cameras aimed in his direction. "The lifeless body of the driver of a rented armored vehicle was found this morning by a city employee. The man, whose name is being withheld pending notification of relatives, had delivered a shipment of goods to a secure holding facility at a vacant local bank. Preliminary investigation by this department indicates that the shipment, meant for the new Salem International Museum, is intact and that no robbery has taken place. The man's personal belongings, as well, appear to be undisturbed. The driver had been shot at close range. The security cameras at the bank location captured some images."

Chief Whaley paused, looking confused for a moment before the security video rolled. Just as Pete had described it, the soundless picture showed the man and the bank employee, whose faces were deliberately blurred, carrying several boxes into the back door of the bank. The chief described, haltingly, but accurately, what we were seeing. We saw the driver approach the truck and disappear behind it. We saw fall leaves on the ground. We saw the bank employee leave via the front door of the bank and get into his own car. The chief said that the truck had not moved, nor—as far as the cameras could tell—had anyone approached it until the city worker saw the truck this morning and found the body. Chief Whaley made a request for anybody who had knowledge about the matter, or anyone who had surveillance videos showing the armored car in question, to call a posted number. Then, not even pausing for the shouted questions from the assembled press, the chief scurried back inside the building.

Scott did a fast—for him—roundup of the known facts of the case, then turned the program back to Buck Covington, who more or less repeated what Scott and the chief had just said, then turned to the national news.

"So," I said to Pete, "nobody really knows what the heck is going on. No wonder the chief didn't take any questions. He has no answers, does he?"

"Looks like you've got that right. We have a perfect setup for a major robbery, but nothing seems to have been stolen." Pete gave a small sigh and shake of the head. "The company that owns the rental armored car is completely reputable. The driver was scheduled to travel to a Boston museum early this morning, so he'd scheduled a two-day rental. When he didn't show up at that museum this morning, they called the rental company, and they called us. That was just about the time the city worker found the truck and the body. The driver's record is as pure as the driven snow. Not even a traffic ticket. So far, we have almost nothing to go on."

"You have a dead man who saw something he shouldn't have seen, or heard something he shouldn't have heard," I reasoned.

"Or was just in the wrong place at the wrong time," Pete finished the thought for me.

CHAPTER 4

Although I had the rest of the holiday weekend off, Pete didn't have such an easy schedule. On Thursday morning, he was awake and out of bed first, as usual. I heard the radio playing country music, smelled the coffee, pulled on a robe, and made my sleepy way to the kitchen. "Good morning, my love," I said, heading for the shower. "There are some cinnamon rolls in the bread box."

"Found 'em," he said. "Want yours toasted?"

"Yes, please." I paused at the bathroom door. "I've been thinking about the person in the boots."

"The vision person," he stated. "What are you thinking?"

"I'm thinking I'll tell River about him—or her. Maybe she can make some sense out of it," I suggested.

Pete wasn't a big fan of what he called "River's hocus-pocus." Surprisingly, he agreed. "Might as well. We don't have anything else to go on."

"She doesn't claim to know exactly how to interpret visions," I reminded him, "but she says they're something like dreams."

"That makes as much sense as anything else about this particular can of worms," he said. "Sure. Give River a shot at it."

"I'll call her this afternoon," I promised. Having once worked that midnight-to-two-in-the-morning schedule myself, I knew better than to call my friend before late in the day. Anyway, I had plenty of homework to fill my day. "This morning I'll email our acceptance to our next-door neighbor's invitation for Friday night too," I told him.

After sharing coffee and store-bought but very tasty cinnamon rolls, I kissed my husband goodbye, opened my laptop on my prized, 1970s-era, clear Lucite kitchen table, emailed the acceptance message, then assembled the assorted lined index cards I'd already scribbled notes on, and prepared to get to work. I was immediately interrupted when O'Ryan strolled into the kitchen from the sunroom and posed expectantly beside his special, but empty, red bowl. I filled it with his favorite dry cat food, put a bowl of water beside it, and waited until he seemed to be comfortably hunched over what might have been his second breakfast. Aunt Ibby has an identical red-bowl setup in her kitchen too. He seems to maintain a healthy weight, so we don't worry about his eating habits much.

"Well, cat," I addressed him, "thanks for the booted vision you made me watch. Any suggestions about what the heck it means?"

He didn't even twitch a whisker—just turned, his bottom facing me, and strolled into the living room. I hadn't expected an answer anyway. I often talk to O'Ryan. He's usually a really good listener, and sometimes just talking something out with someone—or some cat—results in some answers.

I'd begun making notes on my ever-present index cards about the various aspects of my debut museum show documentary. I had some lines cribbed from Wikipedia about the old China trade—which apparently marked the beginnings of relations between the United States and East Asia, right up to U.S. relations with China today. I'd noted a program overview on Egyptology from the American University in Cairo because of Mr. Pennington's mention of the place, and I had several cards about the Mystic Seaport maritime museum, hoping to grab some ideas from their popular coastal attraction.

I had a short list of names, phone numbers, and emails of people who might be helpful in tracking down persons, places, or things that might prove useful in the endeavor. Aunt Ibby had given me a few of the contacts—mostly women friends of hers who were associated with my city's varied historical associations.

An unfamiliar sound came from the living room. I put down my pen and sat up straight, listening. It was a soft bumping sound. *Bump. Bump. Bump.* I didn't have to wait long for an explanation. The very smart—but impatient cat—had helped himself to the floor plan tube, and with his pink nose and carefully sheathed claws, had figured out how to propel the long, awkward-shaped package from one room to the other. He selected a bright patch of sunshine on the kitchen floor, dropped the tube, and sitting in a quite ungainly position, proceeded with his morning cat-bath routine.

I had to laugh aloud. "Okay. You win." I pulled the papers from the end of the tube and spread the two sheets onto the floor in front of him, glad that I'd Swiffered the floor the night before. "Look them over. I have work to do." I returned to the table and began to type, sneaking a look at the cat from time to time. I hoped to get my scattered thoughts and observations into some sort of cohesive form to present to the publicity people at WICH-TV before giving the floor plans another look. Mr. Doan had asked for a general outline of what my documentary would cover so that P.R. would be able to prepare some promotional material for the potential audience. He'd even suggested that the station might use some of the early videos, as the museum was in the process of filling the cases and hanging the paintings, as brief "teasers" before the entire presentation was ready. A glance at O'Ryan told me that he was through studying the sheets. He'd stepped gingerly away from them, returned to the red bowl, checking to see if he'd left anything in it, and walked away toward the sunroom.

"Crazy cat," I muttered, rerolled the plans, pushed them back into the tube, and returned to my own work. I was beginning to warm up to the entire project. Before long, my unfocused card collection had yielded nearly a dozen doublespaced pages of what I thought would pass as a darned good overview of *Seafaring New England*—all the way from Elias Hasket Derby's *Grand Turk* right up to the sinking of the *Andrea Gail* in the "perfect storm" of late October in 1991.

I have to admit it—the idea of being in front of the cameras again held a lot of appeal for me. It was what I'd been trained for, what I'd spent most of my adult years doing in one form or another. While my overview whirred its way through the printer, I thought about what Pete had said about beefing up my wardrobe for the new position. I had no need to economize on my personal clothing allowance. Between the money I'd inherited from my parents and the insurance from Johnny's accident, and thanks to investment advice from Aunt Ibby's financial advisor, I was, by most standards, a fairly wealthy woman. It had taken a while for me to admit that fact to Pete, but he had no problem with it. "That's great," he'd said. "You mean, when we have kids, we don't have to worry about their college educations?"

I looked at the Kit Kat clock over the table. It was much too early to call River, but there'd be plenty of time to do a little fall fashion shopping. A couple of good business suits—pants and skirts both—would serve the purpose, along with a few coordinated blouses and shirts. The promised WICH-TV green jacket would go with everything. I needed shoes too. I peeked into the sunroom, where the cat lay snoozing on the bentwood bench. "What do you think, O'Ryan? Maybe I'll even get a new hairstyle and shoes—lots of shoes." O'Ryan opened one eye. "I'll have to practice walking in high heels—it's been such a long time since I've worn them to work. I'll need some ankle boots too, to wear with the pants." Boots. It brought a mental picture of the ones I'd seen in the mirror. "Those feet could very well have be-longed to a woman," I told the cat.

"Mrrrup," he said, in a bored-cat tone of voice.

"On the other hand," I told him, "since there's nothing size-wise to compare those legs and feet to, they could just as well belong to a man." I shook the mental picture away. "Enough about the darned vision. River will help me with it, and for now, I'll just head for the shops and treat myself to a fresh new fall wardrobe."

I tossed on a NASCAR jacket and headed out-side to our designated parking area behind the house. By then, O'Ryan had already left via the sunroom cat door, and I presumed he was heading down Winter Street to check out his other red bowl at Aunt Ibby's. I climbed into my almost-new, completely tricked-out with every accessory known to the auto industry Jeep Wrangler. It was a far cry from my previous vehicle, a gorgeous Corvette convertible—but certainly more practical—and as Pete said, it was a lot safer for those kids whose col-lege education we didn't need to worry about.

I drove directly to Colette's, my favorite fashion boutique, where they knew my size and my taste and where I could be sure they'd have all the latest looks. I wasn't disappointed. Within two hours, laden with a couple of armloads of bags, cartons, and shoe boxes of varied shapes and sizes, I headed back to the Jeep, a smile on my face and a seriously abused credit card in my purse, and piled my haul into the backseat. I could hardly wait to get started on my new on-camera career. I headed home to Winter Street and parked the Jeep in my regular space, then attempted to gather all those various-shaped purchases into both arms while kicking the Jeep door shut. Thankful that it hadn't rained lately, I stooped to retrieve two bags and a box from the ground.

"Here. Let me give you a hand, Mrs. Mondello." The male voice startled me. I looked up at our next-door neighbor, Michael Martell. Our shared backyard spreads out behind both dwellings, with no dividing fence or foliage separating the two. *The same as the attic.* Smiling, he bent and scooped up the articles easily.

"Thank you, Dr. Martell," I stammered. As soon as he smiled, he looked like the photo on the back of all the mystery novels he'd written under the pseudonym of Fenton Bishop—just a little bit older. The "doctor" title stood for Martell's PhD in education. In addition to teaching classes in creative writing at the Tabby under the Fenton Bishop pen name, he'd also become a regular guest at Aunt Ibby's weekly meetings with her mystery book–loving girlfriends, Louisa Abney-Babcock and Betsy Leavitt. The three women fancied themselves as amateur sleuths: a sort-of senior citizens cross between the *Golden Girls* and *Charlie's Angels*—and they take themselves very seriously, meeting every week to watch *Midsomer Murders*.

"Michael," he corrected, flashing the smile once again, and waiting while I gathered up my remaining purchases. "We're neighbors now. And I'm delighted that you and Detective Mondello will be joining us on Friday." I closed the Jeep's door, and we walked together toward the sunroom on the back of my half of the house.

"Please, call me Lee." I acquiesced to his first-name idea, then made an awkward move to fish the key to the sunroom from my purse, nearly dropping another bag. I pushed the door open with my foot and gratefully deposited my burden onto my much-loved bentwood bench, and he placed his armfuls carefully onto the coffee table. "And thank you again for showing up just when I needed a helping hand. Pete and I are looking forward to talking Salem history with your other guests."

He bowed slightly and walked toward the door. He glanced down. "I see O'Ryan has cat-door access to both of his homes. That's nice."

"Yes." I held open the attractive French door to the sunroom—with its cat door that exactly fit the center bottom pane. "My aunt and I share custody—or perhaps he shares custody of us."

"I've been thinking about getting a cat for myself. I may be in the market for a cat door exactly like yours. I know it will fit since our houses are alike." He looked thoughtful as he stepped outside. "I think a cat will be good company."

"I've enjoyed reading about the antique-store cats in your Antique Alley Mysteries," I told him. "You obviously know a lot about them."

"Research," he said. "I've never actually *owned* one."

"We don't own cats," I corrected, then quoted somebody else's wisdom. "Dogs have owners. Cats have staff."

"I'll remember that," he promised, laughing softly. "Cats have staff. Very good, Lee."

After he'd left, I carried my new wardrobe additions up to the bedroom and hung them in my closet. I looked at the alarm clock on the bedside table. It was time to call River. I had questions.

CHAPTER 5

I was glad to hear my friend's voice. "I didn't wake you, did I?" I asked.

"Nope. Just having a nice cup of hibiscus tea. What's going on?"

"I need to talk to you about a vision I had," I said. "Maybe you can help me make sense out of it."

"The darn things never make sense, do they?" A silvery giggle. "But they are kind of like dreams, so tell me what you've got."

I described the booted feet and the disturbed fall leaves. I told her what I thought the connection was to the news story about the murdered driver. "I'm especially concerned because Mr. Doan has assigned me to do a documentary about the museum the driver's cargo was intended for."

"My camerawoman, Marty, told me about the new gig. It sounds like something you'll have fun with—even if it starts out with a dead guy in a leaf pile," she said. "Tell me more about what the boots looked like. Boy boots or girl boots?"

"Hard to tell. They're black, not shiny. Plain— nothing fancy about them. Pete even has a pair. I do too—not black, of course." River knows about my feelings on black. I even try not to step on the black squares when I cross the black-and-white-tiled floor in the WICH-TV lobby.

"Yep. I have some too, only mine are silver," she said. "Now that it's officially fall shopping time, they're in a lot of the fashion ads."

"I know. I did some shopping myself today. Clothes for being on camera again."

"It's been a while."

"Tell me about it."

"Okay. I've got my dream book in front of me," she said. "Let's see what it has to say about boots. And leaves, while we're at it." There was a pause, and the sound of pages flipping. "Okay, here we go. Boots can mean a powerful movement, like boldness in your position. Sounds like the new job is a good move, maybe." Another pause. "Uh-oh. Boots also can be a metaphor for 'getting the boot.' Planning on getting kicked out of some-where?"

"I already got kicked out of my regular field re-porter job," I grumbled. "Do you think I'll get booted out of this one, too, before I even start?"

"Not a chance. Let's take a look at leaves. You said they're fall leaves, right? It says here that brown leaves mean sadness or loss," she read. "It was all sadness and loss for the poor driver, wasn't it?"

"Yes, it was. Anything else?" I asked.

"How about this? Leaves can be a symbol of fer-tility, growth, or openness?"

"That sounds better, but it's pretty nonspecific, isn't it?"

"Yeah." Another giggle. "The cards are way better than dreams. More specific. I haven't got time for a reading right now, but I can stop by your place on my way to work. Like around eleven tonight? Will you guys still be up?"

"I can't promise that Pete will be, but I'll be watching Buck's show. I still get some kind of perverse kick out of seeing what news stories I missed covering during the day."

"I have a feeling that what you're covering in your new job might be just as much fun for you," she suggested. "Maybe 'growth or openness,' like the leaves said."

"I've learned to trust your feelings, River," I told her. "You're probably right. I've already piled up a stack of topics that need more research. Things that, until now, I've never given much thought to."

"See? There's growth right there," she assured me.

"I was talking to my neighbor about that this morning," I recalled.

"About growth?"

"No, about research." I knew River had read a few of Michael Martell's mystery books. "The antique-store cats in the Fenton Bishop books are all the result of research. He's never actually owned a cat."

"No kidding. He had me fooled. Those might be some of the most catlike kitties I've ever seen in books," she said.

"I know. I was surprised too," I admitted. "But now that he has a house of his own, he's planning to share it with a cat—for company."

"How are you getting along with him? The new

neighbor?" she asked. "Does his—um—past bother you?"

"A little. I mean—he *did* murder his wife, even if he didn't intend to. But as Pete says, he's 'paid his debt to society.' Aunt Ibby and the Angels trust him completely, and his classes are some of the most popular ones the Tabby offers." I shrugged. "Actually, we have an invitation to his housewarming on Friday. Some of the important people who head up the *Seafaring New England* committee will be there."

"Have you accepted?"

"Yes. I thanked him this morning when he was helping me carry the results of my shopping spree into the house."

"So, he's a helpful neighbor who likes cats. Sounds good. I'll see you tonight around eleven for a quick reading."

"See you then." I went downstairs, back to the waiting laptop, and stared at the screen for a long, nonproductive moment. The cardboard tube holding the rolled-up plans for the placement of the various show components of the museum was still on the kitchen counter, where I'd placed it after the cat's perusal. I retrieved it, opened the tube once again, and, snapping the laptop shut, spread the first sheet onto the table. It showed the central street-level room, with several alcoves radiating from the center. Some, although not all, of the alcoves had names printed on them—noting, I guessed, the origin of the items to be displayed in those spaces. The print was neat, but tiny. I pulled a magnifying glass from among the rubber bands, paper clips, and other necessities in the cabinet's "junk drawer." I recognized the names of a number of small museums, some displays specific to certain New England states, and a few marked "private collection." A name I'd seen in print very recently popped out at me: "Sullivan collection."

Michael Martell's note had mentioned that a Kitsue Sullivan would be among the housewarming guests. A coincidence? Not likely. I wished I'd saved the note. I searched my memory, recalling that she was descended from one of the early Salem shipping families. I'd known several Sullivan families during my growing-up years in Salem. Maybe she was someone I'd known back then. The kids I'd gone to school with hadn't talked about their ancestors any more than today's kids did. I rolled the papers up again and returned to the laptop. Facebook might yield some information. Sure enough, she had a personal page. If the photograph at the top of the page was a recent one, she looked to be a little younger than me. A quick scrolling yielded the usual birthday notices, pictures of pets, smiling family poses, and a meme or two. I didn't see anything indicating that she might be in possession of some museum-quality artifacts. Was this Kitsue Sullivan the person Michael wanted me to meet?

Maybe, I reasoned, there was more than one Kitsue Sullivan. I shook my head in disbelief. There were plenty of Sullivans in Salem—I was sure of that—but more than one named Kitsue? I doubted it. In fact, I'd never heard of *anyone* named Kitsue before. I was tempted to message her, but I decided against it. I'd meet her on Friday anyway, and that particular question would be answered soon enough. I even thought about calling Aunt Ibby, whom I think knows everybody who ever had a Salem library card, but I decided against that too.

I cleared the table of papers and laptop, and with them, my unanswered questions. Pete would be home soon, and it was high time I thought about dinner preparations. I'd already decided on Pete's mother's secret recipe for lasagna—secret because it consisted of packaged lasagna noodles, canned spaghetti sauce, frozen meatballs, and deli Parmesan cheese—something most Italian wives do not admit to. A salad and a nice loaf of Virgilio's Italian bread I'd driven all the way to Gloucester for would be welcome, along with the usual ice cream for dessert.

I was still busy chopping tomatoes and shredding lettuce when I heard the sunroom door open. Pete and O'Ryan had arrived together—the cat a few steps ahead of the husband. He put his arms around my waist and gave me a quick kiss on the cheek. "You look so cute when you're being domestic," he whispered.

"I'm trying to get the hang of it," I admitted.

"You're doing great," he said. "How was your day?"

"I took your suggestion about shopping and bought myself a few proper historical documentary executive director outfits," I explained. "Actually, I bought so many that our next-door neighbor had to help me carry them all in!"

"Martell?"

"Sure. I dropped a few packages getting them out of the backseat, and he was there like a shot. I guess he was in his half of the yard and saw me struggling," I reported. "He said he was pleased that we're coming to his housewarming, By the way, he's planning to get a cat."

"So, the shopping trip was successful?"

"I think so. I hope you'll like all my choices."

"You know I will. I think you look beautiful all the time."

"Aw, shucks." I laughed. "Hey, I talked to River today—about the vision."

"Helpful?"

"Maybe a little. She checked her dream book, and the answers were kind of vague. Like, the boots can mean a powerful movement—as in the new job. But they can also mean getting fired, as in getting the boot," I told him. "And the leaves can mean both sadness and loss or growth and openness. See what I mean?"

"I never know what to think about River's hocus-pocus," he said. "It goes right over my head. Or in one ear and out the other."

"She thinks a tarot reading will be a lot more specific, so she's going to drop by tonight around eleven on her way to work," I said. "You don't mind, do you?" The timer buzzed, and I pulled the very good-smelling and not-at-all-bad-looking lasagna from the oven.

He gave a good-natured snort. "Not as long as I don't have to pretend to understand it." He hung his jacket over the back of a Lucite chair. "I'll probably be asleep anyway. Want me to toss the salad while you heat up the bread?"

I handed him the salad utensils. "One of the names Martell mentioned in his invitation shows up on the floor plans Mr. Pennington gave me. Sullivan. It marks a private collection to be displayed on the ground floor."

"Sullivan," he repeated. "I remember that. An unusual first name. Kitsue."

"Right. I'll be interested to talk to her Friday night," I said.

"So will I." He put the salad bowl on the table. "Some of the artifacts in the armored car were from the Sullivan collection."

That was a bombshell. I knew from the floor plans exactly where that collection would go. I could hardly wait for Friday night to arrive.

CHAPTER 6

Pete decided to stay awake to see what River would come up with in the tarot reading. I was surprised, because he usually avoids "River's hocuspocus." It's not that he disrespects what she does—far from it—she's been right so many times I'm sure he's become a reluctant believer, but he's still uncomfortable talking about it. Kind of the same way he views my scrying "gift."

River arrived at our front door a little before eleven, wearing an orange and black Harley-Davidson jacket tossed incongruously over a magnificent, full-skirted hunter-green velvet gown. She wore a coronet of green velvet leaves intertwined with silver stars, long black hair falling loosely over her shoulders. "Getting cool out there," she said, shedding the jacket and putting it on the couch. She held up the familiar silk bag that I knew housed the tarot deck. "Want to do this in the kitchen? The light is better there."

"Sure thing," I said. "Pete is out there now, making coffee. He's going to join us. That dress is amazing."

She pulled the skirt of her gown in close as she sort of wedged through the doorway and managed to fit the voluminous skirt into the chair and under the table. "Thanks. It's for the Celtic tree month of Vine. I got it at a yard sale. I feel like Scarlett in the dress made out of draperies, but I think the audience will get it."

O'Ryan had already curled up for the night in our upstairs bedroom earlier, but he'd dashed down the stairs at the sound of her voice. He loves River.

Pete greeted her. "Hi, River. Thanks for coming over so late. Lee is really concerned about seeing things in that old mirror. You know, about the boots and the leaf pile. I hope maybe you can help."

"I'm always glad to try," she said. "Some of my regular private clients have been calling, texting, leaving me messages at home and at the station. They're worried about a killer with a gun walking around loose in Salem. Are you cops any closer to catching him?"

"We have the driver's name. I guess there's no harm in telling you. The media already has it. He's Walter Wyman, twenty-six years old. Unmarried and lives at home with his parents. He's been with the armored car company for a year and a half. No problems. No accidents. No police record."

"I heard on the news that nothing was stolen

from the truck. Is that true? He got killed for nothing?" Her big eyes widened. "For nothing?"

"It's unlikely that he got killed for nothing." Pete used his patient cop voice. "We just have to figure out why whoever shot him did it."

River removed the tarot deck from the silk bag and handed it to Pete. "Shuffle, will you, Pete?"

He accepted the cards and did as she asked, then leaned back in his chair. She placed the deck in front of her and then put the Queen of Wands, the card she always uses to represent me, in the center of the table. The queen sits on a throne. She has red hair and hazel eyes, and there's a cat in the foreground. River bowed her head, and Pete and I did too. She rested her hand lightly on top of the deck. "I consecrate this deck to bring light wherever there is darkness. I consecrate this deck for guidance and wisdom for myself and others for the highest good for all concerned." Reshuffling the cards, she began the ten-card arrangement she uses most often for the call-in show. There were six cards in the form of a cross, and four more in a vertical row beside it. All the cards were faceup. She'd placed the second card across the Queen of Wands. She tapped it lightly with one finger. "The Ace of Wands," she said. "Here we see eight falling leaves, floating from a wand toward a castle on a hill. The usual interpretation is that this card symbolizes a new beginning." She looked up at me, grinning. "In your case, that would be the new job."

"Leaves. Not sadness or loss, like the dream book said?"

"Nope. Only if the card was reversed," she explained. "Then it could mean a spoiled venture, maybe a setback in a project. See? I told you the cards are way better than dreams."

"I believe you."

Pete leaned forward, interested. He watched her hand as she tapped the next card—the Three of Pentacles—showing a sculptor carving on a building that looked as if it could be a church. "This one speaks of skill and ability. Sometimes it refers to a member of some guild or fraternity."

"Like the East India Marine Society?" I asked, thinking about Mr. Pennington.

"Could be." She moved on to the next card. "The Four of Pentacles, reversed," she recited. "Here we see a man holding tightly to the gold he's worked hard for. His booted feet are planted firmly on pentacle symbols. This reversed card can mean the loss of some earthly possessions."

"Booted feet." I almost whispered the words. "Boots." The reading continued. "Here's the Three of Wands," she said. "See the young merchant watching his ships returning from across the waves? He's holding tight to his wand, secure in knowing his results are on the way." River pointed at me. "Looks like you can look forward to cooperation in your new venture. Besides, watch for help from a successful person."

"I will," I promised. "I know quite a few successful people." The remaining cards offered messages like "Growth through effort and hard work," and "Don't become superstitious." The most interesting one to me was a reversed Seven of Swords. Even Pete perked up when he heard the meaning of that one: "A thief might return what he has stolen."

River returned the cards to the silk bag, and we gulped the last of our coffee and cookies. She donned the biker jacket, and we walked with her to the door and said good night. We'd missed part of the eleven o'clock news, but Pete switched on the kitchen TV while we washed and put away our cups and plates. Scott Palmer was in the coveted on-the-right-hand-side-of-the-news-anchor seat. A color photo of a smiling, young dark-haired man wearing a Red Sox ball cap appeared on the screen. "Twenty-six-year-old Walter Wyman had been driving armored cars for a local company for over a year. His driving record was perfect, and he was well liked by his employers and fellow drivers. Yet, his lifeless body was found yesterday beneath a pile of leaves at the site of a secure facility housing some of the artifacts destined for Salem's new International Museum. He had been shot at close range." The photo faded away, and Scott lowered his voice, then gave his trademark long stare into the camera. "No motive for the crime has been established. It appears that nothing was stolen from the vehicle, and the young man had no known enemies. Staff inside the secure and soundproof building did not report hearing any shots. Salem Police are asking others in the vicinity to report any unusual activity or sounds of a gunshot at about eight yesterday morning, and to turn over any relevant security-camera footage." A phone number flashed at the bottom of the screen, and Scott went on to show an interview he'd done with the man's sobbing parents. I had to look away. That was one part of field reporting I'd always tried to dodge.

Scott left the news desk, and after a commercial,

Buck Covington brought on a sports correspondent who gave a rundown of some late baseball scores. There was a promo for *Tarot Time with River North,* and Buck announced that he'd be shuffling the cards for the popular late-night tarot reader—something he did occasionally and something her regular viewers absolutely loved. Buck knows how to do some of those fancy Las Vegas shuffles. He then announced that the scary movie for the night was *The Black Phone.* I'd seen it before. It's a horror movie about a kidnapped boy who hears the voices of his captors' previous victims on an old telephone. Too creepy to watch this late at night, we decided. Turning off the TV, we went upstairs, and the two of us climbed in beside O'Ryan on our big bed.

"What River said was kind of interesting," Pete whispered, not wanting to disturb the cat. "I wonder if any of it will turn out to be right."

"We'll see," I whispered back. "I'm never surprised anymore when it does."

"Interesting," he said, "how both the boots and the leaves turned up right after you'd asked her about them, isn't it?"

"I know. And the cards were well shuffled—you even shuffled them yourself, so you know it was just the way they fell."

He was silent for a while, and I thought he'd fallen asleep. "Lee," he whispered, "how about the part where the thief returns what he's stolen?"

"I wondered about that too," I said. "Does it ever happen?"

"Oh, sure. Sometimes as part of a plea deal. But most of what River said—I mean, like the boots and the leaves and the merchant seeing the ships.

All of that seemed to be about your museum thing, don't you think so?"

"Yes. The reading was for me. So, the cards would answer *my* questions and give *me* advice."

"That's what I thought." Another long pause. "The part about the thief returning what he—or she—stole. How does that fit in when nothing was stolen?"

The room was quiet then, except for the softly snoring cat at the foot of the bed. I lay awake for quite a long time, just thinking.

CHAPTER 7

My first thought on waking up on Friday morning was, *I have the day off!* I was alone in the big bed—cat and husband both missing. The smell of coffee and a Taylor Swift somebody-done-somebody-wrong song drifted upstairs. I shrugged into robe and slippers, ducked into the bathroom for a fast, cold-water face splashing and tooth brushing, and hurried down the back stairway to the kitchen.

Pete, of course, *didn't* have the day off, and he was showered, shaved, and dressed for work. "I'm having waffles," he said. Want some?" He held up a box of frozen Eggos.

"Sure," I said, pulling open a cabinet door and reaching for the maple syrup. It's the real thing—not the sugary, fake kind. We stock up on it when we go up to the New Hampshire Motor Speedway for the annual NASCAR races. Pete put another plate on the table and popped a couple more of the waffles into the toaster while I poured myself a mug of coffee.

"What do you have planned for today?" he asked. "Are you going to have a look at the museum building?"

"That's exactly what I have in mind," I told him. "I won't have Francine with me yet, but I'll take some pictures with my phone if they'll let me in."

"If the station's press card doesn't work, give me a call. I'm sure one of ours will." He grabbed our hot waffles and put them on our plates. "It looks like this new job is going to keep you busy."

I smeared mine with butter and poured on the syrup. "I'm halfway beginning to like it already. I'm sure I can get involved with the museum and still keep up with my program director duties. I know I'll be working extra hours, though." I frowned. "That cuts into our time together. I'm sorry."

"My schedule already cuts into our time together," he said. "And this armored car case will keep me busy too. We'll work it out. No worries. We'll always find time for each other."

"We have a date tonight, anyway," I reminded him.

"The Martell housewarming," he said. "Should we bring a gift?"

"Uh-oh," I said. "I spent all yesterday afternoon shopping for myself and never gave it a thought. Of course, we should. Good thing I have the day off. I'll get something."

"It's going to be a varied group, isn't it?" Pete observed. "The Indian professor and the Sullivan woman and your aunt and Pennington, along with us. I'll bet some of his students will be there too."

"I wouldn't be surprised to see some more of

the East India Society people there too," I said. "I wish I'd been invited as a field reporter, with a mobile unit and a soundman. That would rate a late-news spot for sure. As it is, I won't even be able to take notes."

"Afraid not," he agreed. "Scribbling on lined index cards might seem impolite. You'll just have to listen carefully and write your notes out as soon as we get home."

"I can do that. At least I can ask them for business cards," I said, then realized I didn't have any of my own yet identifying me as 'historical documentary executive director.' "I'd better stop by the Quick-Print place and get some with my new title."

"You've got another busy day lined up." Pete gave me a quick kiss. "Sorry to stick you with the dishes, but the chief's called a meeting for this morning. Gotta go." He cut through the sunroom to our parking-space area—which gave me my first bright idea of the day.

The cat door. Martell had said he'd be in the market for one exactly like ours. Why not buy one for his housewarming gift so it could be installed and ready for his cat? I'd stop by PetSmart on my way to the A&P-turned-museum building and pick one up. Brilliant! I wondered if they gift-wrapped. I actually hummed as I rinsed the breakfast dishes and put them into the dishwasher, then hurried upstairs to dress for the day.

By nine o'clock, I'd showered, dressed, fed O'Ryan, made the bed, pushed a dry Swiffer around the kitchen for a token cleaning, hung my station ID press pass around my neck, and stepped out into the backyard. A quick glance at the adjoining property told me that the Lincoln was missing. *Our neighbor must have an early class.* I remembered with pleasure my time as a television production instructor at the Tabby, pleased, too, that I knew enough about television production to turn in a better-than-average documentary when my days as historical documentary executive director were over.

I pulled the Jeep out onto Winter Street and headed for the closest Quick-Print store. I wouldn't need the cards for very long, so I ordered the minimum five hundred. Reasoning that I'd saved money on the printing, I opted for some artwork to dress them up—adding a drawing of an old-time sailing vessel—and arranged to pick them up in an hour. Next on the list was the cat door.

I grabbed the last cat door with the correct dimensions, learned that they didn't gift-wrap and stopped at the nearby dollar store for colorful paper with little houses on it along with a stick-on bow and an appropriate "good luck in your new home" greeting card.

It was nearly ten when I parked behind the museum-to-be. With a few barely dry business cards in my card case, and my press pass prominently displayed on my chest, I shielded my eyes and peered through the glass-paned door. I didn't see any activity inside, but I knocked briskly. Mr. Pennington had said there was painting going on, so I knocked a little harder, hoping a worker would hear me.

Someone did. A pair of dark eyes, shielded with both hands exactly the way mine were, peered back at me. There was a pause. I stepped back, heard the *click* of a lock, and faced a painter. I could be sure he was a painter because the white overalls, paper hat, and grinning young face were all liberally spattered with off-white paint. "Hi," he said, sticking out a paint-speckled hand. "You must be the lady from the television station. Rhonda told me to be on the lookout for you, and here you are!"

"Hi," I said. "That's me, all right. I'm Lee Barrett." I shook his hand. "And you are . . . ?"

"George Washington," he said. "No one ever believes me, but so help me, it's my real name. Come on back. I'll show you what we've done so far. This place is going to be fabulous." I followed George into a large, almost-round room I recognized from the floor plan I'd studied so recently. There were people on ladders here, some with rollers, some with brushes. The off-white paint looked bright and smooth. "These are the *real* painters," George said. "I'm just a volunteer. I bring them stuff and take out the empty paint cans and clean brushes."

"All important duties," I said.

"I know," he agreed. "I don't know much about painting, but I'm here every day. I volunteered because volunteers get to visit the exhibit as much and as often as we want—without paying."

"Good deal." I fished a business card from my purse and handed it to him. "I'm going to be around a lot too. Starting Tuesday, I'll be filming a documentary about the museum—from the way it looks now, right up until the opening week of the show."

"Wow. You've got a great job." He cocked his head to one side. "Hey, I remember you now. You used to be a reporter. I used to see you on the news sometimes." He put my card into the big pocket at the top of his overalls. He pulled another card from the pocket and handed it to me. Besides an off-white paint fingerprint, it contained information. *George Washington, Handyman,* it read. *Odd jobs. Painting. Carpentry. Yard Work,* along with his phone number, email address, and website information. "Just in case you need any help around your place. Rhonda says you have a new house. Rhonda is one of my favorite people."

"She's one of mine, too. Can we take a look into the alcoves around the edges of this room?"

"Sure. Some of those are all finished. The designers were here, measuring the spaces where they'll be putting glass cases or hanging paintings." He pointed to the space over an arch leading to one of the alcoves. "There's going to be a real carved figurehead over that door."

I could picture it. We walked together through the arch. No spatters here. Everything looked clean and bright. Droplights had been installed, and crown molding added a classical touch to the walls. It was becoming obvious that whoever was backing this project had seen to it that it was going to be a first-class destination—something Salem could be proud of.

When I'd studied the floor plan, I'd noted that the Sullivan alcove was the second one on the left-hand side of the main room. I walked toward it, George Washington at my side. "Some of the alcoves are ahead of the others as far as the painting and lighting are concerned—especially the ones with true local connections. Like, one family has already had glass-fronted cabinets built into the wall. They have a lot of dishes, I heard. Another one has a giant ship model their great-grandfather built."

We stepped into the one I was pretty sure was

the space marked Sullivan on the floor plan. There were some extra touches evident here. Paneled wainscoting reached about a third of the way up the wall. A delicate-looking crystal chandelier hung from the high ceiling, and I could picture family portraits in orderly rows above the top chair rail. I turned in a slow circle. There was plenty of room here for display cases too.

"She turned around just like you did, Ms. Barrett, looking at everything. The lady who's in charge of this one," George said. "Ms. Sullivan."

"Really? Is her name Kitsue?"

He shrugged. "That's her. I haven't talked to her yet. Just saw her when she came in yesterday."

The rest of my morning tour was a confidence-building experience. Even in the museum's bare-bones state, I saw the possibility of some excellent documentary material. While some of the spaces were near completion, others were just plain off-white, four-walled spaces, waiting for the distinguishing touches that would mark their special place in New England's maritime history. At the rear of the room, a simple staircase, built against the wall with one hand railing, led to a white paneled door opening onto the second story of the building. It was, as Pete had described it, like a big, open attic. I was pleased to see, though, that some preliminary work was being done. Workers on stilt-like extensions scrubbed dingy gray–painted walls in preparation for their new incarnation.

George pointed to the far end of the room. "That's where there'll be a stage. It'll be a real stage, with curtains and all, because they're going to have movies and lectures and some plays about Salem's history." *No wonder Mr. Pennington is so in-*

terested in this project. Undoubtedly the drama department of the Tabby would have some serious involvement.

"This won't be part of the regular museum tour, though," George continued. "They'll be renting it out for private parties, wedding receptions, special movies, and the plays I told you about. There's an old A&P freight elevator in the basement that comes all the way up to this floor," George said. "They're going to fix it up so people can use it to get up here. There's a rickety old staircase too, but it's not safe. They've got a *do not enter* sign on it." He pointed again toward the stage. "I heard they're going to show *The Perfect Storm* movie," reminding me that New England still produces the strong breed of men and women who seek to make a living from the sea. The sad tale of the *Andrea Gail* out of Gloucester had happened within my memory.

By the time we'd finished, and George had seen me out and locked the door behind me, I'd begun to believe Mr. Doan had chosen wisely when he'd picked me as executive director of the whole shebang. I could hardly wait to call Francine to tell her that this was going to be really fun, and that the fun would start bright and early on Tuesday morning.

CHAPTER 8

It was a little past noon when I left the museum-to-be, and I was hungry. As long as I was already downtown, I decided to stop at the station and see what I might be able to do to ensure that my Tuesday morning shoot would go smoothly. At the same time, I'd double-check on my current program schedule—but first I'd stop in at Friendly's, just across Derby Street from the station, and have one of their great cheeseburgers. I parked in my regular spot in the company parking lot and walked across to the restaurant. It was lunchtime, so all the tables were filled, but I don't mind sitting at the bar, especially if I'm in a hurry. Wouldn't you know it? Who came in right behind me and grabbed the barstool next to mine but Scott Palmer.

"Hey, Moon!" he said, "Fancy meeting you here. What's up?" When I had that nighttime show I'd dressed up like a fortune-teller and used the name "Crystal Moon." Scott sometimes still calls me Moon, and sometimes so does camerawoman Marty. I don't mind it.

"Nothing much," I said. "I'm just dropping by to check on my program schedule."

"Can't stay away from the place, huh? How's the new project going?"

"That starts right after the holiday," I told him. "Francine and I will start filming first thing Tuesday morning."

"Doan must think it's important." He put on a sulky face. "You get Francine and the new mobile unit, and I have to work with Old Jim and the Volkswagen van until you get finished."

That crack about WICH-TV's backup videographer annoyed me. I'd always loved working with Old Jim. Francine Hunter was tops in the field. Everybody knew that, but Old Jim had an eye for details—important details—that some of the other camera people, including Francine, sometimes missed, and I told Scott that.

"Oh sure," he backtracked. "The old guy is okay. I mean, it's not him. It's more the converted VW that's a pain. Did you see the interview I did with Walter Wyman's parents?'

"I'm sorry, no," I lied, remembering that I'd deliberately turned it off. I find Scott's manner of intruding on people's grief disturbing, but Mr. Doan says the audience likes it. I know I could never do it. I was sure I'd be much more comfortable reporting on the adventures of New England's long-dead heroes of the sea. I remembered George Washington's reminder that the Salem International Museum would be showing *The Perfect Storm* and that the relatives of the lost crew of the *Andrea Gail* were still around. I hoped it wouldn't occur to Scott to interview any of them.

I gobbled down my cheeseburger faster than I'd meant to, and only finished half of my Pepsi. Having my mouth full meant I didn't have to chat with Scott very much. I paid my tab, tipped Leo the bartender, and headed for the door. "So long, Scott," I said. "See you around."

"Wait a sec, Moon," he called. "You don't happen to have an invite to the wife killer's little party tonight, do you?"

Who told him about that? "Party?" I stalled, playing dumb.

"Yeah. He must have invited you. You practically live together."

"Why do you ask?" I tap-danced around the question.

"Can you get me an invite? I want to interview the Indian guy." He tossed some money onto the bar and joined me at the door. "I did a little investigating. I just found out this morning that he's really famous. He gives lectures at Harvard and Yale and places like that. He even gets invited to the White House sometimes. I already asked Doan. He says I can have a whole hour if I can get him to talk to me. He says an interview like that would really class up my act."

It certainly would! "Sorry," I said. "I don't know Dr. Martell well enough to ask him a favor. You've interviewed him before. Why not just call him yourself?" I knew the answer perfectly well. When Michael had first been hired to teach at the Tabby, Scott had absolutely ambushed him with questions about his two identities—Dr. Martell, the popular teacher, and the mystery writer, Fenton Bishop. Scott had actually suggested the man had a "Dr. Jekyll and Mr. Hyde" personality, with Mr. Hyde being a killer. I could hardly imagine Michael Martell even speaking to him, let alone welcoming him into his home.

"Yeah, well, it was worth a shot. I'll walk you across the street." Together we walked to the station and into the lobby, where I tried not to step on the black tiles. Scott's question had started my own thoughts about Professor Sant Bidani. I'd become so fascinated by the idea of meeting Kitsue Sullivan that I hadn't taken the time to study the Indian man's significant background. I planned to do a fast search as soon as I got home so at least I wouldn't sound like a complete doofus when I got to meet him at the party.

The ride up to the second floor in Old Clunky was a silent one, Scott checking his phone, me trying to get my mind back onto my program director duties. Rhonda, with her usual organizational skills, had printed out notes for each of my shows. *Shopping Salem* had an in-studio back-to-school teen fashion show planned for Labor Day and just needed my okay, and for Tuesday, a long-planned-for back-to school lunch demonstration would feature Wanda, our versatile weather girl who'd recently taken first place in *Hometown Cooks*, beating out top cooking show hosts in a national competition. Ranger Rob and Katie the Clown had the holiday off, and there'd be a cartoon show in its place. For the rest of the week, *Ranger Rob's Rodeo* would feature educational toys from his biggest sponsor, The Toy Trawler—Salem's only ship-shaped toy store—and Captain Billy Barker himself would be on hand to demonstrate how to use a drone.

"When you get through with the program schedule, Doan wants to see you in his office," Rhonda said, then winked and smiled. "Nothing serious. He's in a good mood. He just wants to see how you're doing on the documentary project. Francine says she'll have the mobile unit gassed up and ready to roll on Tuesday morning, any time you say."

"Eight o'clock on Tuesday morning, then. I'll be waiting for her in the parking lot." I walked to the partly open door marked *Manager* and gave a brisk knock.

"Come in. It's open," he said. "Good morning Ms. Barrett—I can't get used to the Mrs. Mondello handle yet."

I stepped inside the purple-carpeted room. "I'm just getting used to it myself," I admitted. "You wanted to see me?"

"Have you had a chance to look over the museum? Is the place ready to photograph yet?"

"I was there this morning. It's taking shape nicely," I said. "One of the volunteers was working as a painter. He gave me a tour, and this evening I'll be meeting a couple of the exhibitors—a woman who comes from an old Salem maritime family and has a private collection of memorabilia to display. Also, I'll be speaking with a professor of Indian culture who specializes in commerce of the seventeenth and eighteenth centuries."

"Good start, Ms. Barrett. That must be the Indian fellow Scott intends to interview. Are your programs all set?"

Lots of luck with that interview, Scott. "All set, sir,

and Francine and I will get everything underway early Tuesday morning."

"Good to hear. Rhonda has your green company jacket ready. Pick it up on your way out."

I stopped to thank Rhonda for the jacket—and for all her help. I told her I'd met George Washington at the museum and that he'd been helpful. "He says you're one of his favorite people."

"And he's one of mine," she said. "What a good guy. Always ready to give anyone a hand."

"His card says he's a 'handyman'," I told her.

"He has cards, now? Well, good for him. I hope he can drum up some business." She pointed at me. "What about you and Pete? Got any odd jobs that need doing around the house? He built a simple bookcase for me."

"Not really." I thought about the paint-spattered overalls, decided that if I hired him, it would surely be for something other than painting. "Say, do you think he could install a cat door?"

"Does O'Ryan need another one?"

"No. I have a friend who's thinking of getting a cat. He's going to need a door installed fairly soon."

Rhonda assured me that George could handle it. I left the WICH-TV building with a new jacket and a good feeling about both my jobs and more confidence in myself than I'd felt in a while. I also had the housewarming gift and the gift wrap in my car, and the business card of an installer in my purse. It had been a good day's work.

I arrived home before Pete did. I hadn't made any dinner plans, and figuring there'd be some kind of repast offered at the housewarming, I put some crackers and cheese on the counter just in case we might want something to nibble on. I used the time to wrap, tie, and stick the bow onto the cat door box, and signed the card "Mr. and Mrs. Pete Mondello." I used my best penmanship and loved the look of the words. Putting the finished product in the center of the table, I stood back to look at the effect.

"It looks darn near professional," I said aloud, "if I do say so myself." O'Ryan strolled in through his own sunroom entrance and immediately jumped up onto one of the Lucite chairs. He reached out a wide yellow paw and tapped the package ever so lightly. "What do you think, O'Ryan? How do you like the idea of having a next-door-neighbor cat?"

He gave what sounded like an affirmative "Mrrow," gave another gentle tap, and headed for his red bowl, which was empty. "Oops. Sorry about that." I filled the bowl, and hearing the sunroom door open again, turned to greet my homecoming husband with a kiss. A nice long one.

"Did you get to visit your museum today?" he asked, when we finally stepped apart.

"I did," I told him, "and they're making good progress. Francine and I will get started for real on Tuesday morning. How about you? Have you learned anything more about Walter Wyman?"

He reached for a cracker and a slice of cheese, opened the refrigerator, and pulled out a couple of cans of lime seltzer water. "We got some interesting footage from a security camera about a hundred yards away from the bank. It looks as though Walter had broken a company rule that morning. There was somebody in that armored car with him—not an employee. Having riders is strictly against company policy."

"Wow. Can you identify the person?" I helped myself to a cracker and cheese and popped open a seltzer. "Man or woman?"

"Hard to tell. The person is wearing dark, red-rimmed sunglasses and one of those damn navy-blue hoodies." He looked at the Kit Kat clock. "It's six thirty. Question. What's the dress code for this shindig we're going to? I see you've got the present all wrapped up. What are we giving him? Should we start getting ready?"

"That's three questions!" I laughed. "I'd say 'business casual.' I bought a new dress. Simple navy rayon with a matching light wool jacket. I'll wear my mother's pearls with it and my new navy slingback pumps. I think slacks and jacket for you. Maybe no tie? We have more than an hour to kill before we have to get dressed. And we're giving him a cat door. Could you see the hoodie person's face at all?"

"Just the top quarter. Hair and eyebrows. It looks sort of like a girl. A cat door? Are we sharing O'Ryan?" The cat in question left the red bowl, snapped his head around, and gave me a wicked cat stare.

"Of course not!" I assured both cat and husband. "Now that he has a house, Michael is planning to get a cat of his own. He mentioned that he'd need a door for it, so I bought one just like ours so it will fit in his French door. How like a girl?"

"It's the hair sticking out around the edge of the hoodie. Kind of frizzy. Girly. He writes about cats in those books of his, doesn't he?"

"Yep. He knows a lot about them. There are cats in all the antiques shops in his Antique Alley books," I said. "Aunt Ibby has read most of them to O'Ryan. He's okayed the gift. I asked him earlier. Is she blond or brunette—the girl in the armored truck?"

Pete didn't question the fact that I'd talked it over with the cat. "Blond," he said. "And frizzy."

"Have you checked with Wyman's friends and family to see if any of them can recognize her?" I asked. If *I* was investigating the murder, that's what *I* would have done—in a polite way, of course. Not like Scott Palmer's heavy-handed inquisitions. "Or maybe it was just a hitchhiker he felt sorry for," I suggested.

"We've made some still shots of her—or him—we're not sure yet. No one we've shown them to so far has come up with any kind of ID. Damn hoodies. Whoever the blonde is, Wyman must have picked her—or him—up pretty early in his run." He shook his head. "The chief's request for people to report surveillance camera footage showing the truck resulted in a pile of calls. She showed up in the passenger seat of Wyman's truck about two blocks away from the armored truck company's lot."

"Probably not a hitchhiker, then," I said. "He must have had a reason for picking her up. I'm betting she's not a stranger to him. What's your guess?"

"I'm not paid to guess," he told me gently—as he had many, many times before. "I'm paid to gather facts."

I stuck my tongue out at him, refilled the cheese plate, and repeated my opinion. "She's a girl," I said, "and she's not a stranger to him."

"No tie?" he said, building a double-decker cheese and cracker sandwich for himself. "I like that idea. How about my gray slacks, blue jacket, and white shirt?"

"Perfect."

"With a tie in the jacket pocket just in case," he added.

"*Semper paratus*," I agreed.

We followed the agreed-upon dress plan, then stood together in front of our full-length mirror. It was one of the favorite pieces I'd brought from my old apartment. The oval glass on the swivel-tilt cherrywood stand reflected us, both smiling, his arm around my waist. "We look good together," he said.

"We *are* good together," I declared.

CHAPTER 9

We went out our front door, Pete carrying the gift, and walked the house-length to the mirror-image of our own entrance, then pushed the doorbell. We'd had ours rigged to chime "It's a Wonderful World," but Michael's gave the standard two-tone *ding-dong*. Our host answered the door, with a welcoming "So glad you could make it."

Music and muted voices issued from within. I spotted a few familiar faces right away—some I'd almost expected to see—a few other Winter Street neighbors, and the drama instructor from the Tabby. Martell's living room, to the left of the front hall, the opposite of ours, was furnished in excellent vintage mid-century modern. The sofa, which must have been over three yards wide, was in a gorgeous Danish style with what had to be a teak base and velvety-looking boldly striped upholstery. A long, geometric, glass-topped coffee table,

NOW YOU SEE IT

elegant in its simplicity, held a stack of gift-wrapped packages and a handsome dish garden of succulents. The painting above the sofa might have been a real Martin Rosenthal oil. We had a brief awkward moment as Pete glanced around, trying to decide where to put our oversized oblong box. Dr. Martell, who wore a white shirt and no tie under his beige suede jacket—which also might have been vintage—graciously took it from Pete's outstretched arms and leaned it against a teak end table with a murmured, "Thank you. You didn't need to."

Still marveling at the perfection of the room, I reached for my phone. "Dr. Martell . . ."

"Michael," he corrected.

"Michael," I began again. "May I snap a photo of this room to show to Mr. Doan? Someday when the station does another 'tour of Salem homes' show, perhaps you'll let us feature this one."

"I'd be flattered," he said. "Take all the photos you like as long as the folks in them don't mind."

I asked permission from the few people there and tried to exclude them anyway. I was only interested in the amazing room itself.

Aunt Ibby and Mr. Pennington arrived together shortly after we had, and the four of us migrated to the kitchen, where we met several of Michael's students—each of whom was clearly delighted to have been invited. "Did you know that Professor Bidani is going to be here?" one of the young women gushed. "He spoke to our world history honors class, and he is just marvelous." Another nodded agreement and added, "And he's so handsome!" I peeked into the nearby sunroom, where a small vintage bar, Formica with atomic designs and a wonderful old jukebox with flashing lights had attracted a few of the guests. They all had their backs to me, so I snapped several shots there too. Doan was going to love the Salem House Tours idea.

I'd been right about food being available. White-uniformed waiters and waitresses circled among the guests with pink Melmac trays laden with assorted finger foods and silver trays bearing flutes of champagne. Our neighbor had done a bang-up job of introducing himself to the neighborhood. The next *ding-dong* of the doorbell brought a flurry of conversation. One of the guests of honor had arrived. Professor Bidani was all that the adoring students had promised, and even more than the Wikipedia account of his career I'd read earlier had hinted at. He was handsome, articulate, and charming. Michael took special pains to introduce each of the dozen or so people who were present to the man personally. With one hand on my shoulder and the other on Pete's elbow, he gently propelled us forward. "Allow me to present my next-door neighbors, Mr. and Mrs. Mondello. Peter and Lee. You'll be seeing Mrs. Mondello often in the coming days," he said. "She will be directing a television documentary on the *Seafaring New England* exhibit. Mr. Mondello is with the Salem Police Department."

"How interesting," he said. "There is a police museum in my birth city of Kerala, on the Malabar Coast of India. Perhaps you will visit there one day. Meanwhile, I hope to introduce some quite amazing articles in a display planned for the *Seafaring New England* exhibit."

Michael left us to answer another *ding-dong* of the summoning doorbell. As he walked away from us, I couldn't help noticing his black leather ankle boots. Professor Bidani hailed a passing waitress. "Our host has made a special effort to introduce some Indian sweets." He indicated the dainty triangular pastries on the tray. "These are called *kottayam churuttu*. My mother used to make them, but I understand that now you can buy them online." He graciously posed for a picture with the pastries. We, along with the students, added the crispy triangles to our plates. He was right. They were delicious, and I wondered if Aunt Ibby had the recipe.

The conversation in the adjoining living room grew a bit louder. Maybe the other special guest, Kitsue Sullivan, had arrived. I hoped so. Her personal connection to Salem's history and the long-ago China trade held great intrigue for me. My guess was correct. When Michael Martell returned to the kitchen, he was hand in hand with a very attractive young woman. Asymmetrically styled, straight black hair complemented her fair Irish complexion. The slight almond tilt to her brown eyes gave a mischievous look to the classic oval-shaped face. She had what I call "smiley eyes"—eyes that looked as if she was smiling even if the lower half of her face was masked somehow. I've wished for eyes like that. I wished I could wear my hair straight like hers, too, but these curls cannot be tamed. Michael introduced us once again as Mr. and Mrs. Mondello. Her handshake was firm, her smile genuine.

"I've been looking forward to meeting you in person, Ms. Barrett," she said. "I've always enjoyed watching you on television, and I'm thrilled that you'll be doing the documentary."

"I've been looking forward to meeting you, as well," I told her. "I understand you're a direct descendant of one of Salem's early seafaring adventurers to faraway lands."

"Yes. Captain Edward Anthony Sullivan. I'm proud to say he was my four-times-great-grandfather." I liked her at once. She turned a bright smile in Sant Bidani's direction. "Great to see you again, Professor Bidani," she said, then explained, "We met at the museum. We were each checking out our allotted spaces." She gave a teasing grin, then shook his hand. "He's got center stage, but I like my alcove, so it's okay." She moved on, pausing to greet others in the kitchen. I heard her ask Michael, "Has my sister arrived yet? It was so kind of you to let me invite her to tag along at the last minute. Her work keeps her out of town so much that she spends very little time in Salem anymore." She spoke to each of the students and to my aunt and Mr. Pennington, then practically danced away back to the living room.

"Want to see what's going on in the other room?" I whispered to Pete, noticing that some of the people who'd been sitting on the couch had joined us in the pink-and-gray, chrome and Formica–themed 1950s kitchen, and a few of the students had already followed Kitsue Sullivan to the adjoining sunroom.

"Let's sit on that couch, Pete," I said. "I want to see if it's comfortable as well as authentic." There was already an older couple we knew from Winter Street on one end of the long sofa. We said "Hello" and "Mind if we join you?" and sat beside them, leaving plenty of room between us for another guest or two. I took a tiny bounce as we sat. "Yep. It's comfortable."

Pete gave a wave at the growing pile of gifts on

the coffee table. "He won't open these while we're here, will he?" he asked, with a surreptitious peek at his watch. "It would take all night."

"Nope. He won't," I told him. "It's not like a baby shower, where everybody brings a present. You open housewarming gifts after everybody leaves."

"Good," he said. He switched to quiet cop voice. "This is a perfect spot for watching people. Backs to the wall. We can see anybody who comes in the front door and then see who they talk to, how they act."

"Is that a professional point of view? Are you looking for anything in particular?" The observation surprised me.

"In a way, yes," he said. "Had you noticed that a good many of the people here, as well as the guests of honor, are somehow connected to your museum show?"

"Now that you mention it, yes."

"So was Walter Wyman, and not in a good way."

I dropped my voice to match his near-whisper. "Are we looking for anything in particular?"

He half-smiled at the "we," and shrugged. "Just fact-gathering."

I realized I'd been fact-gathering too, but my observations had been about mid-century home furnishings, Indian cuisine, asymmetric hairstyles and housewarming gift etiquette. Murder hadn't crossed my mind for even a nanosecond.

Another ding-dong issued from the front door. Michael entered from the kitchen and, nodding and smiling to each of us as he passed by, hurried to admit another guest. The bell dinged again before he got there. Pete turned his head to focus on the entry hall. So did I. So did the couple at the other end of the couch.

"Impatient," commented the Winter Street neighbor woman.

"Indeed," agreed her male companion as the front door opened.

"Welcome. Come in," came Michael's hearty voice. "You must be Kitsue's sister."

"Fiona," she said. "Fiona Sullivan."

"I'm Michael Martell. I'm so pleased you could join us." He drew her into the living room. "Folks, please meet Fiona Sullivan."

The men stood. We all said, "How do you do?" The woman nodded. "Hello," she said, and, facing Michael, "Is Kitsue here?"

"I believe she's in the sunroom. Come along. We'll find her."

Pete and our couch-mate gentleman sat as Fiona Sullivan and Michael Martell whooshed past us—but not before I'd had a chance to make a few observations of my own.

Fiona was about the same height as her sister. No makeup. She hadn't brought a gift. She wore a white Aran knit sweater and acid-washed, boot-cut blue jeans, and she carried a large black leather purse. Her ankle boots were also black. Her short, bright blond hair was what might easily, if unkindly, be described as "frizzy." Without asking permission, as they passed, I grabbed a quick picture.

It didn't take long for us to excuse ourselves, leave the handsome couch, and follow our host and the newest guest toward the sunroom, where Kitsue Sullivan and two of the students, their backs to us, studied the record selection on the gorgeous 1950s Wurlitzer jukebox. I didn't feel the need to ask permission, since no faces showed, so I took another picture. "Surprise," Fiona called. We eased ourselves into the group and watched as the sisters embraced, exchanging joyous greetings. Martell once again performed introductions, and before long, with hardly any prompting, we learned that the two women had been born ten months apart. Fiona was the older, at twenty-seven.

"Ten months apart," Kitsue declared with a laugh. "That's what you call 'Irish twins.' "

"Our grandmother Kitty Sullivan wound up with the pleasure of raising both of us." Fiona's laugh was exactly like her sister's, and they shared the same almond tint to their warm brown eyes. "Our mum took off when we were three," she said, "and we were too much of a handful for Da to handle all by himself."

"He tried. Lord knows, he tried." Kitsue pulled a serious face, and the two went into a gale of sisterly laughter. I experienced a brief passing moment of regret that I was an only child. "So he shipped us off to Gram's house in North Salem," Kitsue reported. "She had plenty of room, so it was a good plan."

It was Fiona's turn to make a face. "Good thing she had plenty of room. It was stuffed to the rafters with antiques."

"Except for your room." Kitsue giggled. "It was steampunk *before* there was steampunk. All wheels and gears and a table full of your smelly science experiments." Her sister made no reply, simply smiled and looked away.

"Kitsue," I said, "Dr. Martell says you girls are descendants of one of Salem's early voyagers to China and that you'll have some primary source written material to share in your exhibit."

"Our four-times-great-granddaddy's letters and

papers," Fiona put in. "Kit has all that stuff, including dolls and dishes and dresses and God only knows what else. I guess it's a good thing she took care of it—I would have tossed it all out years ago."

"True," the younger sister agreed. "I'm the hoarder in the family."

"Kit even has four-times-great-grandma's old shoes and her cereal bowl." Fiona giggled and make-believe punched her sister's arm.

Pete entered the conversation. "I understand you don't visit Salem very often. Has the city changed much since your last visit?"

My cop husband was in information-gathering mode. The simple question was gleaned from an overheard comment between Dr. Martell and Kitsue about her sister coming to the party at the last minute. Sort of an eavesdropped comment, actually. If Fiona chose to answer it, her answer could establish how long she'd been away, possibly where she'd been, and by noticing the changes in the old city, might indicate what her interests were. Would she comment on the proliferation of witch shops? The explosion of trendy new restaurants? The loss of some historic venues?

Fiona took a moment, appearing to think about her answer. "To tell the truth," she said, "I haven't missed the place a damn bit, and I won't stick around for long this time either. I just wanted to see Kit and help out with that horse and pony show she's gotten us mixed up in."

"Well-played," was my grudging inner comment. The woman had answered Pete's question without telling him anything new except that she had no love for her hometown.

CHAPTER 10

We left at a time my aunt would call "fashion-ably early." Not the first to leave the party, but not among those who'd still be at the bar at ten o'clock. When we said our "good-byes," Aunt Ibby and Mr. Pennington lingered in the kitchen chatting with a couple of fellow movie buffs.

The evening was pleasantly cool, and a three-quarter moon shone through tree branches illu-minating our pretty street. We were barely out the door when I voiced the question, "Well, what do you think about Fiona? The jeans? The boots? The frizzy hair? Coincidence?"

"Remember, my love," he said gently, "the boots and jeans exist in a mirror, and you've told me plenty of times that you never know what the vi-sions mean. Besides, a half dozen people there tonight wore jeans, and at least three had ankle boots A tiny glimpse of hair that stuck out from under a dark blue hoodie isn't much to go on either. Anyway, remember the gray-haired lady who was next to us on the couch? She has frizzy hair too."

I thought about his non-answer. "Overprocessed and a bad perm," I said. "It seemed to me that Fiona turned away whenever she saw the camera."

"Did she? There were a lot of people moving around. Did you ask to take the picture?"

"Of course. Nobody at all ever said no to the pictures all evening, but she just turned her head away every time. I think we should try to learn more about Fiona."

"I think so too. Fiona hasn't been in Salem for very long. I'll circulate the hoodie photo again and see if any of Walter Wyman's friends know who she—if it is a she—is." We strolled toward our half of the house. "It's still early," Pete observed.

"Only nine thirty," I agreed.

"I'm still hungry," he said. "You?"

"Those tiny sandwiches weren't very filling," I agreed.

We'd reached our front steps. "Have we got anything good in the refrigerator?" Pete's voice was hopeful.

"A little bit of leftover lasagna and maybe some cooked carrots."

"Want to go to Greene's?" he asked. Greene's Tavern was one of our favorite places. It's in one of Salem's oldest waterfront neighborhoods—a cozy place with a big stone fireplace and comfortable booths, a few big-screen TVs, and good pub grub—pizza and nachos and hot dogs and some good local craft beers along with the usual brands. The owner, Joe Greene, is dad to one of my first

TV Production students, Kelly Greene. I'd stayed in touch with her, and I knew she still took some classes at the Tabby and sometimes worked evenings at the tavern. I was interested to see if she'd met Professor Bidani yet.

"Love to," I said. "Your car or mine?"

"Let's take your Jeep. I like driving it." We cut through the side yard, climbed into the Jeep, and headed out into the moonlight in search of something good to eat. Greene's did not disappoint. I'd just finished the last bite of my hot dog with mustard and relish, and Pete had a nearly empty plate of chicken wings in front of him when a breathless Kelly slid into the booth and sat opposite us.

"Whew. Busy night. I've got a few minutes to sit down and catch up with what's going on with you guys," she said. "I've barely seen you two since the wedding. Lee, I heard at school that you're doing a documentary."

"I am. Did you hear about it at Professor Bidani's lecture?"

She looked surprised. "No. He was in the history department. I'm taking creative writing this year. Fenton Bishop is my teacher. He talks every day about the documentary you'll be doing. He wants all of us to go to the museum as soon as it opens. He wants us to write about Salem history—leaving out the witches—concentrating on the old days, when Salem was the richest city in America because of the sailing ships."

"Michael Martell—Fenton Bishop is our next-door neighbor," Pete told her. "Interesting man."

"He sure is. I love his Antique Alley books. I just finished reading *The Purloined Painting*. Have you read it?"

Pete shook his head and looked at me. "Lee?"

"I don't think so," I said. "He's written so many. What's it about?"

"It's the one where the antique shop owner buys a painting from an old friend and then finds out it was stolen from a museum and it's worth millions."

"Maybe I ought to read it," Pete said. "I'm in charge of security for Lee's museum, and I'd be interested in how they messed up and the painting got stolen in the first place."

"It's not *my* museum!" I laughed at the idea. "I'll be sure to read it anyway, but between the Salem police and the insurance companies, I don't think a mouse could get past all the alarms and cameras and security gadgets that will be in place when the museum opens."

"It's only a story." She stood up. "Gotta get back to work. But you guys be careful. The old friend in the book gets murdered. Can I get you some more wings, Pete?"

"No thanks, Kelly." He pushed the plate toward her. "This was plenty. We were at a little party earlier and the food was good, but the portions were kind of dainty, if you know what I mean."

"Oh my gosh. I'll bet you were at Bishop's— Martell's housewarming party because you live next door." She sat down again. "Right? A couple of my classmates were invited because their parents are friends of his. How was it?"

"It was nice. His house looks fabulous. All kinds of great vintage furniture. Hold on a sec. I've got a few pictures." I turned the phone in her direction and scrolled through the images. "Check out the living room," I said, "and wait until you see the sunroom, and the pink-and-gray, fifties-style kitchen. I'm going to try to get my boss to do a feature on the place."

Kelly "oohed" and "aahhed" in all the right places. She pointed to the screen. "Oh, look, there's Fenton Bishop himself. Who's the blonde?"

Pete and I both focused on the camera. "Where?" Pete asked, as I turned it to face us.

"Her name is Fiona Sullivan." I took a close look at the shot. The woman was partially facing Michael Martell and about three-quarters of her face showed in the photo. "She's Kitsue Sullivan's older sister."

"I read about Kitsue in the *Salem News*. Something about old letters from sea captains or something like that. I love her name. Kitsue. So cute." I turned the phone back in her direction. "Look at that jukebox," she said. "You can tell by the books he writes that he knows a lot about antiques. And cats," she said. "He sure knows a lot about cats too."

"He's going to get one of his own," I told her. "We gave him a cat door for his housewarming gift."

"That's so cool," she said. "Can I get you two anything else? Another dog, Lee?"

I patted my tummy. "I couldn't eat another crumb. Thanks, Kelly. It's always good to see you."

"We'll take the check and go along," Pete said. "And I'll take special care about the museum paintings. We wouldn't want any million-dollar artwork to get—um—purloined."

"I'm sure they'll all be safe with you guys on the case." She cleared the table and favored us with a big smile. "Be right back."

We watched her walk away. "As soon as we get

home," Pete whispered, "let's blow that picture of Fiona up and see how it compares with the hoodie girl."

"Absolutely "

"You know something, Lee?" Thoughtful cop voice. "Like Kelly said, that Fenton Bishop book is only a story, but in *our* museum case, there's already been a murder."

He said our *museum case*. Murder or not, that made me smile.

CHAPTER II

The lights were still on at Aunt Ibby's house when we drove down Winter Street, but we didn't stop. It would have been interesting to get her take on Martell's party—and the guests in attendance—but as Pete pointed out, she'd probably feed us, and neither of us needed more food. Anyway, she does some training of volunteers at the library on Saturdays, so she'd probably be heading for bed soon.

"I'll call her in the morning," I promised. "I have the day off, you know." I couldn't help rubbing it in, knowing Pete had to work. "But," I added to soften the blow, "I'll take another trip over to the museum, so it'll count as a workday."

"Chief Whaley's going to be in at noon," Pete said, apparently not minding my lighter schedule. "I'll run our pictures of Fiona and the hoodie girl by him and see what he thinks. Our forensics team has equipment that measures facial features within the fraction of an inch. There's room for error, of course—especially with the sunglasses and the hoodie. It's a shot in the dark, but it could be the break we've been looking for."

"It would connect Fiona to Walter for sure—even if nothing was 'purloined' from the truck." I said, enjoying using the old-fashioned word.

We parked the Jeep behind the house as usual and entered via the sunroom door. O'Ryan was curled up on the bentwood bench's soft cushion, and he looked up in annoyance when Pete clicked on the overhead light. "Oops. Sorry, old man," Pete apologized, turning off the light. "We're just passing through. We'll be in the kitchen if you want to join us."

We were clearly both anxious to get on with our own photo-comparison experiment. I enlarged my photo of Fiona and Michael and printed it, then edited Michael out of the frame and printed that one too. Meanwhile Pete accessed his fuzzy surveillance Hoodie Girl shot, and using the trusty magnifying glass from the junk drawer, we took turns examining them.

"What do you think?" I asked, passing the glass to him. "There's nothing really distinctive about Hoodie Girl's eyebrows, is there? Besides, anybody can change their whole look with a pair of tweezers or a brush full of hot wax."

Pete cringed slightly at the hot wax mention, but he didn't comment on it. "I know. Too bad we can't see Hoodie Girl's eyes through the sunglasses. Both of the Sullivans have distinctive eyes," he said. "Fiona called them 'Irish twins.' If it wasn't for the hair color, they'd look like real twins, don't you think so?"

"You're right," I said. "Hey, look, O'Ryan has decided to join us." The cat hopped up onto one of the other Lucite chairs, putting his forepaws on the edge of the table. "Want to look at the pictures, O'Ryan?" I asked, putting the three printouts in front of him.

Turning his head from side to side, he seemed to be studying each one. At least it seemed that way to me. Pete gave a headshake, a sigh, and an eyeroll. "What do you expect him to do? Choose the most important one?"

"Only if he wants to. Which *is* the most important one, O'Ryan?"

The cat looked at me, then at Pete, and put a big yellow paw on the picture of Hoodie Girl.

"Random pick," Pete said, moving the pictures around on the table, changing the order. "See if he'll pick the same one again."

Of course, he did. Three times, actually.

"So, he likes Hoodie Girl best," Pete grumbled. "What does that mean?"

"Beats me," I admitted. "Just that she's the most important part of our case so far."

"So far," he echoed. "And we don't even have the murder weapon yet."

"But do you still think it could be Wyman's own gun?"

He shrugged, glancing sideways. "I believe it was, and it's still missing."

By this time, O'Ryan, possibly bored with the game, got down from the chair and scampered into the living room, probably on his way to the upstairs bedroom. I wasn't bored at all. "Hoodie Girl is connected to Walter Wyman," I reasoned. "It doesn't make sense that she was just a hitch-hiker. He doesn't seem like the kind of man who'd risk his job for a stranger looking for a ride."

"What if she's a stranger who was willing to pay a lot of money for a ride?" Pete asked. "What if it was enough money to be worth taking a risk?"

"Does that stranger have to have some kind of a connection to the museum?" I asked.

"I think so. Yes," he said. "Then the question is, 'When did she get out of the truck?'"

"Did Walter make any other stops between the time Hoodie Girl shows up on the surveillance tapes and the time he got shot?"

"There's nothing like that on his work order. If he stopped anywhere else, he did it on his own," Pete said, "and that was unlike him."

"Seems so," I agreed, realizing that Pete was actually discussing an ongoing case with me—something he'd felt unable to do ever since we first met. Was it because we're married? Or because I'm no longer a 'reporter'? Either way, I knew I loved this new part of our relationship, and that I'd treat it with great care.

I tucked the magnifying glass back into the junk drawer, closed the laptop, carefully put the photos into an envelope, and went upstairs. O'Ryan was, as we'd suspected, already asleep at the foot of the big bed. We changed into our individual sleeping attire—frothy pink nightie for me, boxers for Pete—fluffed up the pillows, and pulled up the covers. "Want to turn on the TV and catch the end of the late news?" Pete kept his voice low so as not to disturb the sleeping cat.

"Yes, let's. I'm still wide awake. Must be the hot dog." The TV came to life, volume low, and Buck Covington's handsome face came into view above a *Breaking News* banner. "They seem to be calling darn near everything 'breaking news' lately," I said, "whether it's important or even new. I think I'll ask the graphics people to come up with something else—or why not just read the prompter and let the viewer decide?"

What Buck told us then, though, *was* both new and important—to me, anyway. "WICH-TV has learned that in the matter of the recent death of Walter Wyman, the armored truck driver whose body was found behind a closed local branch bank, police examination of the dry leaves that covered the body has revealed a spent bullet."

I sat up straight. "No kidding!" Pete lay down flat and stared at the ceiling. "Damn!"

The screen showed the original shot of the pile of leaves they'd shown right after the body had been found. I realized that my boots-and-leaves vision had shown that exact picture—but with the boots added. "Did you know that?" I asked Pete. "About the bullet being found?"

"Yeah. The team sifted through all the leaves in the area. I mean, like every dumb leaf. A single bullet showed up this afternoon. Most likely it's the one that killed Wyman. Damn!" he said again. "I wonder who leaked this. Forensics isn't even through with it yet." This was something he hadn't chosen to share with me, so I didn't press for information, just watched the screen and waited to see if Buck would tell us more. He didn't add to the story—just advised everyone to stay tuned to WICH-TV for more on this ongoing murder investigation, then tossed the program over to the sports announcer with the latest national baseball scores. I waited to see if Pete would add to the story. He didn't—he just sat up straight in bed, punched the pillows behind him into shape, and exhaled an exasperated sigh. "Want to see if River has a good movie on tonight?" he asked.

"Might as well," I agreed, now even more wide awake than I'd been before—and not blaming it on the hot dog anymore.

As usual, Buck gave a quick promo about River's show, then added that he'd be on hand to shuffle the tarot deck. Whenever he did that, it boosted her already-significant audience. *Tarot Time with River North* sometimes beats one of the national late-night comedy shows. The commercials began, and my imaginary program director hat was firmly in place. I counted and timed and calculated the revenue involved, noting which one might be a possible sponsor for one of my other shows, and almost missed the announcement of the late movie.

"Tonight's scary movie is *The Bad Seed.*" Buck read the title with a lighthearted tone. I'd seen it before on the classic movie channel, and as I remembered it, there was nothing lighthearted about the plotline of a sweet, innocent-looking, little blond-haired girl whose mother, there was good reason to suspect, might be a psychotic killer.

"Have you seen it?" I asked Pete. "It's a nightmare-inducer. I don't think it would set well on top of champagne, hot dog, and those Indian pastry things."

"I'll pass," Pete said and turned off the set. I was still wide awake, and I could tell he was too. My mind was reeling with so many thoughts. I wanted to talk about Walter Wyman and the bullet the police had found in the leaves, and about the museum connection to his death and the undisturbed cargo he'd had in the armored truck, and River's reading about the boots and leaves and about a blond girl in a hoodie and about Irish twins.

"What kind of bullet?" I spoke into the darkness.

"Nine-millimeter," Pete answered. "Same as I use in my off-duty gun. Same as Walter Wyman used in his gun. But one is enough to match up with a weapon."

"If you had the gun," I said.

"We're sure it was his. He used to do some target shooting with it, so we have other bullets to compare. It was his," he repeated. "Don't worry, babe. We'll get the guy—and we'll get whoever it is who leaked the story about the bullet too. That really ticks me off."

"I could tell," I said, snuggling a little closer to him. "I'm not worried—just curious. Like, why would someone kill an armored truck driver when nothing is missing from the armored truck? They must have killed him over something else. Even something that has nothing to do with the museum at all."

"Maybe." Thoughtful cop voice. "Maybe Hoodie Girl *was* just a hitchhiker, and *she* has nothing to do with the museum either. And just *maybe* Hoodie Girl has the missing gun."

That possibility had occurred to me, too, and I didn't like it—didn't even want to think about it, and I told him so. "I don't want to think that," I said. "But hey, maybe the leaves in my vision only mean 'fertility, growth, and openness,' and the boots just mean I'll get fired again."

CHAPTER 12

Sometimes on Saturday mornings, if we both have the day off, we cook breakfast together. Pete didn't have the whole day off, but he didn't have to go on duty until noon, so we decided we'd make blueberry pancakes. Of course, we used pancake mix and canned blueberries, but the general effect was delicious, and we had that real maple syrup to top it off.

We carried our coffee mugs and plates out to the sunroom, where the rays of morning sun had yet to reach. "Everyone liked how Martell's sunroom has a theme," I mused. "Do you think ours needs one?"

"It has a theme," he said. "It's full of things we like to look at. Your carousel horse, my Patrice Bergeron–signed hockey stick, your bentwood bench, the footstool my nephew Donnie Jr. made for me in shop class. I like it the way it is—and I'm sure we'll keep adding to it." He was absolutely right. Actually, I'd been thinking lately about buying a small ship model to go on the coffee table.

"I like it here too," I agreed. "Since you have the morning off, want to come with me to the museum and see how the painting and fixturing is coming along? There might even be some displays in place."

"Yes. I heard yesterday that private security people are already on duty there now. I'd like to take a look at it with you." That was exactly what I wanted to hear. We'd each dressed casually. Pete would come home later to change from jeans and a New England Patriots sweatshirt into work clothes, and since I didn't expect to be on camera any time soon, I wore jeans, too, with a white shirt, blue cardigan, and sneakers. We took separate cars, in case one or the other had to leave, and found parking spaces next to each other right behind the building. I held my press card up to the window in the door, and Pete opened his wallet and displayed his badge. Once again, George Washington admitted us. "Hi, George. This is my husband, Pete Mondello. "

George offered out a freshly paint-spattered hand to Pete. "Detective Mondello has been here before. Glad to see you both. There's been a lot of progress since you were here last, Ms. Barrett—I mean Mrs. Mondello." He waved his arm toward the main room. "Professor Bidani is here already, checking on the giant glass tube they're installing."

Giant glass tube? "Let's check that out," I said, heading for the main entrance, Pete close behind me. We could hardly miss it. A gigantic, round glass column stood in the center of the round raised platform I'd seen earlier. The thing was about eight or nine feet tall and had a normal-sized door in it. I recognized Professor Bidani, pacing around the perimeter. "Amazing," I breathed. "But what the hell does it do?"

"Glass rocket launcher?" Pete joked. "Let's ask him."

Professor Bidani noticed us almost immediately and stepped down from the carpeted platform. "I see questions in your eyes," he said. "A spectacular display case, isn't it?"

"It certainly is," I agreed. "What will it display?"

"It's a brand-new museum concept," he explained. "The glass shell is of shatterproof-, bullet-proof-tempered glass. The display piece itself will go inside. It's a spiraling column of Lucite shelves, each shelf featuring jeweled items from several periods of Indian history. And to make it extra-special, the whole thing revolves on the base. Quite high-tech. It will contain the treasures of maharajas over the centuries. Can you picture it?"

"No wonder you rated center stage! People will come from all over the country to see it. Will WICH-TV be permitted to film the installation?" I asked, almost breathlessly.

"I don't see why not," Bidani said. "There'll be special security measures in place as soon as the jewels begin arriving from the other museums. There'll be special lighting, too, to display them to the best advantage. I'm quite excited about it."

"I am too," I assured him. "What an honor for Salem this is going to be—and an honor for me to be able to document it."

Pete had begun to walk slowly around the column. I knew he was concentrating on the security aspects involved. It isn't every day a maharaja's fortune in jewels gets to be housed in an old A&P building. This was big-time. "Will guards be posted here in the room—day and night?" he wanted to know.

"Yes, indeed. And also, the tube and spiral can be moved to the next exhibition quite easily by truck, and the jewels themselves will be securely transported by special courier."

"Holy cow! What is it?" The female voice came from behind us. Before I could turn around, another voice called out, "Wow!" The Sullivan sisters had joined us.

Professor Bidani, smiling, arms outstretched, welcomed the two. "Come closer, Kitsue and Fiona. Come and see the latest in museum-display fixtures. You know the Mondellos? I've just begun explaining to them how it works." There was a fast exchange of greetings, and the two women joined us at the carpeted base of the not-yet-revolving, sparkling glass column.

"It's amazing, Sant." Fiona, carrying the large black leather bag we'd seen at the party, began a slow walk around the structure, much the way Pete had. *She's on a first-name basis with the professor.* Kitsue followed her older sister, circling the thing. Pete joined me a few feet away from the action, as I focused my camera on the center platform, wishing with all my heart that I had Francine and the mobile unit crew here to film this properly. I wondered if the spiral shelves would be installed by Tuesday. And what about the jewels? When could we expect them to arrive? So, I asked.

"The spiral is due for installation tomorrow," Professor Bidani explained, "but the jewels will not be in place until a short time before the opening of the museum. They span the centuries—all the way from the early seventeenth century up to the twentieth century."

Kitsue had joined us, while Fiona gazed up toward the top of the glass shell, and the professor backed up on his narrative and explained the workings of the Lucite spiral and the various shelves that would hold the jewels.

"It's wonderful, Sant," Kitsue told him. *First names all around.* "Ours is a much simpler display, of course, but I think once everything is in place, it will tell an important story of Salem's seafaring past that people will appreciate."

"It will, indeed, my dear," the professor agreed. "From the photos you've shared with me, the items you and your forebears have preserved are gems and jewels of Salem's rich maritime history."

"Photos?" I interrupted, apologized for interrupting, and said again—"Photos?"

"For the museum's guidebook," Kitsue explained. "Fiona took them for me over a month ago, before we packed everything up. She's an expert photographer, you know." *No, I didn't know.*

"Would it be possible for me to see them?" Fingers crossed. "It would save me so much time if I could write down some brief descriptions of some of the major items before I begin to prepare the narrative for the documentary."

"Sure. We even wrote up some brief descriptions to go with the pictures. You're welcome to see both." Kitsue flashed the smiley-eyed grin. "Give me your number, and I can send the whole package to you. How would that be?"

"Perfect," I said, fishing in my purse and handing her one of my new cards. "Thanks so much. When I was here last, your alcove looked as if most of the cases and fixtures are in place. It won't be long before you'll be able to fill them up with your treasures—or as Professor Bidani says, your gems and jewels." I returned her smile—even though I'm not blessed with those smiley eyes.

"Some of them are already here," she reported. "We're here again with Fiona's tool bag." She glanced around the room. "Now, where did my sister get to? She's the one with the tape measure."

Fiona's "tool bag"? Pete and I exchanged glances.

"I think she just ducked into your alcove." Pete pointed to the second arch on the left.

"She doesn't think I need to include every little thing," Kitsue explained. "She's such a minimalist. But I think a good museum display is a little bit cluttered—like somebody's attic, you know? I'd better go and find her." She turned and faced us before she entered the alcove. "I think my four-time-great-grandma's shoes are beautiful."

I made a mental note to look up what women's shoes looked like in the mid-1800s, then tugged on Pete's sleeve. "Want to go up to the second floor with me and see what's happening up there?"

"Sure," he said. "Stairs or outdoor elevator?"

"Stairs will be fine. There was a lot of work to be done last time I checked it out." The lighted sign that read *Stairs* was at the rear of the main room. Pete, with his hand at my elbow, steered me to the narrow staircase. "So, Fiona carries tools?" I prodded.

"Seems so," was the casual-cop answer—complete with subject change: "Does the second floor look too much like an attic?" Now there was concern in his voice.

There was clearly not going to be a discussion about purse contents. So, I answered the question. "Not too bad, and they were getting ready to paint it white up there. That will help a lot." When we reached the top step, I was more than pleasantly surprised. Dingy gray walls were now white, and at the far end of the room, a stage had been built and blue velvet curtains made it look like a proper theater. Rows of folding chairs were in place, awaiting an audience.

"Know what?" Pete said. "I wouldn't be surprised if they'll want to show your documentary up here."

I hadn't thought about that possibility, but I was quite sure Bruce Doan would like the idea, and I must admit, I liked it too. There were glass-topped cases here, as well as a long floor-to-ceiling display window. A disturbing note was the dismembered parts of mannequins lying at the bottom of the window—heads and bodies and arms and legs awaiting costuming. I tried to picture the finished product—seaman's uniforms, women's period dresses, perhaps with colorful murals in the background. The body parts were hard to unsee. "Okay," I said to Pete. "Let's go back downstairs and see how the Sullivan girls are doing."

Fiona was still where we'd left her, chatting with Professor Bidani, but now he'd opened the door to the glass column and the two stood just outside, looking into the empty space. "Kitsue is probably in the alcove. Let's go see what's going on in there."

There was a lot going on—or there had been since I'd last seen the alcove. There were several glass-topped display cases lined up along the three walls, and paintings, portraits, and even framed pieces of clothing brightened the white walls. Kitsue wasn't alone in the room. George was there, helping her center a glass-topped showcase beneath a framed portrait of a woman.

"Hello, Lee—and Pete. It's coming along nicely, don't you think so? Fiona did the wainscoting, and look. George helped me get my great-great-great-great-grandmother Sullivan's cloud collar positioned just right." She thanked George, then handed him what appeared to be a cash tip as he left the alcove.

I joined her in front of the case and looked over her shoulder. The item I saw was circular, with scalloped edges and a hole in the middle. The fabric was of creamy-colored, aged-looking silk and was embroidered all over with the most delicate of tiny stitches. "A cloud collar?" I asked.

"The collar went on over her head, covering the top of her dress. See how the edges look like clouds? She made this herself. She made the one that's on her wedding dress too. It's even more intricate than this one. It was an important part of a Chinese bride's wedding dress." She looked up and pointed to the portrait. "See how beautiful she looked?"

A Chinese bride? I looked at the portrait. The brass plate on the frame read *Li Jing Sullivan 1825–1882.* The woman was seated. She wore a fanciful, crownlike headdress of flowers, and her gown was in layers of red and gold, topped with a cloud collar like the one I was looking at in the case. She was, indeed, beautiful.

I managed to say so. "She is beautiful. May I take a picture?"

"Of course. You sound surprised." Kitsue looked

at my face. "Didn't I mention before that she was Chinese?'

I looked at Pete. He was clearly surprised too. "You didn't mention it," I said, snapping pictures of the cloud collar and the portrait. "She is absolutely fascinating. Please tell me all about her."

"Well, as you can imagine, a mixed-race marriage like that one—an Irish American immigrant and a young girl from China—was highly unusual in old Salem. But it was a true love story. Edward Sullivan had been a fisherman in Ireland. He came to America and got a berth on one of Joseph Peabody's ships. Before long, he became a captain of another Peabody ship and made several trips to China. That's where he met Li Jing. Her daddy was a merchant. They fell in love, and he convinced her to run away with him aboard the ship. The story goes that she made many voyages with him, and that, in time, Edward's papers tell us, 'because of her sweet nature and generous heart, she was eventually accepted into Salem society.' " Kitsue smiled her lovely smile. "She was called Li—spelled *L I*—same as you are, Lee."

"I like that," I said. "I understand that you have Edward's papers and letters?"

"Lots of them. Most of the grandmothers all the way down the line have been hoarders—like me. I'm sure some things have been lost, but my own grandmother, Kitty Sullivan, made me promise I'd take care of all of it. So I have."

"Kitty?" I said. "Is that who you're named for?"

"Only half. My other grandmother is Suzanne, So—Kitsue."

"And Fiona? That's such a pretty name too."

"We're not sure about that. Grandma said she might have been named for an old girlfriend of Da's."

"You're close with your grandmother."

"Yes. She's never made any secret of the fact that I'm her favorite. I'm the sole heir to all this"—she waved an arm, indicating all of the alcove—"and more. It will be mine to preserve for future generations to enjoy." She flashed a mischievous grin and whispered, "I used to eat my breakfast cereal out of a white jade bowl worth a million dollars."

CHAPTER 13

Following that jaw-dropping remark, Fiona rushed into the room, bearing the leather bag and a professional-looking tape measure—the kind that winds itself up, not the yellow cloth kind like the one in Aunt Ibby's sewing basket. "Okay," she said, "let's make sure everything lines up right." Pete excused himself then, saying he had to go to work. A quick side-hug, and he was gone.

Kitsue patted the top of the display case containing the cloud collar. "See if this is centered, will you? George and I just eyeballed it, and I know you like things just so." We were obviously not going to hear any more about the women's four-times-great-grandparents just then—or about that jade cereal bowl. Fiona knelt beside the case and began measuring—sideways and up and down.

"Not bad, Kit." Fiona nodded approval. "Not perfect, but not worth moving it. Anything else?"

"Maybe you could put some chalk marks on the floor where the TV is going to be, and there's going to be a small desk near the entrance to the alcove where we can display brochures and put our purses and stuff," Kitsue answered, then spoke to us. "Fi has put together some films and still pictures of a few generations of the family. We'll show it on a continuous loop for the visitors."

I was enthused by the idea. "The more I learn about what's going to be right here in the Salem International Museum's very first show, the more excited I get about documenting it!"

"Your documentary is going to be a big hit." Kitsue spoke with confidence. "I hope you'll put a lot about the Sullivans in it."

"How could I not?" I asked. "You have a great story and plenty of beautiful things to back it up."

"Fi," Kitsue addressed her sister again. Fiona looked up from where she knelt on the chalk-marked carpet. "I told Lee we'd send her a set of the pictures you took for the museum catalog. Okay?"

Fiona appeared to be thinking it over, but after a moment she stood, and answered with a semi-reluctant, "Sure. Why not?" Another pause. "Doesn't WICH-TV have a budget for professional photos?"

It was my turn to pause. "I'm quite sure I can arrange payment for any of your work I use in the documentary," I told her. It was a subject that hadn't come up during my discussions with Bruce Doan. I'd ask next time I was at the station. Fiona nodded acknowledgment of my words, then carried the tape measure to a display case on the other side of the alcove.

"Is this the case where you want to put the old

shoes?" She faced her sister. "And do you still want to put the framed wedding dress right over it?"

"That's right," Kitsue answered. "I think they're absolutely beautiful together, don't you?"

That brought a shrug and an eye roll. "Yeah. Sure. Whatever you say." Fiona released the tape with what sounded to me like a defiant *snap*. I wished that Pete was still there. I wondered how he'd assess the relationship between the Sullivan sisters. Sometimes they seemed to have an enviable sisterly bond—one that I admired—but when it came to the historical aspects of their shared ancestry, it seemed to me they couldn't be further apart.

I shook the random thought away. I was here to create a documentary, not to analyze sibling rivalries, and the remark about the wedding dress intrigued me. "You couldn't possibly be talking about Li Jing's dress, could you?" I pointed to the portrait of Captain Edward Sullivan's beautiful long-ago bride.

Kitsue clapped delighted hands together. "Actually, we are. It's pretty threadbare, and the moths have nibbled on it here and there, and somebody must have hung it in the sunshine, because it's light-struck in places, but I've had it professionally cleaned and framed and I'm so pleased with the result. They did a wonderful job. It's definitely recognizable as Li Jing's dress."

Fiona's laugh was short and unfunny. "You ought to be pleased with how it turned out. Damn cleaning and framing of the ratty old thing cost a fortune." Kitsue didn't respond to the remark, and neither did I. Fiona's words just sort of hung there in the fresh paint–smelling air for a long moment, before Professor Bidani tapped on the side of the arched entrance to the alcove.

"Excuse me, ladies—Fiona? Could you come back with your tape measure? I need to be sure that the collapsible spiral will fit through the door. If it doesn't, we may have to adjust the angles of the shelves."

Fiona's features went through a remarkably fast change—from sullen and sulky to beatific joy—complete with those Sullivan smiley eyes. "No problem." She snapped the tape measure closed, raised one hand to pat her hair, picked up her bag, and joined the handsome Indian man at the alcove's entrance. "Glad to help." Kitsue and I exchanged glances as we watched the two disappear around the corner of the arch.

I searched for something to say—something to break the awkward silence. *The wedding dress!* Of course, the amazing fact that generations of Sullivan mothers and grandmothers and great-grandmothers had managed to find room in their homes—in their lives—to preserve the treasures soon to be displayed for the pleasure of the viewing audience of *Seafaring New England*. To my mind, seeing Li Jing's wedding dress alone would be worth the price of admission. "I can hardly believe that the wedding dress will be here in this room," I told Kitsue. "Now, please tell me about the shoes. Did they belong to Li Jing too?"

"Yes," she said. "I'm sure they were hers because they're so small. If you can come by tomorrow, I'll have them unpacked and ready to display. Of course, the professional display lady does the actual placement of everything. You saw what a perfect job she did on the cloud collar."

"I'll make a point of being here," I said. "Will the wedding dress be ready to hang too?"

She smiled. "I can hardly wait to see it in place myself."

I was about to leave, to drop by the station and make final plans for Tuesday with Francine, when I dared to ask Kitsue another question that had been on my mind. "About that million-dollar cereal bowl—were you kidding?"

"Not at all. It might be worth even more than a million dollars—and yes, I've been eating my breakfast cereal out of it, on and off, for most of my life."

"There's got to be a story behind that," I insisted. "Are you going to tell me about it?"

She tiptoed toward the arch and peeked around the corner. "Just making sure Fi isn't on her way back. She doesn't like to hear about it."

"A million-dollar cereal bowl," I marveled. "How can that be?"

"To tell the truth, until a year or so ago, I had no idea it was truly valuable." She dropped her voice. "I was watching one of those *Antiques Roadshow* programs, and there was a bigger version of my bowl. They called it a 'brush pot,' but it had soldiers, and trees on it, just like mine—and they said it was worth two million dollars. So, I took my bowl to an appraiser, and they said I should insure it for at least a million—so I did."

I couldn't resist a low whistle. "Wow. What makes it so valuable?"

"For starters, it's made out of a solid piece of white jade, and that's really rare." She kept her voice low, her eyes on the archway. "Besides, Li Jing brought it with her from China when she ran away from home to marry my four-times-great-granddaddy, Edward Sullivan."

"And now it's yours." I remembered she'd told us that she was her grandmother Kitty's "sole heir."

"Yes. My grandmother Kitty showed it to me when I was only three years old. It was—and still is—the most beautiful thing I have ever seen. She gave it to me outright for my tenth birthday. The carvings, the soldiers on horseback, the forest and the trees . . . perfection. You'll see it for yourself when the wall-hung china cabinets get installed."

I thought about the love and kindness my Aunt Ibby had shown me when I came to live with her, barely past three years old myself. I remembered the special privileges she'd given me, probably because my own parents had died so tragically. Maybe Kitsue's mother leaving when she was only three moved the grandmother to allow such a special indulgence. "She let you eat your cereal from it." I made the statement, knowing I was right.

She grinned. "Cap'n Crunch."

I thought about my own favorite childhood breakfast bowl. It was made from some kind of hard plastic and bore a colorful likeness of Big Bird. I was pretty sure—no, positive—that Aunt Ibby still had it stashed somewhere. Would my own children enjoy eating Cap'n Crunch from it? Would *their* children even know who Big Bird or Cap'n Crunch were? Would plastic still exist? A couple hundred years from now, would my bowl be a valuable antique? It was something to ponder. I promised Kitsue again that I'd be back the next day, waved good-bye to Fiona and the professor on my way out, and headed the Jeep toward the station.

I parked in my usual corner spot beside the sea-wall. I was pleased to see Francine's truck in the lot. I'd been looking forward to talking over the assignment with her, knowing it would be fun working together again. I rode Old Clunky this time, being careful to avoid looking at the shiny brass door. I'd seen things I didn't want to see on that polished, reflective surface more than once.

As soon as I approached the glass door leading to the second-floor reception area, I saw Francine inside. She spotted me at the same moment, and we practically flew into a happy hug. It had been a while since we'd had the opportunity to work to-gether—ever since my so-called promotion to pro-gram director. "Is it true?" she asked. "Are we going to be together for a whole documentary? That will be amazing!"

"It's true," I promised. "I'm pretty sure it could involve a couple of weeks before the museum opens. Of course, I still have to keep the program-ming moving, and you'll have other assignments too—but I have the feeling we'll be seeing a lot of each other from now on—and I couldn't be hap-pier."

Rhonda, watching our reunion, spoke up. "Hey, Lee. Doan said if you showed up, he has some questions about the museum show. Think fast. He saw you come in."

"Let's both go in," I suggested to Francine. "And let's both think fast."

"I'm buzzing him now," Rhonda said. "Go on in." Francine and I approached the door marked *Manager*. I tapped, waited for the "come in, it's open," and we stepped inside. "Rhonda says you have some questions for us," I began the conversation. He invited us to sit down, then leaned forward across his big desk.

"What I need to know from you, Ms. Barrett, is—how big a deal is this museum going to be—in the big picture? You've had a look around. Is it going to attract a lot of attention? Will people be lined up to get inside?"

"From what I've seen so far, sir—it's going to be a real blockbuster," I said, meaning every word. "Six months might not even be long enough before it moves on to Mystic."

"You two are all set to go on the documentary?"

We nodded in unison. "I can hardly wait to get started on Tuesday," Francine said.

"Good. Now, understand, I'm all in favor of you girls spending your time making the little video—you're on the payroll, anyway. What I need to know is, would it be worthwhile for the station to put some *real* money behind it? To be a sponsor?"

I'd seen the list of companies who'd already signed on as sponsors of the event. It was impressive. Banks, hospitals, hotel chains, a big local shopping mall. That seemed to me to represent big bucks. If I said "yes," what if the whole thing turned out to be a big flop? I didn't want to be responsible for Bruce Doan not getting his money's worth of anything. Francine backed off immediately, claiming she hadn't even seen the place yet.

"Well, Ms. Barrett, is it, or isn't it?"

"It's going to be a good show, but nothing is certain." I knew I sounded hesitant. "I mean, we're still in hurricane season. What if it got shut down for weather reasons? What if there was another pandemic? There are no guarantees. But here's an idea. Why don't you buy a full page in the show catalog? They'll use it here and in Mystic and Newport. Everyone who comes to the show will see it. It'll be full of fabulous photos. I've met one of the photographers. She's even willing to let us have some of her photos for the documentary for a reasonable cost. I can have her call you."

"Good thinking, Ms. Barrett," he said. "I don't want to risk the station's money on uncertainties. A catalog is something real, something you can hold in your hand. I like it." I liked it too. The station would be well represented without breaking the bank, I'd be able to make Fiona Sullivan smile because she'd be getting paid for her pictures, and—not incidentally, it might focus some attention on my documentary.

"While I'm here, I want to double-check on my programs," I told him, "and Francine and I will make sure the mobile unit is ready to roll on Tuesday." Sudden inspiration. "By the way, if you want an occasional standup from the museum site, we'll be ready to do it on short notice."

"Another good idea, Ms. Barrett," he said. "Let's do that. It might tie in with Scott's investigation into the murder of that Wyman fellow who was transporting museum goods."

While I loved the idea of even short reports from the field, I wasn't crazy about "tying in" with Scott Palmer's murder investigation. I put on a fake smile, and Francine put on a real one. "That sounds great, Mr. Doan," I said.

CHAPTER 14

I did as I'd promised, making sure everything was in order for the rest of the holiday weekend programming while Francine checked cameras and sound equipment. I reminded Rhonda to get the rates for museum catalog ads for Mr. Doan. Francine and I said good-bye to one another in the parking lot, with wishes for a happy holiday weekend, hugs, and a good-luck fist bump. Francine drove away in her truck, and I'd just unlocked the Jeep, when the converted VW van rolled past me, with Old Jim at the wheel and Scott Palmer leaning out of the passenger door window.

"Hey, Moon! Got a minute?" The van skidded to a stop, and Scott climbed out, not leaving me time—or space—to get away.

"What's up, Scott?" I asked, still holding on to the Jeep's door handle.

"You might be able to help me figure something

out." He held a large book in his hand. I saw the word *Witch* in bold print and recognized it right away as a Salem High School yearbook, not dissimilar in appearance to my own. *A yearbook?* I was interested.

"I'll try," I said. "Whose yearbook is it?"

"Walter Wyman's mother let me borrow it. I wanted to find out what kind of kid he was, you know? Like, what were his interests? All that stuff. She told me some personal things too. Like, he was a happy person. He loved his job. He was seeing a girl. You know. The cool human-interest details that my viewers love." I had to give Scott credit for doing that kind of research into what was basically a murder investigation.

"He must have been a good kid," I said, letting go of the car door handle and moving toward Scott. "No problems?"

"Right. Good student, ran track, member of the chess club, all that stuff." He held the book forward, open to a page full of pictures of students whose names began with *W*. I recognized a young, smiling Walter Wyman, with a list of his high school accomplishments beneath his picture. "So young," I sighed.

"Yeah. Sure. Young." He ruffled through the pages. "But I found out something else you might be able to help me with. See, last Friday, when I was trying to wrangle an invitation to Fenton Bishop's little house party, I got hold of the guest list from one of the caterers. A name turned up of somebody you might know. So, take a look at this." He held the yearbook forward again, this time opened to a different page—one with photos of Walter's classmates whose names began with *S*.

I recognized Kitsue Sullivan right away.

"Kitsue Sullivan," I gasped, taking the open book from him. "They were in the same class in high school."

"Right. So, you know her, right? Do you think you could get her to talk to me about him?"

My first thought: *Does Pete know about this?* I reached for my phone even before I answered Scott's question. "I know her, Scott, but I'm going to ask you to hold up on this until I talk to Pete. Remember, Walter Wyman was murdered, and so far, the killer is still at large. Let's not get a young woman involved at this stage. It could be dangerous for her—and for you too."

I hit Pete's number, holding up one hand, signaling Scott to wait a minute. "Pete? Did you know that Walter Wyman and Kitsue Sullivan were classmates at Salem High School? No? Well, Scott Palmer found their yearbook, and he wants to talk to Kitsue. I asked him to hold off until you check it out." I listened to Pete's reply, then spoke to Scott again. "Pete says he'll get right back to you. I'll text him your number. I guess you have to return that yearbook."

"I told Walter's mother I'd return it tonight."

I wanted to get a better look at it, and I knew where I could get a copy to study at leisure. Sometimes having an aunt who's a research librarian is very handy. I knew the library had a collection of Salem High Yearbooks back to the 1940s. My next call would be to Aunt Ibby. I texted the promised number to Pete, said good-bye to Scott, climbed into the Jeep, and hit Aunt Ibby's cell phone number, hoping she'd be at the library. She was. I explained what was going on, gave her the year I was interested in, then added, "Her older sister would have graduated a year earlier. She might have known him too. Could you get both yearbooks for me?"

She promised to bring both books with her when she left the library at five o'clock. I could hardly wait to get a good, long, careful look at them. Funny how the human mind can shift gears so readily. Mine had made a fast U-turn from cloud collars and maharajas' jewels all the way back to a body beneath a pile of leaves and a pair of jeans-clad legs and black ankle boots. Funny, too, how the two Sullivan sisters were connected to my museum documentary project, as well as to Pete's—and now Scott's—ongoing murder investigation.

I fully expected Pete would call me back after he finished talking with Scott. I'd just turned onto Essex Street when my phone buzzed. "Okay, babe. He agreed to hold off on talking to Kitsue Sullivan until I do it first. I complimented him on getting the information, and I had to agree to keep him in the loop if the yearbook connection turns up anything important. Now I need to get one of those yearbooks."

I told him about Aunt Ibby's promise to have the one he wanted on hand at five o'clock, along with the one from a year earlier with information on the other Sullivan sister.

He was quick to reply. "How about I drive over to the library? Do you think I could pick them up right now? It could be important."

"I'm on Essex Street right now," I told him. "just down the street from the library. I'll call my aunt, grab them, and bring them over to you."

"That'll be perfect. I'll be watching for you."

My ever-efficient aunt said she'd already pulled the yearbooks and checked them out. There was an empty parking space right in front of the library. I pulled a dollar bill from my wallet and looked around for the multi-space meter where you put in your money and your license plate number. *To heck with this. I'm in a hurry, and I'll only be inside for a minute.* Risking a parking ticket, I stuffed the dollar into my sweater pocket, ran up the stairs into the stately, old brick building and straight to the front desk, where she stood, books bagged and ready to hand off as I raced past, said "thanks," and zipped back out the door.

No ticket. I headed the Jeep toward Margin Street, where I knew Pete would be watching from his first-floor office window. Sure enough, I saw him there as I parked beside the building, the bagged yearbooks, unopened, on the seat beside me. I wanted so badly to take a peek at those pages—but I resisted the temptation and hurried to the front door of the police station. Pete was already there to meet me. "Come on back to my office," he said, "and let's see what we've got here."

It didn't take long for us to see what we had— even a fast look at the pages turned up some pretty darn interesting points. Both the Sullivan sisters were at Salem High during the same years Walter Wyman was, so it was entirely possible that one or both of them were acquainted with him. Pete pointed out that at the time of his murder, Wyman still lived with his mother—at a North Salem address. Kitsue had told us that she and Fiona had been raised in North Salem. Had they been neighbors as well as classmates?

I was busy making notes on my always-present

index cards. "See if Wyman's mother lives at the same address she did when he was in high school," I scribbled. "Find out exactly where the Sullivans lived too."

Walter's yearbook page told us he'd been on the career tech education track, and he had studied automotive technology and woodworking. Kitsue Sullivan had studied humanities, including the fine arts. Fiona had taken the career tech path, too, although a year earlier than Walter, and had apparently majored in secretarial skills. She'd also taken sewing during her junior and senior years, along with—not surprising, since we'd seen her tool kit—both woodworking and arts and crafts. With such divergent studies, and different graduating classes, Pete and I agreed it was highly unlikely that any of them had ever been in the same classroom at the same time.

"If they all lived in North Salem, they could have ridden on the same school bus," I suggested.

"That's possible, but I doubt school bus route records go back that far," Pete said, "and anyway, maybe somebody drove them to school. I wonder if they ate lunch together."

"No way to check that," I knocked down that idea. "I kind of doubt any of them sat at the 'popular kids' table.' " No class officers or star athletes or prom king or queens among the three."

We flipped pages back and forth in near silence for a while. "Clubs?" Pete murmured. "Walter was in the chess club. How about the girls?" I checked Fiona's page, and Pete looked at Kitsue's.

"Fiona was in the science club for four years and in the photography club for her last two," I reported.

"Kitsue was in the drama club," Pete said. "That's the only one I see listed under her name. Let's take another look at Walter's high school achievements." I pushed the Kitsue book in his direction. He turned once again to the *W* names and within seconds uttered a soft "Aha!"

I moved closer and looked at the page. "Aha what?"

He tapped the page. "Photography club his senior year. Same year Fiona was a member." It was our first real connection between the Sullivans and the dead driver. I made a note of that on a separate index card. We passed the books back and forth for a while longer, each of us making a few random notes.

"I'll make copies of the relevant pages and run them by the chief right after you leave," Pete said. "You'd better take the books home. We'll take another look at them tonight, then you can give them back to Ibby to return to the library."

"Good plan," I said. "I've already done my museum visit, met with Francine, and adjusted my holiday program schedule. I'm going to stop by the grocery store and pick up something for dinner. Any special requests?"

"Surprise me." He glanced around to be sure no one was watching, then gave me a kiss of longer duration than might be expected from an on-duty police officer.

CHAPTER 15

Hugging a grocery bag in each arm, I stepped over a pacing cat in the kitchen doorway, parked my purchases on the counter, and tossed my blue sweater onto the comfy wicker chair by the window where I like to sit to watch the weather and O'Ryan likes to sit to watch the birds. I pulled on an apron—one of my wedding shower gifts—with Kiss the Cook embroidered in orange on hot pink and got straight to work chopping, braising, stirring, pouring, sifting, mixing, timing. By the time Pete arrived home, our kitchen smelled really good. I'd followed Betty Crocker's recipe for beef burgundy, and so far, simmering on the back burner, both looks and aroma were perfect. I'd also tried my luck at corn bread from *The Tabitha Trumbull New England Cookbook*, Aunt Ibby's adaptation from a recipe by the wife of Oliver Wendell Trumbull, the founder of Trumbull's Department

Store—the venerable building now occupied by the Tabby.

I'd set the Lucite table with plates, soup bowls, tumblers, and silverware, with a bouquet of grocery-store fall flowers in the center—just to make it festive. I stacked the yearbooks on the kitchen counter with the Fiona book on top, and I put a few index cards and a couple of pens there, too, just in case we found something else worth noting about the Sullivan sisters and their possible connection to Walter Wyman.

"Everything looks amazing," Pete said when he arrived. "It smells amazing too. It's great coming home to all this—and to you." Another nice, long kiss, which could have delayed dinner if the stove's timer bell hadn't announced the corn bread was done. Reluctantly, I grabbed the pot holders and pulled the cast-iron skillet from the oven. "If you want to ladle out the stew, I'll cut the corn bread," I told him. O'Ryan strolled in from the sunroom and sat expectantly beside his red bowl. "And whoever finishes first gets to feed the hungry cat," I added.

Husband, cat, and I proceeded to thoroughly enjoy our dinners—even though some of the conversation necessarily revolved around murder. "What did Chief Whaley think about the yearbook connection between the Sullivan sisters and Walter Wyman?" was my first question.

"He was actually really impressed with what we've found," Pete said. "He even said to tell you 'thanks' for getting the yearbooks so fast."

"Wow. A compliment from the chief." I'm always surprised when Tom Whaley has a kind word for me. Our relationship from the first day we en-

countered one another has been a series of misun-
derstandings, screwups, and all-around bad vibra-
tions—but over time, things have gone a bit more
smoothly. "I plan to return them to Aunt Ibby later
tonight." We both looked toward the counter,
where books, index cards, and pens lay. "I thought
maybe we could take another peek through them—
see if we missed anything important—or at least
interesting."

"I'm glad you did. I've been thinking about that
too. Chief says we might need to talk to Wyman's
mother again—to see if she remembers the Sullivan girls at all. But he wants to put it off for a day
or so. It seems that Walter's funeral is Monday, and
he doesn't want to intrude since we don't actually
have anything new to go on."

"I didn't know that—about the funeral. Chief is
right. Another day or so won't make a lot of differ-
ence, I guess."

"Let's hope it doesn't." Stern cop voice. "We're
dealing with a killer—quite possibly an armed
killer at that. Walter's gun is still missing."

"Maybe I should go to the funeral," I suggested,
but hesitantly. "I'd like to see who shows up."

Pete grinned. "Did I ever tell you you'd make a
good cop?"

"Only about a million times," I said. "I think I'm
better at being a cop's wife." I had no desire to be
a part of the police department, but I had, not too
long ago, taken an online course in criminology.
Pete had taken it, too, but he'd continued with the
course and obtained a degree. I'd learned just
enough to be nosy when it came to any kind of
crime in my little world. The death of the armored
truck driver had made me very nosy, indeed, espe-

cially since the murder victim had been shot immediately after delivering goods to be displayed at the venue I'd been assigned to document. "So, you think it would be okay for me to go to Walter's funeral?" Pete helped himself to another bowl of stew and another triangle of corn bread.

"If you want to. But won't it be awkward for you? It's not as if you've ever met the man."

"He was a recent part of my *Seafaring New England* story," I insisted. "A small, sad part."

"Are you thinking maybe Fiona or Kitsue will be among the mourners?"

"Exactly," I said, slathering butter onto my corn bread. "Wouldn't you show up for a classmate's funeral?"

He shrugged. "Maybe. If I knew the person. I had classmates I'd never even met. Didn't you?"

I had to admit he was right. "Yeah," I said. "I guess I'm just nosy."

We finished our meal in companionable silence. I cleared the table. "Want ice cream and Sara Lee pound cake?" I still hadn't attempted homemade desserts.

"Sure. Then let's have some coffee and dig back into those yearbooks."

"You read my mind," I said, and before long, dishes (and red cat bowl) were in the dishwasher, leftovers plastic-wrapped and refrigerated. I poured the coffee, and Pete put the yearbooks, cards, and pens on the table. We were prepared to go to work, when O'Ryan hopped up onto one of the vacant chairs.

"Looks like we're going to have some help," Pete said, watching as O'Ryan stretched out a big yellow paw and tapped the top yearbook. It was the one with Fiona's picture and information in it. Pete pushed the book closer to the cat. "Here you go, big boy. You work on this one while Lee and I see what new information we can find in the other one."

I knew Pete was kidding about O'Ryan working on the Fiona book, but I watched as the cat nuzzled the edges of the book, his pink nose twitching with interest. Pete pulled his chair closer to mine and opened the Kitsue book to the page with her picture on it. The graduating class had apparently gone for conformity. The boys were all pictured in tuxedos—white shirts, black ties, and black jackets, and the girls wore boat-necked black tops. The only individuality showed in necklaces and earrings. Kitsue had conformed, wearing a simple gold cross on a slim gold chain. I couldn't tell about earrings—her long, straight black hair covered her ears.

"Hey, let's take another look at Fiona's yearbook," I said. "Weren't they all matchy-matchy in that one too? I can't imagine Fiona didn't find a way to be different."

"Good idea." Pete reached across the table, gently dislodging O'Ryan's right forepaw, which he'd managed to fit between the pages partway through the book. "Sorry," Pete told the cat. "I didn't mean to interrupt your browsing. We'll give it back in a minute."

"What page was he looking at?" I asked—too late. The book was firmly closed when Pete slid it down the table toward me.

"He wasn't really looking, just messing around with the pages. Here. Let's take another look at teenage Fiona."

I doubted O'Ryan had been "just messing around." Although he loved being read to, he rarely paid attention to books of any kind unless they were important somehow. I gave the cat an apologetic pat on the head. "Don't worry. We'll give it right back to you." I told him, and opened it to the pages where students with names beginning with *S* were pictured.

"Wow!" I exclaimed. "When we looked at the book before, I didn't compare her picture to the other girls on the page. Maybe I should have." The dress code for Fiona's senior class had been similar to her younger sisters. Boys in tuxedos, girls in black boat-necked tops. Fiona had found a way to make the photo her own. The sewing class might have been responsible for the custom look of her top. Hers looked like velvet, while all the others might have been cotton or linen, and the boatneck had been converted to an off-one-shoulder effect—just enough to display a butterfly tattoo. The trademark frizzy bleached hair was already there, just a tad lighter than the present do—and giant, gold hoop earrings matched a smaller eyebrow ring. Black lipstick and a black velvet choker completed the look of a wannabe rebel.

"Interesting," Pete said, "but I don't see anything we missed in the notes under the picture. Do you?"

"Nothing new," I agreed. "Secretarial and sewing classes, photography and science clubs." I pushed the book back in front of O'Ryan. "Here you go. We even left it open to her page for you."

Can cats do an eye roll? I'm quite sure they can't, but the expression on O'Ryan's face told me that if he could have, he would have. He gave the open book an impatient tap of one paw, then pushed his pink nose against the photos display, effectively turning the page. He did it again. And again. He stopped, looked up at me, and meowed—long and piteously.

"He wants help turning the pages, Lee." Pete reached for the book and slowly turned page after page while O'Ryan and I looked on. He paused after each page, waiting for the cat's reaction. He passed the *S* group, the *T* group. There were no *U* or *V* names.

"Oh. Look. He's up to the *W*s." I patted O'Ryan's head again. "You've got the wrong book, dear cat," I said gently, not wanting to hurt his feelings. "Walter Wyman is in Kitsue's book." I closed that yearbook and picked up the other one. "See?" I pointed to Wyman's photo.

I got the eye-roll look again, and a dismissive "meh." He hopped down from his chair and walked—no, stalked—across the floor to the wicker chair, then plunked himself down on the cushion.

"You've ticked him off somehow," Pete said. "I guess he's going to sulk and watch birds."

But he didn't sulk. Or look for birds. He pulled my blue sweater close to himself and efficiently picked my pocket. With the dollar bill I hadn't put into the parking meter clenched in his mouth, he returned to the table, back up onto the chair, placed the bill on top of the closed book, and sat—giving me an expectant look.

"What?" I said. "You're giving me my own dollar? For what?"

"I've got it," Pete yelled the words as he opened Fiona's book to the *W*s. He pointed to a tuxedoed young man. "Smart cat!"

I got it then too. O'Ryan had given me a bill with a special dead president on it. Pete and I spoke the name together. "George Washington."

My brilliant cat—the witch's familiar—had found something we'd all missed. The painter—woodworker—museum volunteer—had been a classmate of one—or more likely, both, of the Sullivan sisters.

CHAPTER 16

I rewarded O'Ryan with one of his favorite kitty treats, told him over and over that he was the smartest cat in the world. "Want to go down to Aunt Ibby's and return the books?" I asked.

"Let's," Pete said. "We need to tell her how helpful they've been. But first, I'll make a copy of the George Washington page."

"Make one for me too," I said.

I put my sweater back on while Pete ran two copies, handed one to me, then tucked the books under his arm. We headed out the front door, O'Ryan trotting along beside us as we walked down Winter Street to my aunt's house. There were plenty of lights shining from her windows, so I knew she was at home. I used my house key. "It's me," I called, dropping the yearbooks onto the seat of the hall tree where she'd see them on her way out the next day. Bad move.

I purposely hadn't looked directly into that damn mirror, but even a corner-of-the-eye, passing glance could catch the swirling colors and the flashing lights. No boots or leaves this time. I didn't recognize the image at first, but after a moment's reluctant study, I realized I was looking at an aerial view of the old A&P, currently the site of Salem's newest museum. I could even read the faded ghost sign advertising *Eight O'Clock Coffee* at the top of the building. The picture clicked away as soon as I'd barely processed the information— like one of those Facebook things you'd like to save but never can find again. Pete didn't realize this time that I'd been "seeing things," and I didn't want to call his attention to it just then.

"Come on back. We're in the kitchen," my aunt called. O'Ryan had already figured that out, racing through the living room and out of sight around the corner. *We? Were Pete and I interrupting something?* We gave each other questioning looks and followed the cat's path.

We were greeted with enthusiasm by Aunt Ibby and her two besties, dear friend Louisa Abney-Babcock and high school classmate Betsy Leavitt. The three women get together every week to watch *Midsomer Murders*, but I knew the week's viewing date had passed. The three, who were cozily gathered around the big, round kitchen table, like to talk about getting involved in matters that are generally none of their business, and I was pretty sure this extra meeting had something to do with Walter Wyman's murder.

"Please, come join us." My aunt indicated the three vacant captain's chairs. "We've been talking about the truck driver murder." She spoke the words "truck driver murder" as though they were capitalized—something like the titles of Fenton Bishop's mystery book series. I knew he sometimes attended those TV viewing sessions and wondered if he'd had some input into the present deliberations.

Pete and I sat, as bidden, in two of the chairs, and O'Ryan—uninvited—took the third one. "I guessed you might be," I admitted. "Have you three come to any conclusions?"

"Several." Betsy spoke up. "How about this? What if the person who helped him carry the boxes from the vault to the truck is the one who stole his gun, but isn't the one who shot him?"

Pete frowned. "Why would someone do that?"

"Maybe he was paid to get it and gave it to the killer who was hiding nearby." Betsy shrugged, tossing her Farrah Fawcett hairstyle. "I haven't quite figured that part out. Louisa, what do you think?"

Louisa was the Angel the others looked to for financial expertise. Wealthy in her own right, she sat on the boards of several local banks—including the one that owned the vault in question. I was interested in her answer, and I could tell Pete was too.

"I'm not an expert on guns," Louisa said, "so I have no opinion on that part. I have no doubt, though, that whoever committed this crime believes he will profit financially from it. Someone expects to make money—possibly a great deal of money—to take the chance of killing a man to get what he—or she—wants."

"I learned recently that Walter was carrying something in that armored truck that was worth a great deal of money," I said, recalling Kitsue's tale of the million-dollar cereal bowl. "But I doubt he had any way of knowing that, and neither did the killer, I suppose, because nothing was stolen." I related what she'd told me as well as I could remember it. "First of all, I learned that Kitsue and Fiona's four-times-great-grandmother was Chinese." Pete already knew about Li Jing Sullivan, but I was quite sure the Angels hadn't yet heard the story. I paused for the expected surprised comments, then went on to tell them about the white jade bowl. More surprised comments. Aunt Ibby was a fan of those antiques shows and remembered the PBS episode about the two-million-dollar brush pot. "I guess we'll all get to see the bowl when the display people get through with their work." I told them.

"You didn't tell me about the bowl," Pete said. "That's a really good story."

"It is, isn't it? You know, we got so involved in all the yearbook stuff, I forgot all about it."

"It's a great story," Louisa said. "Imagine finding that you've been eating cereal for years from a dish worth a small fortune."

"Cap'n Crunch," I stated, straight-faced, and all three women laughed. "Aunt Ibby," I said. "Your thoughts?" O'Ryan was the first to turn his head, facing my research-librarian aunt. The rest of us immediately did the same, respecting her talent for digging up facts no one else had even thought about. She occasionally claimed that she had a "master's degree in snooping."

"The particular armored truck in question has a window on both the driver's side and the passenger side," she began. "There is another, smaller window behind the one on the driver's side and a door but no window behind the one on the passenger side. That leaves the long, one-window side facing the bank's security camera, effectively hiding any activity behind the truck—unless the shooter's and the victim's feet showed below the truck. I haven't seen those security videos. Pete?"

"The videos we have do not show the area below the wheel well," he said, with a sideways glance in my direction. We both knew I'd seen at least one pair of feet on that leaf-strewn piece of ground, but a scryer's vision was not even circumstantial evidence of a darn thing. And now I had another vision to add to that one—this time a high-above-ground picture of the top of an old grocery store—a vision I hadn't yet shared with anyone.

"Well then, we'll just have to put in some more work, won't we, Angels?" My aunt's tone was confident. "Was there anything of interest in the yearbooks?" she asked. "I've told Louisa and Betsy about your interest in them." I wasn't sure how much Pete wanted to share. I waited for his answer.

"Yes," he said. "We're interested in a couple of people shown in the yearbooks who may have a connection to the dead driver. They were classmates. That's all we have so far."

"That's good," Betsy sounded excited. "Classmates. You know the funeral is Monday. Do you think the classmates might show up?"

"Possibly," Pete said, "Mrs. Wyman chose the holiday for the funeral so that Walter's friends could attend—though their presence wouldn't prove anything except that they may have been acquainted."

Betsy pressed on. "You said you were interested

in a couple of people. Does that mean they're 'persons of interest,' as you policemen like to say? Persons of interest in the murder?"

"No, they are not persons of interest in that sense." Serious cop voice. "Not at all."

I wondered about the tone of finality in his answer—especially since the yearbooks had yielded more than a *couple* of interesting people. Now, thanks to O'Ryan, there were three. In my mind, there were reasons to believe that any one of them might have some sort of connection to Walter Wyman's death—but as Pete had reminded me so many times, he is paid to gather *facts*. The only facts we had about any of the three was that they had all attended Salem High School at the same time as the dead driver had. Period.

At any rate, the Angels had paused in their questioning, so I took the opportunity to bring up another subject. "I've had the opportunity to get a sneak peek at the new museum venue," I said. "The exhibits promise to be even more exciting than I'd dreamed they might be. Documenting the story is a challenge, but so far, I'm enjoying it."

"I've heard there'll be fabulous jewelry from India," Betsy said. "You know how much I love jewelry."

"None of it has arrived from India yet, as far as I know, but according to Professor Bidani, you'll get to see a real maharaja's treasure trove of jewels," I said, "and he has arranged for what may be the most spectacular display piece of the show to house them."

"Lucky you." Betsy pouted prettily. "You two and Ibby and Rupert got to meet him at Fenton's little housewarming. I got a last-minute invitation, but I was on a photo shoot in Boston." Beautiful Betsy, who, like Aunt Ibby, admits to "sixty-something," is still in demand as a model in numerous TV commercials and the occasional walk-on movie part. "Louisa got an invitation, too, but she got there late and the professor and you two had already left. She met the Sullivan girls, though, didn't you, Louisa?"

"I did," Louisa said. "By any chance, Pete, are Kitsue and Fiona your interesting couple of people? I found the two extremely interesting, and it occurs to me that they'd fit the same demographic as the Wyman gentleman. The newspaper said he was twenty-six."

"The yearbooks!" Aunt Ibby spoke up. "Were the Sullivan sisters the classmates you were looking for?"

I didn't see any point in denying that they were. It was a fact, and we would have told my aunt about it anyway. Pete and I spoke at the same time. "Yes." My attempt at changing the subject from murder to museum had made a U-turn. We were all back to square one—the question of who had shot Walter Wyman—and just as importantly— why?

It was obvious the Angels now had a renewed interest in pursuing their own investigation of the matter—using their own sometimes-unorthodox methods. Both Pete and I had learned to respect the senior citizen trio because some of their amateur sleuthing past efforts had been helpful to the professionals. Betsy knows everybody who is anybody in Salem's social circles, and has contacts to rival the FBI or the CIA. Louisa knows how to follow a money trail—and following the money is the answer to solving more crimes than you might imagine. And without a doubt, my aunt Ibby's research skills are beyond legendary. I was glad they were on our side. I told the Angels the yearbooks in question were nearby in the foyer on the hall tree bench, and I had to step out of the way when Betsy, in a swirl of designer silk, hurried to get them.

The Angels' new interest in the yearbooks provided us with an easy exit excuse, so as soon as Betsy returned, we said our "good evenings" and headed back through the living room. I avoided even the tiniest glance in the direction of the hall tree, then realized I was holding my breath as we passed it. O'Ryan had chosen to stay in Aunt Ibby's kitchen, so Pete and I had the Winter Street brick sidewalk to ourselves. Pete unlocked our front door, and I realized as soon as we stepped inside what a pleasure it is to come home—to our very own house.

Saturday had been a busy day for both of us. Due to work commitments and Pete's nephews' weekend hockey schedules, our Sunday churchgoing habits had become quite irregular. We have different home parishes, too—St. Thomas's for him, St. Peter's for me—so we're in the habit of alternating the two saints, and that works fine for us. Sometimes, though, we skip church in favor of spending some quality time together. "Why don't we sleep in tomorrow morning," I suggested. "Maybe we can have a nice Sunday brunch."

Pete yawned and agreed that it was a good plan. He climbed into bed while I did the usual makeup removal and facial moisturizing. I was about to tell him what I'd seen in the hall mirror—the aerial view of the A&P building—but he was already sound asleep. It could wait. Maybe when we went to brunch, I'd tell him about the vision—even though, like most of them, it didn't make any sense.

I slipped into bed, careful not to wake Pete, then lay there wide awake for a long time—thinking about a maharaja's fabulous jewels and a long-ago Chinese bride and a pair of ankle boots and a faded ghost sign for Eight O'Clock Coffee and Cap'n Crunch in a Big Bird bowl.

CHAPTER 17

It couldn't have been a prettier fall day—the kind we don't usually see until October. Colorful trees silhouetted against a cloudless, amazing bright blue sky, temperature hovering in the sixties. Gorgeous. It was too good a day to actually sleep in, and way too early for brunch, so we were up, dressed in jeans and matching NASCAR jackets, fueled with coffee, in the Jeep with Pete driving, on our way down to the Salem Willows Park—one of our favorite places to walk, look at the ocean, and enjoy being together.

We parked at Dead Horse Beach and watched a couple of kids tossing a Frisbee for a sweet golden retriever to catch, then walked all the way to the boardwalk, where the amusement arcade and several of the food stands were still open. We shared a light breakfast from a red-and-white-striped box of the best popcorn in the world, watched the morning harbor ride boats leaving the dock—and in all that time, never mentioned the word "murder."

Eventually, of course, the subject had to come up. It was when we watched the party boat heading for Misery Island. Every summer Pete and I take that trip together, carrying with us a pot of purple pansies to the island to plant on a small dog's grave. We'd done it in the past July, as usual, remembering a pretty little gray schnauzer named Nicky, whose dog mom had been murdered because of a valuable diamond.

"It makes me think about what Louisa said last night," Pete began, "about somebody standing to gain a pile of money—enough to warrant killing a man for it."

"If Walter was killed because of the museum," I said, "there'll be plenty of things there some people would kill for. Like a glass tube full of jewels that used to belong to some maharahjas. Heck, even Kitsue Sullivan's cereal bowl is worth a cool million dollars."

"True, but whoever killed Walter had a shot at stealing it and didn't take anything. If profit is the motive, it must be something other than a jade bowl." Thoughtful cop voice. "The Indian jewels make more sense. There'll be plenty of other expensive stuff showing up in your museum, too, I'm sure."

"Not *my* museum," I reminded him again, "although I'm beginning to feel protective about it— and while we're on the subject of the museum, I had a teensy little glimpse of a vision last night in the hall mirror."

"You did? What did you see?"

"It was just a quick flash of a picture," I told him,

squeezing my eyes shut—trying to bring it back. "I was looking at what I guess you'd call a bird's-eye view of the museum—yeah, like what a bird might see while he was flying by." I opened my eyes. "I could even see the old advertisement for coffee that was painted up near the top."

"The museum building again," he said. "That old place shows up lately a lot more than the scene of the crime does."

"Except for Hoodie Girl," I reminded him. "She shows up at the scene of the crime."

"Not exactly. She shows up *before* the truck is on the bank property."

"Do you think Fiona is Hoodie Girl?" The question slipped out—blurted words I couldn't hold back.

His answer was delivered carefully. "It appears that Fiona was out of town, working, when Walter was shot."

Working out of town. It occurred to me at that moment that I didn't even know what Fiona did for a living. "What kind of work?" I asked.

"She's a sort of design specialist," he said. "She has some private clients, and she also works as a consultant for some of those television shows about fixing up your house. She was measuring a church over in Peabody for new stained-glass windows."

That would explain the ever-present tool bag.

"What about the photo-comparison thing the chief was looking at? Does Hoodie Girl match Fiona or not?" I knew I sounded pushy.

"A lot of similarity, but like I told you, there's room for error. Anyway. I told you. She wasn't in Salem."

"She and Kitsue look a lot alike," I said. "You don't think Kitsue could be under that hoodie?"

"Checked it. Kitsue was at the museum on Wednesday morning, in conference with a picture framer, haggling over price, in the presence of at least several witnesses—including George Washington."

"Is there any way Hoodie Girl could have altered her features somehow?"

"Sure. You can do it with a liquid silicone or latex. Actors use it. It temporarily tightens up wrinkles or makes skin look wrinkled, makes eyes look thinner or wider. You can even pucker up the skin and make a fake scar. I used to do it with glue at Halloween when I was a kid to make me look more like a scar-faced pirate."

"That would mean that Hoodie Girl—whoever she is, if she used the liquid, knew she might have to pass by security cameras and that the hood wouldn't cover enough of her face to disguise her." I was almost talking to myself. Our popcorn was gone by then, and the Misery Island boat was a speck in the distance.

Pete sighed, then looked at his watch. "I'm afraid so. Forensics says it looks like there's some kind of makeup above the eyebrows. Time for that brunch? Eggs Benedict and a mimosa maybe at the Ugly Mug?"

"Makeup," I said—thinking out loud again. "You said there's special makeup actors use. Kitsue was in the drama club. She must know something about stage makeup. What if . . ."

"What if Kitsue was Hoodie Girl?" Pete finished my thought.

"Just how good are those excuses both Sullivan

sisters had for the time Walter Wyman was at the bank?" I was in full nosy mode by this time, pushing my luck with questions I never would have asked Detective Pete back when I was Field Reporter Lee. Now I was a program director and a documentary maker—having nothing officially to with breaking news or murder. Besides all that, I was also now Mrs. Pete Mondello.

He answered right away. "A little bit loose, actually. Nobody was punching a time clock at either the museum or the church. Times were approximate, and after all, the questions were just routine. Nobody seriously thought those girls had anything to do with Wyman's death, anyway. We'll be checking those alibis again."

I figured I'd already pushed my questioning luck about as far as it was going to go, murder-wise. The Ugly Mug was our go-to Sunday brunch place, and I was hungry. "Let's go," I said. We headed back to the beach, where the Frisbee-catching goldens had been replaced by a couple of women launching paddleboards, and within a few minutes we were on our way to Washington Street, where I knew, if I shaded my eyes, I'd bc able to see the top of the old A&P building. Would I be able to see the old coffee sign too? I wondered.

We parked in a nearby city parking lot, and no, I didn't bother look for the museum building. I'd be inside it soon enough. We were shown to our favorite seats near the back of the restaurant. Pete, like most police officers, liked to sit with his back to the wall. Eggs Benedict and mimosas were served and enjoyed as usual, along with light, fun husband-and-wife conversation. We talked about movies we might like to see, a rug we were thinking of buying for the den, and the possibility of finishing off the attic space in our house.

"I like the idea of at least putting up a wall to separate the two halves," I said. "We can decide how to use the space later."

"That's not a bad idea," Pete said. "I wonder if George Washington can handle putting in a simple wall," Pete said. "Then, if we want anything more complicated, like the dormer windows, we can get somebody more experienced."

"Let's see how he does on our neighbor's cat door first," I suggested. "We don't know if that high school woodworking course is all the training he's had."

It was well after eleven when we finished breakfast and started for home. Pete needed to change clothes for work and pick up his own car—along with the copy of George Washington's page in Fiona's yearbook.

Pete went upstairs to change, and I stopped to visit with O'Ryan, who'd found a sunny spot on the floor of the sunroom. I told him once again how smart and clever and beautiful he is—he seems to enjoy hearing the words, which are—most of the time—all true. "I really liked how you showed us the dollar bill," I told him. "Got any more bright ideas today?"

He got up from his warm space, stretched, yawned, and moved to where the footstool Pete's nephew had built was halfway pushed under a black-painted tavern chair. With a little effort, he sat, balancing himself on top of the footstool—its surface too small for the large cat bottom—then returned to his original spot, looked up at me, then closed his eyes.

"What the heck does that mean, smarty pants?" I asked, but he was either asleep or faking it successfully. Never mind. I'd figure it out later. Maybe. Meanwhile, I exchanged my NASCAR jacket for my green WICH-TV blazer, called up the stairs to Pete telling him I'd be at the museum and would see him later for dinner at home—and reminding myself I'd better hit the grocery store again or arrange for takeout.

There were only a few cars in the museum parking lot, which I took to mean that there wouldn't be many people inside. That was all right with me. I'd feel free to poke around more freely, taking pictures whenever I liked, being generally nosy. I knocked, holding the press card up to the glass as usual. The man answering my knock wasn't George Washington and he wasn't paint spattered. This man wore a neat navy-blue uniform marked *Security*. Unsmiling, he checked my name against a list on his clipboard, and after a moment, still poker-faced, he unlocked the door and waved me inside.

"You know where you're going?" he asked. "The place isn't finished yet."

"It's okay, Mr. Thomas," I said, leaning forward, reading his name tag—Victor Thomas. "I'm going to be doing a TV documentary about how a show like this gets put together. The camera crew will start filming on Tuesday. I'm just here to figure out the best way to tell the story." I glanced around. There was no one in the main room, where Professor Bidani's glass tube loomed tall and empty. "Is anyone else here yet?"

"Some folks are up on the second floor having some kind of a meeting, and there's a lady in there unpacking boxes." He pointed to the Sullivan alcove.

"Thank you, Mr. Thomas," I said. "I'll just be wandering around, making notes, maybe snapping some pictures."

"Okay, miss. I'll be around if you need any help with anything." He gave a little salute and returned to his position inside the front door, while I made a beeline for the Sullivan alcove, anxious to get a look at whatever goodies were being unpacked in there.

I peeked around the corner and, not recognizing the woman whose back was to me, gave a little courtesy *knock-knock* on the side of the arched doorway. "Hello," I said. "I'm Lee Barrett from WICH-TV."

She turned, facing me. "Hi, Lee. Kitsue said you might stop by. I'm Priscilla Decker. I head up Kitsue's display team."

We shook hands. "Kitsue is so happy with the work you've done so far," I told her. "Especially the cloud collar and the wedding dress."

"I'm thrilled to have the opportunity to handle these precious items. Today I'll be arranging a selection of the four-times-great-grandfather's personal letters and some old photos in this one." She tapped the top of one of the flat-topped glass cases. "But first, I'm going to put what I think are the best of the household pieces—for instance, the lovely bone-china teapots and the Burmese silver jewelry box and the carved jade pieces—where they'll be safely displayed to their best advantage. I'm working now on getting the lighting just right." She pressed a small button at the base of the indicated cabinet, and a soft, pinkish glow illuminated the empty—so clear it was almost invisible—shelving.

"There's quite a science to it, isn't there?" I said. "I hadn't ever given much thought about display being such an art form."

"It truly is, and on so many levels. From Macy's Department Store windows to the way produce is arranged in your grocery store. Think about it." She gave a wise nod. "There's always room for another pair of eyes, though. Perhaps if you're going to be in the building for a while, you'll stop by again and take a look at my work? I expect Kitsue herself to drop in later today. I hope she'll approve."

"I'll be honored," I said, meaning it, thinking about how tape-measure-particular the Sullivan sisters had been about the placement of those very cabinets and cases. I thought then, too, about the perfection of Michael Martell's vintage-themed rooms and wondered if he'd also used the services of a display lady—or was that the same thing as an interior decorator?

"Back to business," I told myself. "You're here to set things up for Tuesday's first shoot." I was much too easily sidetracked—my mind wandering off to a rock-and-roll-themed sunroom when I needed to concentrate on *Seafaring New England*.

Priscilla had begun polishing one of the still-empty cases with a thick white cloth decorated with what looked to me like pink bunnies. I must have looked surprised. "Cloth diapers," she said. "They make wonderful polishing cloths—washable, super soft, and perfectly padded. When my sister's baby outgrew them, I took them all. I'm going to leave a few here for Kitsue. They're good for polishing cars too."

"Good to know," I said, "for when I have babies."
I told her I'd be back within the hour, then moved
back into the main room, where I once again
walked slowly around Professor Bidani's space
age–looking tube thing, marveling at the stark
contrast to the eighteenth-century goings-on in
the alcove I'd just left. I was sure, though, that
when the fabulous jewels of those long-ago maharajas were finally put in place, the contrasting
centuries would meld perfectly. I strolled into the
next alcove, where there'd been some progress
too. According to the floor plans, this one would
be sponsored by an assortment of local and re-
gional bookshops—both big name and independent ones. There were floor-to-ceiling bookshelves
in place where books, both fiction and nonfiction
in keeping with the *Seafaring New England* theme,
would be for sale throughout the event. There
were already chairs and tables in place for brow-
sers. I could see myself spending time there.

I headed for the stairway leading to the second
floor. When I reached the top of the stairs, I heard
voices, laughter, and music issuing from the far
end of the room, past the rows of chairs. As soon
as I got closer, I recognized one of the voices, one
that would be hard to mistake for anyone else. His
back was to me, but it was undoubtedly Rupert
Pennington. I moved closer, next recognizing my
neighbor, Michael Martell. The two men were seated
in the front row, facing forward to where Kitsue
Sullivan, in a plaid dress with big patch pockets, sat
on the edge of the stage, slim legs swinging back and
forth to the sound of a recorded song with men's
lilting voices.

CHAPTER 18

Kitsue was the first to notice me. "Hi, Lee!" she called. "What do you think?"

Think of what? "The music? Um . . . it sounds very cheerful," I offered.

"It's a Bahamian sea shanty," she said. "The 'Sloop John B'."

"Uh-huh."

Mr. Pennington spoke up. "Oh, my dear Marilee," he said. "We're working on ideas for a play. A special production for the *Seafaring New England* show. It would involve the drama and music divisions at the Tabitha Trumbull Academy, of course." He put one finger up to his lips. "But hush. For now, it's a secret. The idea came up at Michael's housewarming, right, Michael?"

"Yes, indeed, it did, and Mrs. Mondello, I want to thank you and your husband for the most thoughtful gift. I've already found a man to install it. George Washington. He's a volunteer here. Perhaps you know him."

"I do. He's the very person I was going to recommend," I told him. "I'm excited about the idea of a locally produced play."

What kind of production did they have in mind? I wondered. A Salem-themed play? Arthur Miller's *The Crucible*? No. Too witchy for the sea-themed venue. Ditto *Bell, Book and Candle*.

Mr. Pennington went on. "We'll need to find funding for the production, of course, and costuming suitable for the period, but we have Michael to write the story and Kitsue's ancestor's wonderful diaries to help tell the love story, and Kitsue herelf to play the part of great-grandmother Li Jing, with myself"—a modest bow of his head—"as Edward Sullivan. Of course, we'll have to age Kitsue with makeup but that's no problem. Michael is already working on the script. The sea shanties will be appropriate background music, and we're all excited about the idea. There is an outside entrance from the street, so we can close this part of the museum off and charge admission for movies and plays and such, or even rent the space out for private parties. But don't say a word yet. We have to get the approval of the museum board of directors first. Alright?"

It was, I realized immediately, an absolutely fabulous idea. One I most sincerely didn't want to promise to keep a secret. I was, after all, contracted to produce a video of the preparation for the Salem International Museum's first show. *All* the preparation.

"When will you know if the board approves? I have to begin filming on Tuesday," I told them. "I can delay covering this area for a day or so, I suppose. Will it be okay if I sit here for a few minutes and—um—observe?"

"We should know if they say yes or no by Tuesday for sure." Mr. Pennington raised a warning hand. "You won't tell anyone about this yet?"

"I won't," I promised, "until you tell me it's okay."

Kitsue slid herself down gracefully from the edge of the stage and joined me in the front row of the audience seats. "I'll sit with you, Lee," she said. "We're just listening to how different groups interpret the sea shanties. I love the sound, don't you? I'm thinking shanties might make nice background music for the whole event." The soundtrack had moved on to "What Do We Do with a Drunken Sailor?" and I found my foot tapping to the beat. Even if the board didn't like the idea of background music for the whole show, I could surely use some for background in my documentary. I made a note of the name of the singing group.

"A play about your interesting ancestors would be a great addition to the show," I said. "Playing your own four-times-great-grandmother would be exciting for you."

"I hope I get to do it," she said. "I've had some training for it—studied theater arts at Boston University—but I'd love to have some real stage experience."

"I took theater arts at Emerson," I told her, "but television was my aim. I've never done stage work."

"Fi and I both went to BU at the same time," she said. "I did School of Theater and she did Art and Architecture. We day-hopped by train every day.

That got old after two years, so we both quit and went to work." It occurred to me that I didn't know what Kitsue did for a living, and all I knew about Fiona's career was that she'd worked with some television home shows originating in Boston.

"I understand that Fiona is involved in some sort of home design, and she has her photography. What sort of work did you choose?" I asked.

"It sort of chose me," she said. "As Grandmother Kitty got older, it was obvious that she needed help, so I became her caretaker, and I've had a series of part-time jobs to help out. We still live in the old house in North Salem. Fi has her own place in Brookline—strictly minimalist but quite beautiful. So, for now, I take care of Grandma and work a few afternoons a week at one of the witch shops selling T-shirts and candles. Fi's staying in her old room at the house while she's here helping me out with the show."

"The steampunk room," I remembered.

"Not anymore." She giggled again. "Now it's painted white. There's a black futon and a black painted bureau she put together from Ikea. She only kept one of the steampunk pictures—a thing made out of clock gears—and she still has her old table full of science stuff, beakers and test tubes and Bunsen burners and rubber gloves and jars and bottles of herbs and potions." Her tone was affectionate. "That's Fi. We're both hoping that Grandmother Kitty will be well enough to come to see the show when it opens."

"You've got a lot on your plate," I sympathized. "A job and a house and an aging relative, and now you're a part of the new museum."

She smiled that crinkly smile. "Being here, in

this building, with so many creative people, is like being on vacation from all the rest of it."

"I'm enjoying it too," I told her. "I can hardly wait for Tuesday, when we get down to the real job of making the documentary."

"I can tell that you love your work. I wish I loved mine." An apologetic shake of her head. "Not that I don't love my grandmother Kitty. I don't regret a minute of caring for her, helping her. I love both my grandmothers. But the part-time jobs—not so much."

"I understand," I said, not really understanding and trying to imagine what it would be like if someday my take-charge, always-on-the-ball Aunt Ibby couldn't care for herself, couldn't live alone anymore. Would I be as selfless, as brave, as Kitsue Sullivan was? I shook away the unthinkable idea of a diminished Aunt Ibby. "You mention your other grandmother—the other half of your name. Tell me about your grandmother Suzanne."

Another sweet smile. "Our mum's mother. We don't see her very often. Never did, but whenever she came to visit us when we were kids living with Grandmother Kitty, she was kind and loving and always brought us presents from New York City. We found that very glamorous. She was really pretty. Married money. She still lives in the city, still stays in touch with us. Whenever she's in the area, she stays at Fi's place."

"Family is important," I said. "I love watching you and Fiona laughing together about your shared childhoods and seeing you working together on your alcove."

"I know. That's a big part of why I'm so happy about this project—and about being here in this building. Fi's been such a big help to me—and to others too. She's really handy with tools. She can fix things, install chair rails, lay carpet—she's a wonder."

"I hope the play you and Mr. Pennington and Dr. Martell are working on will happen. You looked so joyful, listening to the shanty music."

"I'm keeping my fingers crossed." She held up one hand, fingers crossed to prove the point. "I'd love playing Li Jing. With some good professional makeup, I think I'd look like her, and Fi is a whiz at making costumes. Besides, we still have plenty of old Halloween costumes at the house she can probably rework somehow." She giggled. "I told you I come from a long line of hoarders." Again, I thought about the sisterly bond between the two women, even though they were quite unalike in many ways.

"I'll cross my fingers too," I told her. "Right now I'm going back downstairs to see how Priscilla is doing with your display so far. She seems very capable."

"I think I'll go along with you," Kitsue said. "I hope I'll love it. I have images in my mind about how it should look. But I know images can change."

The kind of images I see sometimes change, and I never love them.

We excused ourselves, leaving the two gentlemen in the front row, and started down the stairs to the first floor. Kitsue and I each stopped short on the bottom step. It was a spontaneous reaction to the changes that had happened in the main room in the short time we'd been upstairs.

"For goodness' sake, look at that." Kitsue pointed to the large ship model on a wheeled dolly being maneuvered into the alcove next to hers.

"I think that may be a model of the great ship *America*. It belongs to the Crowninshield family," I recalled. "Scott Palmer talked about it on TV. There's going to be a real ship's figurehead over the doorway to that alcove too, and a model of an elephant in the main room, along with another ship model even bigger than that one. Kids are going to love seeing the elephant, and I'll bet the museum gift shop will have a pile of stuffed toy ones. Look, there's your sister and Professor Bidani inside the glass tube thing. I wonder if the shelving for the Indian jewels will be installed today."

"I can hardly wait to see those jewels, can you?" Kitsue moved ahead of me, almost skipping toward the round, space-age, display case. I followed, smiling at her enthusiasm. Fiona and the professor opened the door from inside the tube and stepped out of it. I noticed that Fiona's ever-present tool bag was on the silvery floor of the tube. Professor Bidani shook my hand while Kitsue hugged her sister. "Hi, Fi. Hi, Sant," Kitsue said. "We're on our way to see how Priscilla is doing in our alcove. Want to come with us?"

"Of course, I do," Fi said. "Coming, Sant?"

Carefully closing the glass door, the handsome Indian man joined us, and together, we four entered the Sullivan alcove. There'd been a significant change here, too. The soft-pink glow illuminated the long display case, and the almost-invisible shelves displayed their precious wares. I recognized a doll's tea set as Rose Medallion because Aunt Ibby had a vase in that pattern. There were several bone-china cups and saucers, some blue-and-white rice bowls, some delicate figurines, and several sitting Buddhas, of brass and gold and carved wood. A collection of jade figures and cups and bowls filled the center shelf, most of them in varying shades of green. The center item was what I knew had to be Kitsue's beloved white jade bowl. It was an ivory-ish shade with a few tiny streaks of rust color at the base, and it occupied the place of honor in the case. The bowl was centered on a mirror, and a round mirror behind it reflected the carved figures on the back so that the viewer could get the entire effect. The carved figures she'd told me about stood out in sharp relief, bathed in the rosy light. The whole effect was literally breathtaking. Kitsue, with tears in her brown eyes, gave Priscilla an impulsive hug. "It's amazing. Thank you so much." She reached into one of the big patch pockets of her dress, withdrawing a small, triangular, embroidered item. I thought at first it was an evening purse of some kind, but realized, on closer inspection, that it was a tiny shoe. Kitsue dangled the colorful thing from one finger. "I guess you've found the mate to this." She held it out toward Priscilla.

The answer was a confused, "What is it?"

"Four-times-great-grandma Li's little shoe. This one was out being photographed for the catalog and all the others had already been packed. So, I stuck the mate to this one in with the bowl when I wrapped it," she said. "Surely you must have found it."

Priscilla shook her head. "No. I'm sorry, Kitsue. There was nothing in that package except the lovely bowl. Are you sure that's where you put it?"

"I'm sure," Kitsue answered. "I gave the mate to my sister, Fiona, for the catalog pictures. She only needed this one. Isn't that right, Fi?"

"Yes." Fiona reached for the shoe, and balanced it in one hand. "This is the one I used for the photo. I'm sure of it. I remember those little flowers on the left side. I never saw the other one."

"It's quite small," Sant Bidani put in. "Perhaps the other shoe is still in the package wrappings. Did you save them, Priscilla?"

"I put all the wrappings into the big box the letters and photos came in," she said. "I think George picked it up a while ago to put in the trash. I'll ask him to go back and try to retrieve it."

"May I see the shoe, Fiona?" the professor asked. "I've heard of lotus shoes, but I've never seen one close-up."

"Neither have I." I watched as Fiona handed the shoe to Bidani. "How tiny was your four-times-great-grandmother's foot, anyway, to fit into this teensy thing? It must be less than six inches long."

"Her feet were bound when she was a child, weren't they, Kitsue?" Sant Bidani asked. "The lotus foot was fashionable in China for over a thousand years. The shoes were intended to resemble a lotus bud, and it was a cruel way to make a young girl appear attractive."

"According to Edward Sullivan's writings, it was very difficult for Li to walk," Fiona said. "I looked it up when I wrote the copy for the catalog. Poor thing."

"I have several pairs of her shoes," Kitsue said, "but I'd hate it if one of these was lost after all these years of the grandmothers taking care of them, handing them down to the next generation."

"Don't worry, Kit," Fiona said. "It will turn up. With all the stuff you've had to organize, it's no wonder it got misplaced."

"I'm sure your sister is right." I tried to console

Kitsue, who was obviously upset about the missing tiny shoe. "You'll find it."

"In university, I read a book by a Chinese American writer named Maxine Hong Kingston," Bidani said. "I was amused by her observation: 'Perhaps women were once so dangerous they had to have their feet bound.'"

"Good one, Sant," Fiona said. "I'll bet four-time-great-grandmother Li would have liked that."

"I think so too." Kitsue tucked the lone lotus shoe back into her pocket. "Maybe Michael can write it into the play."

Priscilla, Sant Bidani, and Fiona faced Kitsue, as if in one coordinated motion. Fiona spoke the words. "What play?"

"Ooops." Kitsue hunched both shoulders and widened the brown eyes. "I'm not supposed to tell."

"Come on, Kit," Fiona demanded. "You have to. Is Michael writing a play?"

"He's thinking about it," her sister hedged. "Nothing certain. That's why we're not supposed to talk about it. Right, Lee?"

Did you have to bring me into this? "That's right," I hesitantly agreed. "It's just a germ of an idea. No script, no funding, nothing concrete at all."

"Please don't tell anyone," Kitsue pleaded. "I wouldn't want Michael's idea to get jinxed before it even gets started."

"None of my business," Sant Bidani declared. "I won't say anything."

Priscilla held up her right hand. "You have my word."

Fiona raised one eyebrow and looked at her sister. "A play? Are you going to be in it?"

CHAPTER 19

Silence. Crickets. Nobody spoke. Kitsue looked down at her feet. Sant Bidani stared at the ceiling. Priscilla busied herself by running a cloth over a dust-free display case. I concentrated on the artfully displayed letters in that case—letters Edward Anthony Sullivan had written to his Chinese sweetheart more than a century ago. *Wow. These are great. Michael could use some of these lines in the play.*

Fiona persisted. "You just said Michael could write about the lotus shoes in the play. So, the play must be about Li Jing Sullivan, right?"

Whew. She'd figured that out fast. Maybe Fiona should be a cop!

"Can we talk about it later—please?" Kitsue sounded—and looked—close to tears.

"Okay. Later." Fiona, smiling, headed for the alcove exit. "Come on, Sant, I'll show you how my special formula of clear silicone will bond seamlessly with your Lucite."

The professor nodded politely to Priscilla. "The display looks wonderful, Ms. Decker. I hope mine works out as well. Kitsue, Lee, about the secret—my lips are sealed." He followed Fiona into the main room.

Time for a fast subject change. I was getting pretty good at that. "Kitsue, did Fiona say she has some kind of special formula?"

"Yeah. She's an inventor, along with all her other talents. Who knew that some of the smelly science experiments would turn out to really work? She's trying to get some of her ideas patented, but that costs money, you know. She doesn't want to give her wonderful ideas away like some inventors have done. She needs a lot of money to be able to actually produce all the things she's dreamed up. People will want to buy them, and she'll be rich and famous." Kitsue sounded confident that her sister's dreams would come true.

Fiona said she has a special formula of clear silicone. Hadn't Pete told me that actors use some kind of silicone to change their faces?

"I'd like to see how her silicone special sauce works," I told Kitsue. "Wouldn't you? Let's go over to the glass tube and watch." We thanked Priscilla again, and she returned to her work while we hurried to catch up with the others.

By the time we'd reached the tall enclosure, Fiona and the professor were inside, and Fiona had picked up her tool kit/handbag. Sant Bidani held two oblong pieces of clear plastic—Lucite, I was sure—one in each hand. The glass enclosure was fairly soundproof, because while we could see

they were talking, I couldn't make out what they
were saying. Their hand gestures, though, especially Fiona's, told us she intended to bond the
two, edge to edge. I'd seen long tubes of silicone
sealant before, when Aunt Ibby had created my
apartment on the third floor of the Winter Street
house. I was interested to see what was special
about Fiona's.

Fiona pulled what looked like a sample-size
toothpaste tube with a long spout on it from her
bag. She took one piece of plastic from Bidani and
ran the spout along the edge. Then she pressed
the other piece to the first one. She held them together for a moment, then held the resulting
piece of clear plastic up for his inspection. From
where I stood, it now looked like one clear sheet of
Lucite. There was no detectible line where the two
were joined.

"Amazing," I breathed.

"She sure is," Kitsue agreed.

"I mean, what she just did there. She made
those two pieces into one." I leaned closer to the
glass, my breath making little fog circles on it.
"That's not the kind of silicone you put on your
skin, is it? I mean, you'd never get it off, right?"

Again, the silvery giggle. "Of course, it's not.
But Fiona invented one for that back when we
were in high school. We used to use it on ourselves
and all our friends at Halloween. She could make
us look like witches or pirates or monsters or old
men or old ladies. You can do all kinds of things
with that silicone stuff. Ask Fi."

By this time, the two inside the cone had seen us
lurking there, peering in at them. They didn't
seem to mind. Bidani waved, and Fiona, still hold-

ing the newly fused Lucite, smiled the identical crinkly smile of her sister.

Kitsue and I both jumped a little when George appeared behind us. "I didn't mean to scare you ladies," he said. "I thought maybe the crown jewels of India had arrived in there. What's going on?"

I felt a bit embarrassed about almost looking as if I had my nose pressed against the window of a candy store, but Kitsue didn't seem to mind. "We're watching Fi showing the professor one of her science projects."

"No kidding." He waved at the two inside the glass. "I hope it wasn't one of the ones that used to blow up." They laughed together, the way old friends, old classmates, do. "I'm just on my way back to your space, Kit." He held forward a cardboard box with an untidy stack of wrinkled brown wrapping paper, white tissue paper, and several kinds of Bubble Wrap sticking out from the open top. "I rescued this out of the trash. I hope it's the right stuff."

Kitsue sighed. "Thanks, George. I appreciate your help."

"No problem," he said. "I'll bring this in to Miss Priscilla." He backed away from us, and after one more look through the shatterproof, bulletproof, tempered glass, we followed him into the Sullivan alcove, where the head of Kitsue's display team, wearing white gloves, reached for the box.

"I'll go over this thoroughly as soon as I have time," she promised, "although I'm not optimistic about finding your dear little shoe."

"I'm really not optimistic, either," Kitsue admitted, "but I appreciate your trying." She stood in the middle of the small room and turned in a slow circle. "I love everything you and the team have done here, Priscilla. It's even better than I'd dreamed."

Priscilla gestured toward a still-empty case. "I'm planning to put the rest of Li Jing's lotus shoes in this case, right under the chandelier—perhaps with some silk cherry blossoms and an old photograph of her that was in Edward Sullivan's papers. She was sitting down with her poor tiny feet showing beneath her long skirt."

"I'll be here on Tuesday with my mobile unit crew from WICH-TV," I said. "I'm excited about the way your space, and the others, are coming along. Some are near completion, like this one, and some are just getting started. That's what makes an interesting documentary—the step-by-step process of putting a major project together. I'll show how it builds from empty rooms to a professional display of fascinating, historical items that tell a story."

Even as I spoke, I thought about the similarities between the steps my TV presentation would document and the steps Pete takes to put together an investigation. He gathers facts, step by step, piece by piece, building toward the completion of an investigation, keeping the provable parts and discarding the questionable information—the same way the curators decide which things in a museum are genuine and which are fakes.

What about Hoodie Girl? How good—how genuine—were the alibis that both Kitsue and Fiona had offered for the day Walter Wyman had died? I was pretty sure Pete knew the answers by now, and

I meant to ask him to share. Meanwhile, was there something I could do? Some puzzle piece I could discover? Even a very small puzzle piece?

What about a puzzle piece as small as a tiny, embroidered shoe shaped like a lotus bud? What if that cruel lotus shoe was somehow missing from a carefully wrapped, clearly marked package that we knew had been securely stored in a vault before its delivery to the museum?

The slanting rays of the late-afternoon sun shone in the big window beside the entrance door. I checked my watch. Too late for a grocery store trip plus prep time for a proper Sunday dinner. I'd call Pete and see what take-out cuisine he'd like tonight. I pulled the phone from my purse and stepped inside the arch of a nearby alcove, the one where the giant ship model had been delivered earlier in the day.

"Hi, Pete. I'm still at the museum, thinking about dinner," I told him. "It's too late for the home-cooked variety. Any ideas for takeout?"

"Hey, since we've been talking about China so much lately, how about some spring rolls and crab Rangoon and pork fried rice and—well, you know."

"I know. Good idea. I'll do it. Hey, I'm standing next to the biggest ship model I've ever seen. Wait 'til you see it. It's not even in a case. There's a waist-high fence around it so you can't touch it, but you can walk all around it and see every detail—even the little sailors. Amazing. This job gets more interesting every day. How's your job going? Did you get to check out Kitsue and Fiona's alibis for the day Walter Wyman died?" I'd sort of ambushed him with the question, but I really wanted an answer.

A pause. A really short one. "Yeah. I did. Neither one of them actually holds up. I mean, they were where they said they were on that day, but the times were pretty loose. Like, Fiona had plenty of time from when she was at that church in Peabody to get to Salem, and Kitsue was in and out of the museum a dozen times that day." He sighed. "Either one of them or damn near anyone else who has a forehead and eyebrows could be under that hoodie."

I knew he was exaggerating, but I heard the frustration in his voice. "I've found a new rabbit hole to go down here at the museum," I said. "It's about a missing shoe. I'll tell you about it over kung pao chicken. Love you."

"I can hardly wait." He laughed. "See you at home. Love you too."

CHAPTER 20

I took a closer look at the ship model of the *Naiad*. It was almost as tall as I am and several feet long. The detail was remarkable. The sails and hatches and ropes and flags and even the miniature painted metal crew members looked real. The framed information card told me about the brig's weight and builder and the name of the master—Nathaniel Osgood. It also told about how, on her arrival home to Salem from Calcutta one Sunday, she'd been struck by lightning and how the second mate, William Griffen, who was on the main topsail yard, was instantly killed and fell into the sea. I leaned closer to the fence. There he was— ill-fated sailor William, just below the highest sail. He appeared to be smiling.

"Kids are going to love this exhibit," I whispered to William, and promised myself that we'd give the brig *Naiad* significant notice in the documentary.

With a backward glance, I left the alcove, passed Professor Bidani's much-more-modern presentation, and returned to the Sullivan area. The lights had been dimmed and Priscilla appeared to be ready to leave for the day. She stood at the entrance, staring down at the box full of wrappings.

"Did you get a chance to look for the shoe?" I asked.

"I didn't," she said. "I'm tempted to take the pile of wrappings home with me, but you know, I'm paid by the hour." Her smile was wry. "I hate to charge the girls anything extra for rooting through trash—especially since I'm quite positive there's no shoe in it."

I had a sudden inspiration. "Here's an idea," I said. "How about I take it home with me? My aunt Ibby has a couple of girlfriends who'd like nothing better than being part of a treasure hunt. They'll think that searching for a missing antique shoe is wonderful fun."

Her relief was evident. "Would you, Lee? That would be such a relief to me."

"My pleasure," I said, knowing I was right about my aunt and the Angels enjoying the challenge of the search. I lifted the box and headed for the front door, where the security guard stood, stony-faced. How was I going to explain removing a good-sized box from a museum full of valuable antiques?

I approached Victor Thomas and set the box on the floor. "This is . . ." I began.

He smiled. "I know. I've already seen it before—when George first brought it in from the Dumpster. It's paper and twine and Bubble Wrap and gobs of sticky tape. George told me there might be a shoe in it. I checked it. There isn't. It won't take a minute for me to check it again." He shook his head. "You museum people are an odd lot." He plunged both hands into the box, scrambling through it like a puppy digging a hole in the dirt. "Okay," he said. "No shoe. Nothing but trash. Good night, Ms. Barrett."

I wished Mr. Thomas a good night, picked up my box, and hurried to the parking lot. I stuck the box into the backseat, climbed into the Jeep, phoned my order to the Ming Dynasty, and left the almost-ready-to-open Salem International Museum site.

One of the great things about Chinese takeout is its extraordinary reheat-ability. I put the neat little containers, with their wire handles and pictures of red pagodas, into the warming oven, knowing that when Pete arrived, all would be ready to eat. I'd ordered extra crab Rangoon and plenty of white rice in case Aunt Ibby might like to join us. I called and asked her, and she accepted, offering to bring wine and dessert. Good deal. I could hardly wait to tell both aunt and husband about the surprise in the backseat of my Jeep. I returned the WICH-TV jacket to my closet and changed into easy-fitting pale-blue sweats.

Aunt, husband, and cat arrived at the same time. O'Ryan entered via the cat door, Aunt Ibby had driven over in her Buick, and Pete had brought home his favorite 2010 unmarked Crown Vic. We waited for Pete to change from work clothes to jeans and hockey sweater, then with rice, meat, and vegetable dishes transferred into wedding china bowls and plates, we gathered around the kitchen table. O'Ryan's red dish contained his usual fare—Chinese spices and salt aren't good for cats.

I couldn't wait any longer to tell them about the missing lotus shoe. I started with a quick rundown on the progress at the museum, about the giant ship model and the display of Edward Sullivan's letters and photos, and led as fast as I could into how Kitsue had pulled Li Jing's little lotus shoe from her pocket and told us she'd put its mate into a package along with her precious white jade bowl. "Priscilla clearly didn't know what Kitsue was talking about," I said. "She'd unpacked the bowl—there it was in the case for everyone to see—and there had been no shoe with it. She was positive about that."

"Then where is it?" my aunt asked.

"That's the big question," I said. "The shoe in Kitsue's pocket was one Fiona had used for a photo for the museum catalog. The mate should have been in the same package as the white jade bowl." I told them about how George had retrieved the box of wrappings and that Priscilla hadn't had time to check them for the shoe.

"That's too bad," Pete said. "There could have been something useful in that box."

Perfect lead-in to my big revelation. "I have the box," I announced. "I told Priscilla that I was pretty sure my aunt and her girlfriends would be happy to look through it—to see if she or George or even the security guard had missed anything."

Pete, cop-faced, didn't say anything right away. Aunt Ibby, green eyes sparking, was ready to run into the yard and get the box that very minute. "The Angels will love this idea," she said. "Who knows what they might turn up, what they might find that nobody else has noticed. This is right up our alley!"

"That's what I thought," I said. "The box is safely locked in the Jeep. It can wait until after dinner."

"It may wait a little longer than that," Pete said. "As long as you have the box, which, if you all recall, was in the armored truck immediately before Walter Wyman was murdered—I'd like the forensics team to take a look at it. *If* Kitsue Sullivan is correct, and she did, indeed, pack one shoe with her bowl, why would anyone remove the shoe and leave a bowl reputed to be worth a million dollars? It doesn't make sense."

Pete was, of course, absolutely right. Why, indeed? I agreed that Pete should take the box in to the police station in the morning. Aunt Ibby reluctantly approved, and then quickly the conversation turned to the murder of Walter Wyman. "The Angels and I believe that whoever killed Mr. Wyman was someone he knew," she said. "To get that close, and to get a ride in his armored vehicle—it had to be someone close to him," she insisted, making her point by pausing her forkful of bok choy in midair. "Mark my words."

"I agree," Pete said. "We're looking at a few possibilities."

"Are the Sullivan sisters still in the mix?" she asked.

Pete hesitated, so I answered. "I'm afraid they are," I said, "and I like them both, so I wish they weren't."

"They're very much involved in the museum, I understand," she said.

"Kitsue is the expert on family history," I said, "and Fiona knows so much about the mechanics of putting together such a project, she's even been helping out other displayers. She actually carries a big leather purse that doubles as a tool kit."

"I know women like those big purses, but one with tools in it must weigh a ton." Pete took a long look at the fairly good-sized hobo bag I'd hung over the back of a kitchen chair.

"Fiona's in really good shape," I said. "She slings that thing around as though it's nothing. She probably works out, in addition to her other talents."

"You said she's a photographer too. Does she do that on a professional level, or is it a hobby?"

"Mr. Doan agreed to pay for her photos," I recalled, "and I guess she's been commissioned to take some of the photographs for the official museum catalog."

"Multitalented," Pete observed.

"I'd say so," I agreed, thinking about the seamless sheet of Lucite I'd seen her produce within Sant Bidani's glass tube. "Her sister says that Fiona is an inventor—that she's trying to patent some of her inventions."

"An interesting woman," my aunt observed. "I'd like to spend some time with her someday. But for now, O'Ryan and I should head for home." She looked at the big cat. "If he wants to come to my house, that is."

"I'll walk you out to your car, Ibby," Pete offered, "and while I'm out there, I'll move the trash package from the Jeep to my cruiser. I don't have to go to work until noon tomorrow, but I'm sure it'll keep until then. Lee is going to the Wyman funeral tomorrow morning, and I plan to sleep late."

My aunt looked at me, her green eyes sparkling. "You're going to see who else shows up to mourn the poor fellow, I imagine."

There was no point in denying the fact. "Yep," I said. "Good night." O'Ryan followed my aunt to the sunroom. "Looks like O'Ryan chooses your place tonight."

"Call me after the funeral," she said.

"You two are such a couple of snoops," Pete said, holding the sunroom door open for aunt and cat.

"I'm going to see what I've got in my closet that's appropriate for a funeral." As the door closed behind them, I picked up the hobo bag and started upstairs.

I surveyed the selection in my closet and decided on a gray three-piece business suit—skirt, vest, and jacket—along with a navy blouse and navy sling pumps. A small navy cross-body bag would hold the essentials I transferred from the hobo. I hung the outfit on the front of my closet door, where I'd be able to grab it without waking Pete in the morning. I knew how badly he must need a couple hours of extra sleep. I went into the bathroom for the usual nighttime preparations, and by the time I returned, Pete was already in the big bed, snoring softly.

On Monday morning, I caught the alarm clock at first *ding*, shut it off so it wouldn't wake my sleeping husband, picked up my waiting wardrobe selections, and tiptoed downstairs. I'd already decided to stop for coffee at a drive-through Dunkin', rather than rattle around in the kitchen, so well before nine I was dressed, made-up, hair tamed and ready for what the day might bring.

I had plenty of time to spare, so with a large coffee—three creams, no sugar—and a cinnamon doughnut, I took a ride to the almost-deserted strip mall where that closed branch bank was located. I wanted to see for myself where the armored truck Aunt Ibby had researched and described so carefully had been parked in relation to the place where Walter Wyman's body had been hidden by leaves. Not incidentally, maybe I'd be able to figure out where those booted feet I'd seen in the mirror belonged in the picture.

I stepped out of the Jeep and walked under the covered drive-through toward the back entrance of the place where Walter had parked. The yellow police tape was gone, so whatever investigation had been going on here was finished. With the tall cardboard cup warm in my hands, I took a long sip of my coffee. The once-busy mall had backed up to a once-carefully-groomed row of hedges and some tall old-growth trees. The few places of business left here were closed—windows dark and empty, the hedges scraggly and uneven. The branches of the trees were mostly bare, like naked, skinny brown arms reaching for the sky, and the pile of leaves everyone had viewed on the news was gone. Marks from a recent raking marked the earth, and the few dried and scattered remnants of foliage blew in the cool morning breeze.

I took a few tentative steps toward where I thought the armored truck must have been parked when Walter Wyman was shot, and with my back to those grasping branches, I tried to visualize the side of the truck. But wait. The hedges and trees would have provided ample shelter for a killer. Maybe the small window on the driver's side of the truck had reflected the person's image. Would Walter have drawn his gun then? Was there a struggle? And what about Hoodie Girl? Had she seen everything?

Was she afraid to come forward? Or was she part of the crime? Had he let her out of the truck before he'd parked the truck here and she had nothing to do with anything?

Once again, I had more questions than answers. I took a few sideways steps until I stood where the rake marks were—where the pile of leaves had hidden the dead man—possibly where the booted feet had stood before—or after—the fact of the murder.

I looked around me. I was all alone here—or was I? I had an uncomfortable feeling. Was I being watched? Were all these buildings actually empty? I took another sip of my rapidly cooling coffee and got back into the still-running Jeep, locked the doors, and headed for Federal Street and the funeral home. I'd be a little bit early, but it would guarantee me a good parking place near the exit so I could leave whenever I wanted to.

I learned almost immediately that my quick-get-away parking space was also a good vantage point for seeing who else had arrived early. One of the first was—who else?—Scott Palmer. Naturally he recognized my Jeep, and smiling sweetly, parked in the next space to mine, then hurried toward the funeral home's handsome front door. Scott, I was sure, would want a front-row seat, while I wanted to be as close to the back as possible.

I finished my by-then-cold coffee, decided to save the doughnut for later to avoid spilling sugar and cinnamon onto my suit, and after what seemed like an appropriate wait, left the comfort of the locked Jeep and climbed the stairs to the funeral home. I slid into the second-from-the-back row, not joining the mourners who were greeting the family members since I didn't know any of them. Scott had no such compunction and sat as close as he could get to the weeping mother of the deceased. I hoped he wasn't secretly recording.

It wasn't long before the room began to fill with people. Kitsue Sullivan came in by herself and joined the folks who were lined up to offer condolences to the family, then sat alone near the front of the room. Before long, in walked George Washington—also alone. He spoke briefly with the family, too, then—at Kitsue's beckoning gesture—he sat beside her. Did that mean they'd been high school buddies, or was their acquaintance a result of recent time spent at the museum? What about Fiona? I wondered if she'd be in attendance—perhaps arriving late, as she had at the housewarming. The service—the celebration of Walter Wyman's life—began. There were hymns and scripture readings and loving words from friends. It was moving and quite lovely. There was an overflow audience, and I was glad to see that he'd made so many friends in his short lifetime.

I was among the first to leave the building, but I stayed in the parked Jeep for a few minutes, just watching, looking for—I didn't know what. My outdoor vantage point was just as good as my indoor one had been. I'd pulled down the visor to help hide my face so I could observe the folks exiting the parking area. I began to feel silly after a while, though, and so I backed up, checking the rearview mirror. There was only the tiniest flash of swirling light and colors. I thought at first that Fiona Sullivan was actually standing behind the Jeep—and that she was wearing a hoodie. I slammed on the brakes, then realized very quickly that I was, once again, "seeing things."

CHAPTER 21

The visions are always startling, often frightening. This one was particularly upsetting, and I sat in the parked Jeep for several minutes trying to figure out why that was so, before—very slowly and carefully—moving onto Federal Street. I reached for the dregs of the now-ice-cold coffee and opened the pink and orange bag containing my doughnut. Getting sugar and cinnamon on my suit was no longer a consideration, and a happy sugar rush would be welcome. I looked at the clock on the dash. It was past noon, so Pete would be at work by now. It was a holiday, though, so the library would be closed, and after all, I'd told my aunt I'd call her after the funeral. She doesn't like to hear about the visions any more than Pete does, but I wanted to talk to somebody about this one. River doesn't mind talking about them. In fact, she enjoys it, but it was too early to call her. Why was Fiona in my vision? Why was she wearing a hoodie? Why wasn't she at the funeral in person instead of in my mirror?

I drove to Winter Street and home, changed out of the suit, and put it in a bag to take to the dry cleaners. Did it need cleaning for just a sprinkle of sugar? Probably not. Maybe I wanted to clean away both the sad funeral and the troubling vision. I changed into comfortable "day off" clothes and phoned Aunt Ibby.

I gave her a fast rundown of the funeral, who'd been there that I recognized, who the officiating clergy person had been. I even remembered to tell her they'd played "Amazing Grace" and used some scripture from First Corinthians.

She asked if I'd heard from Pete yet about the contents of the box. "Not yet. But there is something I'd like to talk to you about. May I come over?'

"You don't need to ask," she scolded. "You know you're welcome here anytime. Day or night. I've always told you so."

"I know that," I said, "but you also told me that it's polite to call first."

"*Touché*!" She laughed. "Sure. Come on over."

I decided to walk to her house. As soon as I reached her front steps, I saw O'Ryan, his pink nose pressed against the glass of the long window beside the door. I used my key and happily received purrs and ankle rubs. Cat greetings are so pleasant and special. I picked him up, gave him a hug, and kissed the top of his head. He relaxed in my arms, so I called out my usual "It's me," and carried him into the living room.

"In the kitchen—as usual," came the answering call. Cat and I followed the voice.

"Something smells wonderful in here—as usual," I said. "What's cooking?'

"Just some pumpkin spice bread. It's that time of year," she said. "Michael and the Angels are coming over this evening to discuss a new project Michael is working on."

"If it's a new play, I already know a little about it," I said, aware of my promise to avoid discussing it. But, hey, if my aunt and the Angels were involved in the same project, I wasn't "telling tales out of school," as my aunt is fond of saying.

"It's a play about Salem," she said, reaching for the cat. "Come here, you big silly. You're not a kitten who needs to be carried around. He's been quite clingy lately." She took him from me and placed him firmly on the tile floor. He stalked toward the kitchen cat door, turned, and—I swear this is true—stuck out his pink tongue at her, then he went out the door into the back hall.

"Now you've done it," I said. "He's annoyed."

"He'll get over it," she said. "He loves me. He's lurking just outside the door. Do you want coffee? I just made it. What would you like to talk about?"

I sat in one of the captain's chairs. "No thanks. I just had some. After I left the funeral, I saw—um—something strange in my rearview mirror."

"By 'strange,' you mean something not real?"

"I'm afraid so. Did I tell you Fiona wasn't at the service?"

"You didn't say that she was. I'd planned to ask you about that."

"I thought it was odd," I said, "since Kitsue and George were there. But when I left, and began to back the Jeep out of my parking space, I looked at the rearview mirror, and there she was."

Aunt Ibby spoke softly. "But not really?"

"But not really," I echoed. "It was so clearly, definitely Fiona that I jammed on my brakes to avoid hitting her, and Aunt Ibby, she was wearing a navy-blue hoodie."

"Like the mysterious girl in Walter Wyman's armored truck."

"Yes. Except that her face wasn't covered, and she wasn't wearing red-rimmed sunglasses."

The oven bell *ding*ed, and she retrieved the hot pumpkin spice bread, put it on a cooling rack, and sat opposite me again. "You haven't told Pete about this—um—this vision yet, have you?"

"I haven't. I'm not sure what to think about it. The darn visions are so inconsistent, so unreliable—does it mean that Fiona *is* Hoodie Girl? Or does it mean something entirely opposite?" I sipped my coffee. "Pete deals in facts, but sometimes—every once in a while—the visions show something factual."

"Mostly, though," she said, "they are pretty obtuse, don't you think? I mean, once you've figured everything out and you look back on it, the vision usually turns out to be relevant, but not anywhere near factual."

She was right. Maybe I wouldn't bother Pete with this one—at least not yet. "I think I'll hold up on this one with Pete," I told my aunt, "and I think I'll see what River has to say about it." That decision made, I felt better, even though the impression the vision had made was still disturbing. "I'm excited that Michael is going to write a play about Salem," I told her, fishing for information. "I'm sure Mr. Pennington is delighted. I expect that the Tabby drama department will definitely be involved." She didn't take the bait.

"I expect so," she said, and deftly changed the subject back to the recently clingy cat. "Has O'Ryan been particularly protective when he's been at your house lately?"

"Not that I'd noticed," I said. "But if he's watching over you, be extra-careful. You know how smart he is. He knows things we don't know." I thought about what Kitsue had said about her grandmother needing help, and once again the unwelcome thought of my aunt becoming needy somehow crossed my mind. I made the thought go away. "I have some housework to catch up on," I told her, "so I'll get back to my place. Thanks for listening."

"You're welcome—I'm always glad to lend an ear," she said, "and I promise I'll be careful. Let me know what River says about you seeing Fiona— the way you saw her."

"I will. Enjoy your pumpkin spice bread meeting tonight."

"I'm sure we will. I'd invite you, but this is strictly a brainstorming meeting. Michael called it."

"I understand," I said—and I did, but I felt like the kid who wasn't invited to the birthday party.

I decided to leave by the kitchen door and found that my aunt had been right about O'Ryan. He was, as she'd said, lurking, curled up on the welcome mat so close that I darn near stepped on him. He scooted inside. "Here comes your guardian cat. See you later," I told her, and opened the outside door to the garden.

CHAPTER 22

I took my time walking home along Winter Street. I wasn't kidding about the housework waiting for me. Between the program director job and the preparations for the start of the documentary, along with normal married life, I'd been making do with minimum dusting and sweeping, and the laundry was beginning to pile up. So I strolled along, wasting time, kicking chestnuts, watching a couple of squirrels chasing each other around and around a red maple tree. I approached our house—and stopped short.

Am I "seeing things" again?

I closed my eyes tightly, then opened them again. Fiona Sullivan—the *real* Fiona—no hoodie—was sitting on the front steps. "Fiona? Hello. Is everything all right?"

She stood, walking toward me. "Hi, Lee. I was at the museum this morning, and there was hardly anyone around. I figured it was because of the holiday, and then I remembered that some people might be at the funeral for that man who got shot."

"Yes," I said. "I was there. It was really well attended. Walter Wyman had a lot of friends."

"Kitsue said she was going. Did you see her there?"

"Yes." *Why are you here?* I wanted to ask her, but I didn't.

"Do you think Kitsue is—well—all right?"

"I don't know what you mean," I told her. "She's doing an amazing job on the Sullivan display."

"Seems that way," she said. "I shouldn't be bothering you about it. Actually, I came here to see Michael, but he isn't home. I knew you lived next door to him, and I saw your car out back, so I've been ringing your doorbell. Nice tune, by the way."

"Thank you." I waited for her to get to the point of this visit. Housework began to look better every minute.

"I'm worried about the missing shoe she's talking about," she said. "That, and a couple of other things."

"I hope the shoe will turn up," I said.

"That's just it. It already has." Fiona reached into the commodious leather bag. "I found it this morning—in her room." The tiny shoe in the palm of her hand was unmistakably the mate to the one I'd seen earlier. Or was it the same one? She must have anticipated my question.

"I wondered right away if this was the shoe she said she'd packed with the bowl." She held it toward me. "And see? The embroidered flowers are on the right side. The shoe I photographed for the catalog has them on the left."

"It was in her room?"

"In her bottom drawer."

What business did you have looking in her bottom drawer? Again, she anticipated my question. "We've always borrowed each other's clothes. We're exactly the same size." She shrugged. "When we were in school, we used to joke that the first one out in the morning was the best-dressed. Today I needed a pair of black tights. She keeps hers in her bottom drawer."

Once again, I experienced that tiny flash of sister-envy, the trust that must come with such lifelong sharing. "I see," I said, wishing, in a way, that I *did* see. "Have you told her yet that you've found it? She'll be so relieved."

"I haven't told anyone." Abruptly, she sat down on the top step again, her short skirt pulling up over her knees, exposing sheer black tights. It seemed quite natural for me to join her there. "I mean," she whispered, "why did she hide it? Why is she pretending it's lost?"

It was, I realized, a perfectly logical question—one without any kind of positive answer that I could see. "She must have a good reason," I suggested hopefully. "Is it possible that this particular pair of lotus shoes is somehow more important, or more valuable than any of the others?"

"I don't know," she said, still keeping her voice low. "I hadn't thought about that. All I know about the shoes is the tiny bit of research I had to do for photo captions." She put her elbows on her knees, cradling her chin with both hands. "Even if they are, why would she hide them? If they were mine, I'd just up the insurance and put a spotlight on them in the display—just like she's doing with that dumb little cereal bowl."

The dumb little million-dollar *cereal bowl,* I thought, but I only said, "You'd planned to talk to Michael about this, though—not me. Maybe he has some better insight into how Kitsue is thinking these days than I would."

"Maybe." Long sigh. "I *used* to know how her mind worked. She's different from me in a lot of ways—I'm sure you've noticed that—but in recent years, we've been apart so much of the time, maybe we've lost that mental contact, that almost-twin-bond we've had for so long."

Twin-bond. Wow! "I don't really know much of anything about the play they're working on together, but I could tell that Kitsue is excited about it," I told her. "I think Michael will help you if he can. I think that his—um—unpleasant past experience has made him quite empathetic. The characters in his books display that."

"No kidding? I've never read any of them. Cozy murder mysteries just aren't my cup of poison." She gave a short, sweet giggle—just like her sister's. "I like Navy SEAL adventures better."

"Nothing wrong with that," I agreed. Another long pause. I decided to push the envelope a tad. "You said there were a couple other things you're concerned about. Besides the shoes."

"She's playing a game we used to play when we were kids, when we both lived in Grandmother Kitty's house."

"A game?"

"A game. A trick. Call it what you like." She stretched out her legs and folded her hands in her lap. "We used to change places—messed with our teachers and even with our poor, long-suffering grandmother. We had these ratty old Halloween wigs. One of them was short blond Dynel, and the other one was some kind of a synthetic pageboy brunette. We learned to shampoo them and style them and wear them—each of us playing the other one's part—sometimes for a week or more."

"That seems harmless enough. It must have been great fun—fooling everybody like that." I had to smile, imagining how they must have laughed together after school.

"It was. But the game can only be fun when *both* of us play. She's styled that old blond wig. It's on a Styrofoam head on her bureau, but the brunette one is still in the box." She raised one hand and covered her eyes. "Don't you see? She's the only one playing. She always tells me how exciting my life is compared to hers—how boring her days and nights have become. I think . . . I'm afraid . . . I wonder—if sometimes she actually believes she is me." A tear rolled down her cheek, and she quickly brushed it away.

I almost put an arm around her, but her sadness seemed too deep, too personal. I sat there, quietly, silently, hoping the moment would pass. It did. She suddenly sat up straight, reached for the leather bag at her feet, then stood. "I've already taken too much of your time, Lee," she said. "I'm sorry to keep you sitting here, listening to me rambling nonsense. You're such a good sport. Thank you. I'd better go move my car before Pete gets home.

Bye. See you at the museum." And *poof!* Like a scene from *Hocus Pocus,* she zipped around the corner of the house and was gone.

What the hell was that all about? I sat there on the steps for a while, trying to process the conversation. Was Fiona convinced her sister was suffering some kind of mental breakdown? I'd read that such things were possible—especially if someone is so dreadfully unhappy with their lot in life that they begin to create a fantasy world. Kitsue herself had told me she wished she loved her work the way I loved mine. Or was Fiona the sister who was imagining things—making more drama out of everyday happenings than they deserved? But what about the shoe in the bottom drawer? That was one thing I knew to be true. Pete would be here before long. I stood, picked up my hobo bag, and unlocked the door to the comfort of home sweet home.

CHAPTER 23

It didn't take long for me to get into housework mode. I told Alexa to play Ravel's *Bolero* and started with the waiting laundry. Opening the louvred door hiding the stacked washer and dryer, I began sorting. With the summer whites all done earlier, I tossed darks and colors into the machine, keeping time to the slow, rhythmic beat of the opening bars of the music, then pushed the appropriate buttons and moved on to vacuuming. As the London Symphony built the hypnotic theme louder and faster, I progressed to kitchen sink, counter, and floor scrubbing, and by the time the music reached its crescendo, the laundry was folded and even the downstairs bathroom was a vison of sparkling perfection. After the crash of the final cymbal, I plopped down on the couch. "Well done," I told myself. "Maybe tomorrow I'll do upstairs."

Pete arrived home to a clean and orderly first floor, my first attempt at a shepherd's pie in the oven, and a freshy showered, neatly dressed, proud-of-herself, but still-puzzled wife. I could hardly wait to tell him about my two visits with Fiona—both the rearview mirror and the front-steps versions of the woman.

Over dinner—I'd used frozen veggies, deli meat, and packaged mashed potatoes, but the pie was pretty good—I told him about the mirror vision and about the real Fiona's story of finding the shoe and seeing the blond wig. "Do you believe her?" he asked.

It was a good question. "I'm not at all sure that I do," I told him, "but on the other hand, she showed me the shoe. I guess I don't want to believe that Kitsue hid it in her bureau drawer. Why would she do that?" I went to the refrigerator and got the ice cream. Rocky Road. "I don't want to think Fiona is making it up," I explained, "or that Kitsue is imagining things. I like them both. I want them both to be well and happy."

"You didn't see Fiona at the funeral?" he asked. "I mean, the *real* Fiona?"

"No. I sat in the back so I could see everybody coming and going. She definitely wasn't there."

"One of our women detectives had a talk with Kitsue and Fiona's grandmother Kitty. Nothing critical—just a query on who lived where back in their high school days. A nice old lady. Sharp as a tack, too, even though she's in a wheelchair because of arthritis. She told our detective that Fiona and Walter Wyman dated for a while back in high school. That makes me wonder why Fiona didn't go to his funeral and Kitsue did."

"Me too," I said. "Today she referred to him as 'that man who got shot.' "

"That seems cold."

"It does. She cried real tears when she was talking about that role-switching game the sisters used to play, but she didn't bother to go to the funeral of an old friend when she was right here in Salem."

"You've spent some time with Kitsue." Pete put a generous scoop of Rocky Road into each of our dishes. "How does she strike you?"

"I like her," I said again. "I like her enthusiasm about her alcove and about the museum, and about Salem's history in general. Her excitement about Michael Martell writing a play is real. She loves the idea of playing her own four-times-great-grandmother."

"Fiona seems to think her sister wants to change places in real life, is that right?" He poured some chocolate syrup onto his ice cream.

"It sounded that way to me, but that's just crazy, isn't it?" I answered his question with a question of my own.

"I deal in facts, my love—not sisterly disputes," he said. "I'd need to see some facts to back up the things Fiona told you. Did Kitsue hide the shoe, or was it somebody else? In fact, was the shoe hidden at all? Did Kitsue really pack it with the jade bowl or not? Is Kitsue unhappy with her life? I've only met her a few times, but she seems pretty upbeat to me."

Again, more questions than answers. Another thought popped into my head. "Hey, maybe Fiona is so pleased with herself that she *thinks* her sister should be envious."

"That's worth considering," he said. "Enough about sibling rivalry. This pie thing was darn good—you're turning into a real cook. Maybe you take after your Aunt Ibby after all."

"Thanks. It turned out I'm not as hopeless in the kitchen as I thought I was after all."

"Baloney! You can do anything you set out to do. You always have. Look at you right now. They ask you to be a program director, and *boom!* You do it. They want you to produce a documentary. *Boom.* You do it. When they wanted a field reporter, you did that too. Even a call-in psychic gig, *boom*, you . . ." He grinned. "You gave it a hell of a good try."

"I did," I admitted, remembering the short, ill-fated "Crystal Moon" phase of my career. "But it was then that I met you, so it turned out just fine."

"It did," he agreed, "and chances are, your two new friends will be okay too." He looked around the kitchen. "Where's O'Ryan? Doesn't he usually check in at about this time?"

"He does," I said, "but Aunt Ibby says he's been kind of clingy lately. He doesn't seem to want to be away from her for very long."

"Well, maybe he's getting old. He's obviously quite attached to her. How old is he, anyway?"

I shrugged. "I have no idea. They say he wandered into the station years ago. Phil Archer remembers when he showed up—a full-grown, healthy cat. He was friendly, surely not feral. Phil says they even advertised him on the air in a missing pets segment. Nobody claimed him. Ariel adopted him, and then he came to live with Aunt Ibby and me. That's all I know about his history. Sometimes I wonder how many lives he's had."

"Speaking of cats, has our neighbor installed his cat door yet?"

"I don't think so. He has George's number. Maybe he's waiting until he actually gets a cat." I reasoned.

"That makes sense. Putting the door before the cat is the same as putting the cart before the horse," Pete joked.

"I guess so," I agreed. "Like, what if some wandering stray cat saw this nice new door and just strolled in and made itself at home in Michael's lovely house?"

"Exactly like O'Ryan did however many lives ago?" It was a good question.

"Yeah. Like that. It might be a good thing," I thought about it. "A found cat can be a *very* good thing. Maybe I'll wish that for Michael."

"Would that be 'putting the cat before the house'?" Another big grin. "He'd probably feel sorry for it."

I couldn't resist. "Do you mean he might put pity before the kitty?"

By then the conversation had deteriorated so completely into silliness that further consideration of the meanings of misplaced shoes or disremembered high school romances went out the window. *Or out the cat door, as the case may be.* We refilled our ice cream bowls, added sliced bananas and strawberry jam to the chocolate syrup—and declared the result just as good as a Baskin-Robbins banana split.

We'd finished loading the dishwasher, wiped down the counters—extra carefully because I'd cleaned them so nicely earlier that day. Pete was about to snap off the kitchen light when we heard

what was the unmistakable sound of *our own* sunroom cat door opening—not with the usual sound
of an easy swing, but with a *wham-bam* slam of a
sound, followed by a loud yowl, then another and
another as O'Ryan raced into the room, ran
around the edges and back to the sunroom, then
repeated the pattern, yowling all the way.

"Something's wrong with Aunt Ibby! Come on!"
I yelled.

"Let's run!" Pete led the way to the front door
and pulled it open. "It'll be faster than backing a
car out."

O'Ryan beat us both to the sidewalk and streaked
out ahead of us. "Wait! I need my keys!" I went
back to the kitchen, grabbed my hobo bag, then
tried my hardest to catch up with husband and cat.
By the time I reached Aunt Ibby's front door, Pete
stood there, impatiently peering into the side window, waiting for the key. O'Ryan was already inside, having accessed one of his several cat doors,
and he looked back at Pete from the lowest pane.
Wordlessly, I turned the key in the lock, and Pete
and I tumbled into the foyer, both of us calling my
aunt's name. O'Ryan had already left his window
post and started across the living room, looking
back at us every few steps. "She must be in the
kitchen," I told Pete. "Hurry." I called her name
again and heard a faint reply.

"Here," she said.

I was right. She was in the kitchen. It was easy to
see what had happened. She lay prone on the
hard, tile floor, beside a step stool I remembered
from childhood. I guess it would be called "vintage" now, with a bright red vinyl seat and two pull-

out steps on a still-shiny chrome frame. I knelt beside her. "What happened? Where does it hurt?" I heard Pete behind me, already on the phone with 911.

"It's my right leg," she whispered. "I can't move it. Can't stand up."

"Don't try to move," I ordered. "An ambulance will be here in a minute."

She wore a wry smile. "I guess this is the part where I say, 'Help. I've fallen and I can't get up'."

"I guess it is," I agreed. "Did you fall from the second step?"

"Worse. I was standing on the seat part."

"Oh, Aunt Ibby. You warned me a million times to never, ever, do that." I scolded her—rightfully. "What were you trying to do?"

"I saw a spider up in the corner. I was trying to spray him." She motioned with one hand to a bug-spray can that had rolled under the stool. "I guess he got away."

A siren howling from outside signaled the arrival of help. Pete hurried to the front door, and within seconds uniformed EMTs took over the scene. With my aunt safely secured to a wheeled stretcher, her right leg encased in a boot-like apparatus and a blanket ensuring her modesty while being carried down the steps and into the waiting ambulance, Pete and I hurried home, climbed into his cruiser, and with red-and-white lights flashing, reached the Salem Hospital ER at the same time as the ambulance.

We spent what seemed like an extremely long time in the waiting room. No, it didn't just seem like it—it *was* an extremely long time before the

ER doctor called my name. My aunt, looking annoyed, was in a wheelchair, her right leg encased in plaster below the knee, extended toward us.

"Mrs. Mondello," he said. "We're going to keep Ms. Russell overnight for observation, due to her age. It's a simple bone fracture involving the tibia. I've set the bone in place and applied a plaster cast to keep it from moving while the pieces grow back together. You can probably take her home in the morning if all goes well. She won't be able to put weight on it for a while. She says she doesn't have help at home. Is that correct?"

"That's correct," I said. Was his tone accusatory? *Does he think I'm a bad niece because my aunt—the most fiercely independent person I've ever known—chooses to live alone with only a cat in a big house?*

"Perhaps"—his tone was gentle—"perhaps that isn't the best option for Ms. Russell for the time being. Can you arrange for assistance for her?'

"Hello!" Aunt Ibby interrupted, green eyes blazing. "I'm right here, doctor. Kindly don't talk about me as though I'm not in the room. I can make decisions for myself, thank you very much."

The good doctor looked surprised. "Sorry, Ms. Russell," he said. "I think it's best that you have some help for a while. Climbing stairs is out of the question."

"That's better," she said. "Maybe I'll get one of those riding chairs that go up and down stairs. That should do the trick."

"That'll take a while to install," Pete said. "Meanwhile, why don't you stay with us? We have a den and a bathroom on the first floor. We can fix it up for you tonight. No problem." He gave a broad wink in her direction. "The kitchen is there too.

You haven't broken your arms. You can still stir and sift and measure, right?"

She had to laugh. "Right. Okay. But just until the stairway ride is in." She pointed to her right leg. "Well, doctor. That's settled. Can I walk on this thing?"

"Not yet. You'll need a wheelchair for a while. The hospital can arrange for a rental. We can fix up a walking boot before too long."

"Fine. All right. I'll stay here tonight. Is there a decent TV in my room?" She raised one eyebrow.

"I'll see to it," he said, turning the wheelchair around.

"Good night then, Lee, Pete." She waved to us as the properly humbled doctor carefully wheeled her away. "I'll phone you in the morning as soon as I'm discharged. Lee, give the Angels a call tonight, will you? Tell them I'll let them know about this week's meeting as soon as I get to your house."

CHAPTER 24

We hurried across the hospital parking lot. "Let's move the bed from the guest room down to the den," Pete said, "and we can put my recliner in the living room, and put one of the lounge chairs in the den, okay? The TV in there is a good one, and she can put her stuff in that little bureau my sister gave us when she redecorated the boys' rooms."

I linked my arm through his, running to keep up with his long strides. "Thank you for inviting her to stay with us," I said, "and for thinking of ways to make her comfortable."

"She's my aunt now, too, you know. You, Ibby, and O'Ryan—I signed up for the whole package." Slowing down as we approached the car, he covered my hand with his. "Best deal I ever made in my life."

On the ride home, we made some more plans

for dealing with this sudden change in our lives. "You know she's not going to want us hovering over her," I said. "As long as she can wheel herself from den to bathroom to kitchen and sunroom, I think she'll be fine staying alone during the times you and I both have to be at work."

"I'm sure she will. I'm hoping the wheelchair will fit through our old doorways," Pete worried.

"I'll bet one or both of the Angels will volunteer to Ibby-sit whenever we need them," I said. "I'll call Betsy and Louisa as soon as we get home, and in the morning, we'll order the stair lift for her house."

Our work was cut out for us. With much pushing and pulling and not a little hysterical laughter, we managed to wrestle bed frame, box spring, and mattress down the narrow front staircase and into the den and swapped the recliner for the living room lounge chair. Pete brought Donnie Jr.'s small cast-off bureau down from the attic. It needed a new paint job. Stencils of baseball bats and balls weren't quite Aunt Ibby's style, but it would do for now.

I remembered to call the Angels, who were each sincerely upset by the news about their friend, and promised to do anything and everything they could to help. Betsy asked if they could come over to see her the following day, and I said I'd check with Aunt Ibby and let her know.

Aunt Ibby's accident had come at a particularly inconvenient time. I'd arranged with Francine to meet her at eight o'clock the following morning to begin our documentary. That meant Pete would have to pick her up at the yet-undetermined time at the hospital, get her settled in her room, and stay with her until I could get away from the museum.

"Don't worry about it," Pete said. "The chief will rearrange my schedule as much as we need to. I'll get it straightened out first thing tomorrow when I go in to work. I might have to work a few extra nights, that's all. He's a big fan of your aunt." It was true. Chief Whaley's wife and Aunt Ibby were longtime friends. "Anyway, the Angels will be happy to come over and help out. Betsy just told you so."

He was right. I tried really hard to stop worrying and to concentrate on my TV wardrobe. I'd already decided to wear the WICH-TV company green blazer with gray skirt, white shirt, and gray pumps for the first day and ease into wearing some of the new outfits and great shoes I'd splurged on as we moved along. I was ready for sleep. I put on my pajamas, set the alarm clock for six thirty, climbed over the cat onto the bed, and didn't even try to stay awake for the late news.

The call from the hospital informing us that we could pick Aunt Ibby up came earlier than we'd expected. It was a little past seven. Pete and I were enjoying our morning coffee, congratulating ourselves on the good job we'd done on the room preparation, and getting ready to leave for our respective jobs. I felt surprisingly calm, considering that although my new business cards identified me as an *Historical Documentary Executive Director* today would mark my debut effort at actually *being* one. The call from the hospital came to my phone.

"Good morning, Mrs. Mondello," she said. "The

doctor has decided it will be all right for you to pick Miss Russell up this morning. Will nine o'clock be convenient for you?"

"Pete," I asked, "can you get Aunt Ibby at nine?" He nodded "yes."

"We can do that," I said. "but isn't that quite early to discharge a patient?"

"The doctor has the paperwork ready. Miss Russell is quite anxious to leave."

I had to smile at that. Aunt Ibby can be very convincing when she wants something. "Mr. Mondello will be there at nine," I promised, then shrugged into my green jacket, ready to leave for my own eight o'clock date with Francine.

"Break a leg, sweetheart," Pete said, then laughed. "Not an appropriate saying under the circumstances, is it? You look gorgeous and very businesslike. Don't worry. I'll fix my schedule with the chief, and I'll have Ibby all cozy in her new room in no time."

I gave him a hug and a quick kiss. "I know you will. Love you so much!"

It felt good to park the Jeep in my same old reserved space beside the seawall. I saw Francine's truck in her usual space and the newest WICH-TV mobile unit parked beside the studio entrance. Tapping my code into the pad beside the door, I entered the long, cool, black-walled room. I heard the chatter of kids' voices coming from the nearby soundstage. The daily influx of "little buckaroos" had arrived for *Ranger Rob's Rodeo*. I love the sound of kids laughing. *Maybe before too long*, I thought, *Pete and I will start raising our own little buckaroos*. I smiled at the idea and opened the green metal door to the staircase leading to the second-floor office.

Francine was already there and greeted me with a hug. Back when I was a full-time field reporter, Francine and I had made a great team—and had shared more than a few hair-raising adventures in pursuit of a good story. "It'll be like old times," she said. "You and me and a camera. What a hoot!"

Rhonda had written "Museum Documentary Lee and Francine 8 AM to?" on the whiteboard. "I appreciate the open-ended time allotment," I said. "We had a little emergency last night, and I may have to do a little back-and-forth between job and home." I told them about Aunt Ibby's accident, and about her staying with Pete and me for a while.

They both know Aunt Ibby, and I knew their words of support and sympathy were heartfelt. They each offered "anything I can do" sentiments, and I told them I wouldn't hesitate to ask for help if we needed it. I meant it too. "Is Mr. Doan in yet?" I asked. "Any final instructions before we leave?"

"He's not here yet, but that photographer woman left an envelope of photo prints for you—along with a hefty invoice." She pulled a large yellow envelope from her desk drawer and handed it to me. "Doan okayed the invoice, said the pictures are excellent and you should use as many as you need to. He says she got a lot of shots of the interior before any work in there began. And that those will be perfect for a before-and-after comparison at the end of the shoot."

So, without being specifically asked, Fiona had anticipated what we'd need and had provided a pricey package that Bruce Doan not only clearly liked, but was willing to pay for. *Fiona loves her work,* was the thought that came to mind. I looked down at my high heels, my neatly pressed green jacket. I loved mine too, especially when I was in front of a camera. Maybe this documentary would convince Doan to give me more assignments like this one. I remembered, too, what Kitsue had said to me. *"I can tell that you love your work. I wish that I loved mine."*

"Come on, Lee. Let's get this show on the road," Francine prompted. I stuck the yellow envelope into my handbag—not the old faithful hobo, but a sweet Jacki Easlick cognac leather tote, and followed her through the metal door, down the back stairs, and out onto the parking lot. I hiked up my narrow skirt and climbed into the passenger seat. "Here we go," Francine said. "On the road again." She gave a satisfying blast of the horn to Scott, who'd just pulled into the lot. I pasted on a big smile and waved as we drove by. *I do love my work.*

We didn't have far to go to get to the museum site. Francine hadn't been inside the building since back when it was a gym and said she was anxious to see what was going on in there. I was anxious to show her. She pulled a shoulder-mounted camera from the side door of the van along with a tripod for closeups. "Let's do a walk-through with this one. Doan likes the immediacy of this new shoulder-mount Sony. He even got one for Old Jim too."

"Whatever you say," I agreed. We each held our press passes up to the window. Mr. Thomas seemed to read each one carefully, then, poker-faced, let us in. Francine adjusted my clip-on mic, then with me leading the way this time, and Francine recording, we stepped into the main room. I took a deep breath, smiled, and faced the camera.

"Hello. I'm Lee Barrett, and we're inside the building that will soon house the Salem International Museum. Less than two weeks from now, the doors will be open to the public to view this new venue's first show—*Seafaring New England*. For six months, visitors will see and learn about the days when ships from New England ports, including many from Salem, sailed the oceans of the world. During the filming of this documentary, we'll be privileged to see the inner workings of producing such an event."

I moved to one side and indicated the huge, still-empty cylinder dominating the center of the room. "For instance, see that very space age–looking glass tube? Before long, it will be filled with displays of fabulous jewels—maharajas' treasures all the way from India, gathered today from museums all over the country." I walked toward the giant ship model. "Here's a display already in place. This is a model of the Salem vessel *Naiad*." I motioned for Francine to move in for a closeup while I told the sad story of William Griffen. She focused on the metal representation of the smiling sailor.

We moved from alcove to alcove, some of the empty ones, some with partial fixtures in place, and the few that, like the Sullivan alcove, were near completion. Thanks to my notes, and Mr. Pennington's floor plan, I was able to give a fair idea of the remarkable scope the city's first event in the rehabbed building would offer to locals and tourists alike. We'd filmed for a couple of hours on the first floor when I signaled to Francine to pause.

"I'm quite sure the photos we picked up from the station this morning were taken well before any of the painting or construction was done," I told her. "It might be a good idea to take a look at them now and see where they might fit into today's segment—like maybe a still photo of the main area before it was painted or carpeted, and a shot of one of the in-progress alcoves when it was first being constructed." I crossed my fingers. "At least I hope that's what we've got. Let's take a look."

We'd left my handbag with the yellow envelope of photos locked inside the mobile unit, so with a brief explanation of our intentions to Mr. Thomas, we made a quick exit and return to the museum-in-progress. The raised, carpeted platform outside the fenced-in area where the ship model was displayed made both a comfortable spot for sitting and a clean, flat area for spreading out the photographs.

I opened the envelope, pulled out the top photo, and placed it on the platform. That was as far as I got. The six-by-nine photo offered a clear shot of the top of the A&P building. It even showed the faded letters of the Eight O'Clock Coffee ad. It was, in fact, the exact picture I'd seen in my vision.

CHAPTER 25

"What's this doing here?" The question slipped out.

"What do you mean?" Francine asked. "It's a really good 'before' picture of the building. I like it."

"Yes, I know," I mumbled. "It's—um—very good. I just didn't expect to see the place from that angle."

Francine picked the photo up, giving it a closer look. "A good drone picture. I enjoy taking them myself."

"A drone picture. Of course." Not that a drone picture is at all unusual, but I'd sure never had a *vision* from that angle before. *What does it mean?*

"Are you okay?" Francine gave me an intense stare. "Are you worried about your aunt?"

Of course, I was worried about Aunt Ibby, but I knew that wasn't what made Francine give me that look. I couldn't very well explain to her the reason the photo bothered me. I slipped the envelope back into my bag and fibbed a little. "If you don't mind, I'd like to give Pete a call—just to see if she's settled into her new room."

"Sure. Take your time. I'll wander around a bit, maybe take a peek into some of those alcoves."

I texted Pete. **Everything OK? How is she doing?**

He answered immediately. **Putting on a brave front. She's hurting more than she lets on. Gave her a pill. She's asleep. I'll stay here until you get home.**

Another hour should do it.

I looked around for Francine. Maybe I'd see the rest of the pictures later by myself, just in case there were any more surprises in there. She was talking to a worker who'd just unpacked the figure-head that was to be positioned over the alcove that already housed the Crowninshield ship model. Installing the figurehead, which I could see already was a beauty—a buxom lady with trailing skirts and windblown hair—would make a good first-day shot. I hurried across the room, passing by the glass tube and the giant ship model. It didn't take us long to get into position. Francine had already had the workman sign a model release, while I did a quick read of the information sheet pasted to the packing carton in which the lady was housed. "This figure, carved of pine, dates from about eighteen-oh-five and may have adorned a Salem vessel," I told the camera. "She makes a fitting entrance to this alcove, which will house important historical items from one of Salem's most distinguished shipping families."

I'd timed things correctly, and within an hour we'd covered a couple of the partly finished alcoves and one of the ones with floor-to-ceiling china cabinets. There, two white-gloved women placed blue-and-white Canton china in neat rows while I read the story of a bride whose husband had died before the wedding gift barrels of the double set of china had even been unpacked—and had never been used. Francine walked around the room, adding some extra angles to areas she'd recorded earlier to make the film editor's job easier, including a snippet of paint-spattered George touching up the baseboards of one of the still-empty alcoves. We hadn't yet entered the Sullivan family display, which I realized was the most complete of all so far. I looked in and saw Kitsue and Priscilla from the display team laughing together. I was happy to see the smile on the young woman's face. Perhaps, at last, she'd found work she loved. I hoped so—and at the same time, hoped there was some good, logical reason for a tiny, embroidered shoe to be in her bottom drawer.

"Kitsue," I called. "We're doing a first-day walk-around for the documentary. May I come in and do a brief interview about the things a visitor will see here? Yours is the most complete of all the exhibits so far. It'll give the viewers a hint of things to come."

She hesitated for a couple of seconds. "Well—I don't know—I guess it would be all right. How does my hair look?"

"Perfect, as always," I told her. Francine joined us, and I made quick introductions. "Kitsue, why don't you stand in front of Li Jing's portrait. I'll tell the audience who you are and ask you to tell us a little about her, about the love story with Captain Edward Sullivan."

Priscilla watched from outside the alcove entrance while Francine positioned herself across from the portrait of Li Jing. Kitsue stood to one side of the painting. "It looks as if your four-times-great-grandma is looking at you," Francine remarked. "Nice. Move a little closer. Okay. Counting." She pointed to me. "Three. Two. One."

I faced the camera, explained what we were about to see, and began the interview. The Q-and-A with Kitsue Sullivan was maybe the easiest interview I've ever done. Kitsue absolutely sparkled. Her answers were succinct and heartfelt, her facial expressions delightful, her knowledge of the subject impressive. She told the love story, touching on the voyages the two had taken together to faraway lands. She described the wedding dress, teased viewers with comments about some of the things they'd see when the museum opened. In short, she nailed it.

Afterward, Francine, Priscilla, and I showered her with compliments. "That was totally professional," Francine told her. "Heck, you could be hosting your own show."

I echoed the idea. "Kitsue," I said. "That was wonderful, and the camera loves you. Have you ever thought about doing something in TV?"

A shy smile and a shake of the shiny black hair. "I don't think about things like that anymore, but thank you. It was fun, Lee. I hope your documentary will be a success." She motioned to Priscilla. "Back to work for us, Priscilla. Let's figure out how to show Captain Sullivan's logbooks and his sextant. I'm beginning to wish we'd picked one of the bigger spaces."

It was time for Francine and me to pack up and head back to the station. We made a fast turn around the main room, thanking workers we'd met, the Canton china ladies, the figurehead-hanging man, George, Priscilla, Mr. Thomas, and Kitsue. I tucked my bag under one arm and Francine's folding tripod under the other. We walked out into the getting-cooler September air. I texted Pete again. **Almost finished. Need to check in with Doan.**

He answered immediately. **The Angels just arrived. Ibby still sleeping. Take your time. We're covered here. Betsy will call you.** What a relief. I felt as though a weight had been lifted from my chest. My aunt couldn't be in better hands.

We took a shortcut down Norman Street to New Derby, Francine and I chattering enthusiastically about the venue we'd just left. "This show is going to be a big attraction for Salem," Francine said. "Have they told you yet what the next one is going to be about?"

"I don't know," I admitted. "It will have to be something world-class, something exciting. I know Florida has had some big ones in the past. Aunt Ibby went to one in St. Petersburg about the *Titanic* that drew more than a million visitors."

"I'll bet this one will do that for Salem," she said. "If all the exhibits are as good as what Kitsue Sullivan showed us, it can't miss." She gave a nod toward the handbag at my feet on the floor of the cab. "I thought we were going to insert some still photos. Have you had a chance to pick any yet?"

"Not yet." I tried to sound nonchalant. "Maybe I'll look them over in my office when I get a minute." I was still shaken by the photo—not because of the subject matter, which made perfect sense—but because I'd seen that *exact* picture in my vision.

I'd never had an experience quite like it before, and I didn't like it. What other surprises might Fiona's pictures hold?

We checked in with Rhonda and read our white-board assignments—Francine was to contact Scott about covering a book signing at the Wicked Good Books bookstore. I was to see Mr. Doan about helping his wife, Buffy, select a venue for the up-coming Halloween party since the Hawthorne Hotel ballroom was already booked.

Why did she wait so long? This wasn't going to be an easy task. I knocked on the station manager's door and waited for the expected "Come in. It's open."

"How did the first day of filming go?" he asked.

"It went absolutely smoothly," I said. "It's all ready for first edits now. I think you'll be pleased."

"I certainly hope so. How did you like the pictures the Sullivan woman took?"

"I think they'll work in nicely," I lied.

He cleared his throat. "Now, about Mrs. Doan's party. We'll need an area big enough to accommodate about a hundred, maybe hundred and fifty people. We'll need a dance floor, of course, and a place to put a band and room for the caterers to set up a buffet." He raised his eyebrows. "Can do?"

"Can try," I offered.

"I have every confidence in you, Ms. Barrett," he said. "Get right on it."

Sure. Right after next week's program schedule and that little museum gig you handed me.

Still shaking my head in wonder at the man's confidence in my limited abilities, I took the ramp down to the news department and my not-so-private cubicle, turned the key, and sat behind my own not-so-private desk. I grabbed a couple of lavender sticky notes—one to remind me to ask Betsy to see if she wanted to set up some kind of Zoom meetings for the weekly *Midsomer Murders* get-togethers, and the second for Doan's impossible dream of a last-minute Halloween party venue— and stuck them onto the window-wall behind my chair. I couldn't put off examining the rest of Fiona's photos any longer. Surely since Mr. Doan had paid top dollar for them, he was going to want his money's worth.

I pulled the yellow envelope from my purse once again and dumped the contents onto the desk, spreading them out, fanlike, the way River sometimes arranged the tarot deck. The drone's-eye view of the building was still on top. I pushed it beneath the next photo, a very good picture of the giant model of the *Naiad*. "This is beautiful," I said to myself, looking closely at the image. "I can even see the smile on poor William Griffen's face." I moved on, one by one, examining the photos, re-alizing they were undoubtedly worth whatever Mr. Doan had paid for them and they would surely im-prove my documentary.

My phone buzzed. Caller ID told me that Betsy Leavitt was calling. I felt my heart speed up. Good call or bad call?

It was a good call. "Hi, Lee. Betsy here. Louisa and I are with Ibby, and everything is fine. We're all having tea, and some Girl Scout cookies we found in your cute cookie jar. You go about your business. Do what you need to do. Don't worry about anything here."

"Oh, Betsy. That's such a relief. Can I speak to Aunt Ibby?" I wanted my aunt to confirm Betsy's words for me. She was on the line in seconds. "Aunt Ibby? How are you feeling?"

"I'm fine, dear. My friends are here, spoiling me, and Pete gave me some kind of happy pills. The leg hardly hurts at all."

I told her I loved her and that I'd be home soon, then said good-bye. I suddenly had a creepy feeling that someone was watching me. In my fishbowl office, that wasn't unusual, and usually the watcher was Scott Palmer. I spun the chair around, and there he was. He smiled and made the familiar "call me" sign. I sighed and hit his number. If I didn't, he'd simply make a pest of himself until I did.

"Nice pictures," he said. "Who's the photographer?"

"Fiona Sullivan." I moved the *Naiad* photo aside, exposing the next one.

"Wow. Great drone shot," Scott almost shouted. "She must have caught the whole main floor in that one, right?"

I picked the picture up, holding it closer to my eyes. He was correct. From one side to the other, the photo showed the main room in detail. "How did she get that one?" I wondered aloud.

"The drones are great. I'm no photographer, but I'm going to get one just for fun. You should try it too." He leaned forward, almost pressing his nose against the glass like O'Ryan does "Let's see it again."

I held the photo up, facing him this time. "It looks like it was taken from the center of the first-floor ceiling."

"Sure. It was. Don't you watch your own programs? That captain from the Toy Trawler explained how they work to a bunch of kindergarten kids this morning on the cowboy show."

I had to smother a laugh. I'd had no idea that Scott was a Ranger Rob fan. "I'm sorry I missed that one," I said. "I'll pull it up from the archives and take a look." I meant that. If Captain Billy could make the little buckaroos understand drone photography, he could probably teach me about it too.

"Can I see the rest of the pictures?" Pleading tone. "You're not going to be the only one covering it, you know. Doan told me the station bought some pictures. If those are the ones he bought, that means I can use them, too, if I need to. Right?"

He was, of course, absolutely right. "Okay," I told him. "Have you had lunch yet?"

Big smile. "Nope. Are you buying?"

"Not a chance. I'm starving. Let's grab a booth at the Friendly, and I'll show you the pictures," I told him. "You can pick the ones you want, and we'll get Old Jim to make prints."

"Want to go now?" he asked.

"Let's go," I said. I wasn't kidding about being hungry, and besides, I wanted to see if he'd learned any more about Walter Wyman and if he'd observed anything at the funeral that I might have missed.

CHAPTER 26

We walked across Derby Street together. Most of the lunch crowd had left the Friendly when Scott and I got there, so there was no problem in getting a booth. We began spreading the pictures out on the table a few at a time, careful to keep them away from our burgers and drinks.

"Whenever you see one you think you can use, put it on the seat beside you so we can get a print," I suggested.

"I guess she didn't get any pictures of the Indian guy's jewels yet, did she?"

"Of course not. They won't be there until it's almost opening day." Scott could be so exasperating. "You knew these were taken a while ago."

"I know." He selected a few pictures from the layout on the table. I spread out some more, put the previously displayed ones on the seat beside me. "It looks like she got quite a few with the Indian guy next to the tube thing."

"It does look that way. I haven't looked through all of them yet myself," I told him. "She's not only a professional photographer, you know. Her sister told me she's also an inventor. She has some ideas she's trying to patent."

"No kidding? What kind of ideas? Like, photography?" He selected a few more photos and put them on his seat.

"Kitsue says she's done some things with silicone," I said, "and I've seen an amazing plastic sealant she's developed that's absolutely invisible."

"I wonder if I could interview her about all that," he said.

"I doubt it. At least not until she's got her patents on these things—and she says that can take a lot of money to do it right," I suggested. "But you could ask her."

"You could introduce me."

"I guess so. I don't actually know her very well. I just run into her occasionally at the museum." I spread some more photos on the table. "I was surprised that I didn't see her at Walter Wyman's funeral. You had a better seat than I did. Did you see her anywhere that day?"

"I saw the cute sister, Kitsue, and that guy, George, who works at the museum," he said. *So Kitsue is the "cute" sister—even though they look so much alike.* I'd never thought of them that way, though apparently a man might. Would a comparison like that one be a cause of conflict between the two? Interesting.

The yellow envelope was nearly empty. Our dishes had been cleared away when I spread the last of the photos on the table. "Look." Scott pointed. "There are a couple more of those drone shots. She must have flown the thing into the Sullivans' alcove. Some of the cases were still empty."

"That'll be a good one for me to use." I picked it up. "I'm trying to show the place as it gets put together from the empty stages up until the show is ready for the public to come in the doors." There was another drone photo. "It looks as if this is another one showing the main room. From the ceiling. You can see right down inside Sant Bidani's exhibit."

"So cool," he said. "What do you say someday you and I take a ride over to that Toy Trawler and let Captain What's-His-Name show us how to work them? Maybe we can get Doan to buy a couple for us."

"Fat chance of that." I laughed. "But it would be fun to learn. Someday. Right now I need to get home and check on my aunt. Thanks for lunch."

We walked across the street together, but while Scott went back into the building, I climbed into my Jeep. I didn't want to risk finding something new for me to do on Rhonda's whiteboard, so, feeling only the tiniest twinge of guilt about it, I headed for Winter Street and home.

As soon as I approached our house, I saw Betsy Leavitt's Mercedes parked at the curb. I turned into the driveway, parked behind the house next to Louisa's new Lexus, and unlocked the sunroom door. I was greeted with gales of, well, "girlish" laughter from inside. It sounded pretty darn hilarious for a supposed sickroom. *Are they having wine with their tea and cookies? Is my aunt sharing those happy pills?*

I hurried to the den-turned-bedroom. "Hi, everybody. Thanks, Betsy and Louisa, for coming over so quickly." My aunt waved to me from her bed, looking as healthy as ever. Betsy sat in the lounge chair, and Louisa had brought a Lucite chair in from the kitchen. Several good-sized flower arrangements were lined up on the floor beneath the window, and another occupied most of the bedside table. "Oh, Maralee," my aunt chirped happily. "I feel ever so much better than I did in the hospital!"

"My goodness, it looks as if you're keeping all the florists in Salem busy," I said, seriously impressed by the floral tributes. I looked at the card on the largest one. It was from the staff at the library. Another was from Rupert Pennington. Betsy filled me in on the other two. "The one with the orange day lilies is from Louisa and me, and the vase with the two dozen roses is from Michael."

My aunt moved her covers aside, displaying the plaster cast. "Look. Betsy and Louisa signed it. Michael will be over later to add his autograph." She pulled a black Sharpie pen from under her pillow. "You can be next."

I accepted the pen and took the opportunity to look above and below the cast. Her recently pedicured toes were somewhat bruised, and her knee looked a bit swollen, but all in all it didn't look bad at all. Louisa stood, offering me her chair. "Sit down, Maralee. You've been working all day. I'll just pull in another of these beautiful chairs from the kitchen." Before I could protest, she darted out the door, returning with the chair and preceded by O'Ryan. The cat, with a loud purr, put his front paws on the edge of Aunt Ibby's bed, with what seemed to me to be a plea to join her there. She patted the space beside her.

"Come on, dear cat. *Mi bed, su bed.*" O'Ryan climbed onto the bed, so carefully, so gently, and lay beside her, her hand resting on his head. Sitting there in my kitchen chair, I looked around the room, thankful that my aunt had these two thoughtful and loving friends, and so many others as evidenced by the flowers. It was a pleasant scene.

"Maralee, dear." My aunt looked up from her cat-stroking. "You did remember that tonight is *Midsomer Murder* night, didn't you? They're showing part one of 'With Baited Breath.' You don't mind if we hold the meeting here, do you?"

I hadn't expected the question. It was becoming apparent that my aunt didn't intend to let a mere broken leg slow down her lifestyle one little bit. "That's the one about the giant fish, isn't it? Haven't you all seen it before?"

The trio laughed in unison. "Of course, we have," Betsy said. "But every time we rewatch an episode, we observe nuances in the detecting methods, hidden clues that lead to the solution."

Louisa agreed. "Going over and over each episode is the most valuable part of our study of each murder, understanding motives, not just discovering the *who*, but more importantly, the *why*. Inspector Barnaby has taught us all so much."

"We're getting really good at figuring out motives," Aunt Ibby offered, "and Michael has been a big help in spotting the tiniest indications of guilt that the ordinary person might not recognize." She gave me a confident grin. "So, it's alright if we hold the meeting here, isn't it? We won't be any trouble at all. The girls will bring all the snacks and wine."

"Why, yes. If you feel up to it, Aunt Ibby, why not?" I agreed, not entirely convinced it was a good idea and not at all sure how Pete would feel about it.

"We'd like it if you'd join us," Louisa suggested. "We'll be discussing the murder of Walter Wyman, and for this meeting, we'll be searching for motive. Perhaps Pete would like to sit in too."

Pete understands that the Angels take their amateur sleuthing seriously, and, in fact, some of their input had been helpful to the police in the past. "I'll ask him," I said, "but he's really busy. Halloween month in Salem brings some extra police work."

The motive for the shooting of Walter Wyman was, so far, the biggest question of all. There had to be one—his death hadn't been an accident. The short-staffed police department didn't have the time or resources to investigate it as they'd like. Was it possible that some amateur-sleuthing womanpower could contribute something of value? It wasn't outside the realm of possibility. I made a quick decision. "I can't speak for Pete," I said. "He may be working late, and I can't promise to watch the whole movie with you, but yes, I'd like to sit in on the discussion about motive. So far, there doesn't seem to be one in Walter's case."

"Wonderful. We'll be back, then, at around eight o'clock tonight." Betsy stood, then leaned down to give Aunt Ibby a kiss on the cheek. "I'll call Michael and tell him the meeting is on."

"We left a casserole in the refrigerator for your

dinner," Louisa said. "We figured you might not have time to cook." *Anyone who has friends like these is truly blessed.* "Should we put these chairs back into the kitchen?"

"Let's leave them here for now," I said. "If you don't mind, Aunt Ibby, I'll move some of your flowers to other rooms and make room for some more chairs in here so that everybody at the meeting can see the TV." I saw Betsy and Louisa out— Betsy to the front door, then Louisa through the sunroom door. Louisa had just left in the Lexus when I heard the sound of a car next door. It wasn't the sweet purr of Michael's well-maintained Lincoln, though—more like the rumble of a truck— one with the whine of a bad alternator. Okay, call me a gearhead. It comes from years of hanging around NASCAR tracks. A beat-up green Chevy pickup had pulled into Michael's yard, and George Washington climbed out of the cab. He carried a box with a picture of a cat on it—my housewarming gift to Michael. He spotted me right away.

"Hey, hi, Ms. Barrett," he called. "I'm here to put in this cat door for Dr. Martell. Thanks a lot for the recommendation."

Sincerely hoping that passing George's business card to Michael hadn't been a gigantic mistake, I returned his greeting and walked over to the adjoining parking area. "I don't think Mr. Martell is home, George."

"That's okay. He'll be along in a minute." He held up a jangling key ring. "He gave me his keys so I can get started right away. He's going to an important meeting later tonight."

I know. It's at my house.

Putting the carton with the cat's picture on the

ground, he unlocked the sunroom door, pulled it open, and inspected the glass panes. "Yes. It ought to just about fit in that center section."

"It's exactly like the cat door in my sunroom," I told him, hoping to make the installation as easy as possible. "Do you think it would be helpful if you took a look at mine before you start?"

"Couldn't hurt," he said. "Wait a sec 'til I get my tools." He pulled a rusty red metal toolbox from behind the passenger seat, then followed me across the yard to my house. I went inside, leaving the door ajar. "Look it over, George," I told him. "Take measurements if you need to. It's exactly the same as Dr. Martell's. The houses are identical, just reversed. Just call if you need me. I'll be right inside."

"Thanks, Ms. Barrett." He pulled a measuring tape—a yellow cloth one—from the toolbox. "I heard that your aunt got hurt. Is she going to be okay?"

"Yes, thank you, George. She'll be fine. Doctor says it's a simple break. She'll be staying here with me until she can get around by herself."

"Great. Tell her George Washington was asking for her."

"I will. Just call me if you need me," I said again.

I hurried to my aunt, who was still awake. O'Ryan had not left her side. "Did I hear you talking to somebody?" she asked.

"It's George Washington. He asked how you were. He's going to put the cat door in for Michael so he's looking at the way ours was done," I explained.

"George is a nice fellow. Not much of a reader, though. Thank him for me," she said. "I can hardly wait to see what kind of cat Michael will choose. Judging from his books, I see him with a Maine coon cat like Theodore in *Death on an Oriental Rug*. What do you think?"

"I think he'll choose a rescue cat," I said, "like Scoobie in *The Antique Hope Chest Murders*. But let's ask him tonight, and when you all discuss the Walter Wyman murder, I wonder if he's found any of those 'indications of guilt that the ordinary person might not recognize' you mentioned."

"I wouldn't be a bit surprised," she said. "Writing all those murder mysteries gives him a way of looking at things with unusual imagination."

The doorbell chimed "It's a Wonderful World." "I'll get it," I said. "Probably more flowers for you." I was right. This time it was a dish garden from the women's club at Aunt Ibby's church. As the florist's van pulled away from the curb, I saw Michael's Lincoln entering his driveway. I stopped at the doorway to Aunt Ibby's room, showed her the plant, and told her I'd put it on the coffee table in the sunroom—and that's what I did.

"Dr. Martell is home," I told George. "What do you think about the job? Do you see any problem with installing the cat door?"

"Nope. Easy. She's going to fit just fine." He picked up the red toolbox. "Want to come over and watch?" He smiled. "You can hand me the tools, like a doctor doing surgery!" It wasn't a bad idea. Michael had parked the Lincoln. I told my aunt I'd be next door for a few minutes and followed George across the yard.

Michael had picked up the cat door box and stood holding it in his arms, beaming happily. "Hello, George, Lee," he said. "I'm excited to get this in place and then to give some nice rescue cat a forever home."

"Like Scoobie," I said.

"Exactly." He seemed pleased that I'd remembered one of his book cat characters. George looked back and forth from me to Michael. I guessed that as my aunt had observed, George wasn't much of a reader. "Scoobie is a cat in one of my murder mysteries," Michael explained.

"Cool," George said. The hinges on the rusty toolbox squeaked as he lifted the top section. "I haven't used this much lately. Not since I banged a few heavy-duty picture hangers into the wall for Kitsue." I held the box package open while Michael removed the cat door from it. It was an all-in-one-piece gadget, so I figured that probably George wouldn't have much room to mess it up.

"Holy crap!" George's face was drained of color. Michael and I turned to face him. "Holy crap!" He lifted a gun from the toolbox. It was still partially wrapped in thick white cloth printed with cute pink bunnies.

CHAPTER 27

Michael dropped the new cat door as if it had burned his hands, grabbed the doorknob, and darted into his sunroom. "Get that thing away from me!" he yelled through the glass. "It can't be on my property. Get the hell out of here with it!"

George hadn't moved—just stood there holding the gun. I spoke softly, understanding Michael's terror. "George. Leave the gun in the toolbox and come over to my side of the yard. I'm calling the police right now. Dr. Martell cannot have weapons on his property." I was quite sure that George knew Michael was a convicted felon and that his Second Amendment rights had been taken away for good reason. Trancelike, George did as I'd told him to. Carrying the still partially open toolbox with both hands, he followed me across the yard and into my sunroom. Pete answered my call right away. I told him what had just happened as well as I could.

"Leave it where it is. Tell George not to pick it up or handle it," he ordered.

"He already picked it up, but it's wrapped in a diaper." I told him.

"A diaper?"

"I'll explain when you get here." I put the phone down, moved the new dish garden aside, and motioned for the silent George to put the toolbox on the coffee table. "Sit down, George," I said. "The police are on the way."

George again followed my instructions and sat obediently on the bentwood bench. I sat facing him, the two of us waiting silently for the police to come and take away the gun protruding from the rusty metal box. I had a strong suspicion that we were looking at the weapon that had killed Walter Wyman. I hoped the police wouldn't arrive with sirens screaming and lights flashing. I didn't want Aunt Ibby—or the rest of Winter Street—to be disturbed any more than necessary.

I watched Pete's unmarked Crown Vic pull quietly into his regular spot in the yard. I learned a few minutes later that two more police cruisers— no sirens, but plenty of flashing lights—had parked in front of the house.

Aunt Ibby called from her room, "What's going on, Maralee?" at the same time Pete came through the sunroom door.

I pointed to the coffee table, then ran toward the sound of her voice. "There it is," I called, as Pete positioned himself between George and the coffee table. "I'll be right back."

My aunt sat upright, both legs dangling over the

edge of the bed. "Get me that wheelchair, Maralee," she ordered. "I want to see what's going on."
The lights from the street outside flashed red and
blue on the windowpanes, and the doorbell began
to chime.

"Wait a sec. I'll get the door," I told her. "George
found a gun in his toolbox." There was no time for
further explanation. I pulled the front door open,
admitting two officers into the narrow hallway.
"Follow me," I said. "Pete's out back." We paraded
through the living room to the sunroom, where
now George stood, hands behind his back, facing
Pete from the opposite side of the room.

Do I stay here, or go back to Aunt Ibby?

Pete answered my unspoken question. "See to
Ms. Russell, Lee," he said. Serious cop voice.
"Then we'll need a statement from you. Another
officer will take Dr. Martell's statement." I realized
then that there must be officers in the second police car, too, who'd be ringing our neighbor's
doorbell. He was not going to be happy.

I crossed the living room again and did as my
aunt had asked, unfolding the wheelchair and
helping her into it, talking in low tones, explaining as fast as I could what was going on. "I have to
get back out there," I said, "to give a statement.
They're going to ask Michael for one too." She
wheeled herself to the window. "Come back and
tell me what's going on out there," she whispered,
then I went back to the sunroom, prepared to do
my civic duty. This time O'Ryan followed me.

Pete asked me to sit down. George remained
standing, as did the officers. One of them held a
small recorder. George was questioned first. In a
halting voice, he told them what had happened,

how he'd come to install the cat door for Dr. Martell, opened his toolbox, and found the gun. He said he'd picked it up and immediately dropped it back into the toolbox.

"Was Dr. Martell present at that time?" Pete asked.

"Yes, he was," George said. "He told me to get the hell away from his house with the gun. He went inside and slammed the door."

My answers to their questions duplicated George's. *I expect Michael's answers will be exactly the same.* With George's permission, they put the toolbox with the gun into the largest evidence bag I'd ever seen. I told George that we could probably provide whatever tools he'd need to finish installing the cat door, then I showed the two officers to the front door with the evidence. I returned to the sunroom, with the cat following my every step, to see if Pete was going to share with me what he expected to happen next. I flat-out asked the question. "What happens next?"

I got the expected answer. "We'll see." I told him about the planned *Midsomer Murders* viewing along with the Angels' current input on the Walter Wyman murder. "It'll be at eight o'clock. Louisa and Betsy brought over a casserole for our dinner, so that's taken care of. Okay with you?"

"Sure, as long as you're sure your aunt isn't doing too much after her injury."

"Want to pop in and say 'hello' to her as long as you're here?" I suggested. "She seems to be her old self, except for the cast. She'll ask you to sign it, I'm sure."

"She's a trouper," he said. Together, we followed the cat back to my aunt's room.

"Oh, Pete, I'm so glad you're here. Will you help get me out of this contraption into a proper chair?" She gave a little side-to-side wiggle to illustrate her discomfort. "Do we have any crutches? I think I could get around just fine with crutches."

Pete didn't try to hide his smile. "I'm sure my sister, Marie, has some. When you have kids who play hockey, you have crutches somewhere in the house. If your doctor says it's okay, I'll ask her for them."

"Good. Now, if I can sit in that lounge chair, I'll be all set to eat my dinner and watch the TV tonight." She wheeled herself to the bedside, reaching under the pillow for her pen. "Want to sign my cast?" She turned toward me. "Maralee, dear. Would you make my bed? It's just not proper to have an unmade bed in the room when there's going to be a man present. Now, will somebody please explain to me what in the world is going on here? Police cars out front? George with a gun?" She handed Pete the pen and folded her arms expectantly.

Pete obliged with his signature while I made the bed. As he assisted her into the chair, he gave a succinct and cop-voiced rundown of the recent gun-related, backyard events. Apparently satisfied with both the explanation and the seating arrangement, she gave another little wiggle—this one a self-satisfied maneuver, unlike the wheelchair performance. She stuck out her injured leg. "Maralee, do you have a footstool I can rest this cursed thing on?"

I understood immediately why O'Ryan had made such a show of balancing himself on the footstool Pete's nephew had built.

"We certainly do," I told her, and hurried back

to the sunroom to get it. With the footstool in place, accompanied by a smart-alecky, *I-told-you-so* look from O'Ryan, I heated Louisa's casserole. It looked and smelled divine, and I hadn't the slightest idea what was in it. I fixed a tray for Aunt Ibby, then set two places at the kitchen table for Pete and me.

Pete gave the food a tentative taste, then dug right in. "This is good. What do you call it?"

"I call it Louisa's casserole," I said, tasting—and immediately agreeing with his assessment.

"Maybe you could make it sometime." His tone was hopeful. "You were going to tell me about the pink and white diaper. You'd seen it before?"

I didn't comment on the odds of my duplicating this particular dinner. "Priscilla, Kitsue's display lady, gave it—or one exactly like it—to Kitsue for dusting, along with a few others. She says they're good for all kinds of cleaning. I remembered it because of the cute bunnies."

"George told us that the last time he saw the toolbox was when he was in the Sullivans' alcove helping with the picture-hanging hardware," Pete said. "Is that how you understood it?"

"Exactly," I said. "I guess this means you'll be talking with Kitsue."

"For sure. So far, the Sullivan sisters have been in the middle of the puzzle, haven't they?" He held up one hand. "All in a circumstantial way, of course."

"Like Hoodie Girl with hair like Fiona's and the missing Chinese shoe from Kitsue's gazillion-dollar cereal bowl," I offered.

"And now a gun turns up," he said, "which may or may not be the murder weapon."

"And it's wrapped up in a dustcloth diaper, which may or may not belong to Kitsue," I finished the thought. "Speaking of Fiona's hair and the missing little shoe, Fiona told me about a couple of strange—but probably strictly circumstantial—happenings at grandmother Kitty's house in North Salem."

"Tell me about it," he said. "Have we got ice cream for dessert?"

"Three kinds." I pulled the half-gallon box from the freezer. "Aunt Ibby calls it 'Neopolitan.' Chocolate, vanilla, and strawberry."

"You can have all the strawberry," he offered. "Tell me about the strange, circumstantial happenings."

I scooped the ice cream into our bowls, vanilla for him, a mixture of chocolate and strawberry for me, and began to relate what Fiona had claimed she'd found while "borrowing" from her sister's bureau. Trying to remember every detail, I told him about the recently styled blond wig and the missing mate to the Chinese shoe Fiona had photographed for the museum catalog.

"Taking a pair of tights out of her sister's bureau without asking, huh? I don't know how girls feel about that, but if it was me, I'd wouldn't like it."

"I don't think I would, either, but then, I don't have a sister," I said. "They're very close in a lot of ways, even though they seem to be quite different from one another. Fiona says they've always worn each other's clothes. They even used to fool people by switching places."

"I might have to talk with the North Salem grandmother again," he said. "Do you know if Fiona has told Kitsue what she found?"

"I don't believe she has." I thought about it. "I don't think she's told anyone except me. Isn't that odd?"

"Uh-huh. It makes me wonder—especially about the blond wig. She knows from the housewarming that you and I are married." He leaned forward, his elbows on the table. "She'd expect you to pass the information on to me. Why does she want the Salem Police Department to consider that Kitsue could be playing the old switching-places game?"

"Hoodie Girl," I said. "She's trying to tell us that Kitsue pretended to be Fiona and hitched a ride with Walter Wyman—that Kitsue is Hoodie Girl, and Fiona doesn't want to be the one who blows the whistle on someone she loves so much—even if her sister turns out to be a killer." Just saying the words aloud made me sad.

"I'm afraid that's a possibility," Pete said. "Of course, it's not the *only* possibility."

"You mean, maybe Fiona really is Hoodie Girl, and she's trying to put the blame on Kitsue." I didn't like that possibility any better than the other one.

"Could be," he said. "It could be that Fiona is simply telling the truth about what she found, and she thinks that somebody is trying to frame Kitsue."

"Like who?"

"Like whoever had possession of the possible murder weapon?"

"George Washington," I stated. "But what's in it for him?"

"What's in it for anybody?" Pete answered my question with another question. "If nothing has been stolen from the armored truck, who benefits from Walter's death?"

"Motive," I mumbled, remembering my online criminology classes. "There has to be a motive."

"Chief always says there are only three reasons for murder," Pete said. "Money, love, and revenge."

I thought about that—tried to make sense out of it—and decided to change the subject. "If this was a murder mystery book," I said, "there'd be fingerprints on the gun that would lead to—to somebody. Then we'd find out why they did it," I reasoned. "When will you know if there are fingerprints?"

"I already know. There aren't." Wry smile. "Life isn't a mystery book, Nancy Drew."

"I know that. Just the same, I'm going to be interested in what Michael Martell has to say about all this," I insisted. "Sad as it is to say, Michael can see it from the point of view of both a mystery writer and a murderer."

"You're right. I'll be listening carefully to Martell and the Angels tonight," he said. "They all tend to think outside the box. Maybe one of them can come up with a motive the department has missed so far." He picked up our dishes and carried them to the sink. "Don't ever tell the chief I said that! By the way, your aunt always makes the food for the TV show. Do we have anything ready?"

"The girls are bringing snacks and wine," I promised. "Let's see if Aunt Ibby wants ice cream."

My aunt did want ice cream—"just a smidge"—and she also wanted to change clothes—"into something more presentable." I prepared the smidge—incorporating all three flavors in one small scoop—then barred Pete from the room while we accomplished a bathroom trip and a change for her into a heather-toned skirt and sweater outfit.

Betsy and Louisa arrived well ahead of the start

of *Midsomer Murders,* carrying between them a
large cooler. Louisa busied herself unpacking it
while Betsy visited with Aunt Ibby, then the two
changed places. Aunt Ibby gave each woman a precise, librarian-like report on the happenings on
Winter Street that day, and all expressed their concerns about Michael Martell's reaction to a gun
being discovered on his property. As time for the
airing of the show drew closer, there was quite a bit
of watch-checking and doorway-glancing going
on. Would Michael join the group tonight? He'd
never missed a meeting since the first time he'd
been invited to sit in. When O'Ryan suddenly
scampered away from Aunt Ibby's chair and a
knock sounded from the sunroom door, there was
a palpable sigh of relief from the Angels.

"I've got it," Pete called. "Michael's here."

There was no way that Pete and I were going to
miss this meeting. We carried the two remaining
kitchen chairs into the bedroom, along with the
tavern chair from the sunroom. A crowded group
of mystery fans faced the TV. Betsy and Louisa
had, as promised, provided snacks and wine and
had even brought along appropriate plates and
glassware. When the opening credits flashed onto
the screen, the six of us balanced our plates of
beautifully decorated petit fours with stemmed
glasses of a lovely fino sherry—ginger ale for
twenty-odd-years-sober Michael—and focused on
the unfolding story. We'd put off the usual pre-
show discussion of current events, waiting for
Michael's arrival, so the topic on all our minds
would have to wait for the station break in the middle of the show. The protocol of these meetings
never varies—even for broken legs or murder.

CHAPTER 28

It was time for the mid-show break. Aunt Ibby, as founder of the group, introduced the subject for the meeting. "We're all aware of the goings-on right here on Winter Street this morning," she said, "although from different perspectives. For instance, I observed the arrival of two police cars from that window." She pointed. "Maralee saw what happened from her own backyard, and Pete arrived on the scene shortly after a weapon was found in a handyman's toolbox in Michael's backyard. The Angels only know what they've heard from me, I suppose, or from others who were not on the actual scene. Maralee, will you begin?"

I recalled, as well as I could, how I'd heard George's truck arrive behind Michael's house, and about the brief conversation we'd had about installing the cat door, and about Michael's arrival—right up until the point when George opened the squeaky top of the red toolbox and yelled, "Holy crap" when he saw the gun wrapped in a pink and white diaper.

"Since George isn't here, Michael, will you take up the story at this point?" my aunt encouraged the writer. If Michael was still disturbed by the earlier happenings, he disguised it well. He began with an apology for using "strong language" when he sighted the gun. I assumed that he meant the words "get the hell out of here," and suppressed a smile when thinking of the much stronger language I'd heard from the Angels from time to time. He began with his own arrival at the back of his house and seeing George preparing to install the cat door, which was still in its carton.

"The door to my sunroom was partly open," he said, "and Mrs. Mondello stood in the yard watching us. Then George opened his toolbox and I saw part of a gun sticking out of a piece of cloth. I ran into my house and shut the door and locked it." He breathed deeply for a moment, squeezing his eyes shut. "I cannot, under any circumstances, have a gun of any kind on my property. I am, regrettably, a convicted felon. My only thought was to get that gun as far away from me as possible." There were murmurs of understanding from around the room.

It was time for Pete's narration. It was brief, delivered in his usual "just the facts" manner. "There was a telephone communication from this address in reference to a weapon having been observed on the premises. I dispatched two cruisers to the scene and transported myself here. I observed a Salem police officer transfer a red Craftsman toolbox and its contents into an official evidence bag."

Betsy wagged her hand in the air. "Pete, is it the gun that killed Walter Wyman? That's what we're investigating here, isn't it?"

"That's not been established as fact yet, Betsy, but it's a likely possibility."

"Details, details," Aunt Ibby interrupted. "Let's assume that it is and get to solving that poor boy's murder. We three"—she gestured toward the other Angels—"have been discussing the case between ourselves, and we all have some thoughts on the matter. I'm sure Maralee, who has been close to the museum, which seems to be 'ground central' for much of our mystery, has things to share, and perhaps Pete can, without violating any police secrets, fill us in on some detail, while Michael, with his author's insight, can help us find the elusive motive for all that's happened."

When it was nearly time for the windup of the *Midsomer Murders* episode, and also time for us to relate Investigator Barnaby's crime-solving expertise to our own current puzzle, I was determined to pay close attention to the fictional story we'd been viewing—not because I expected to find the answers to our puzzle, but because that was the Angels' rules for these meetings, and so far they'd turned out surprisingly well. Among the usual red herrings and unreliable sources, Barnaby had found the answer to his current mystery by uncovering facts that had happened many years earlier. As the closing credits rolled, I stood, preparing to clear away plates and glasses, but Louisa waved me away. "Betsy and I have it handled, Maralee. We brought it, and we'll take it away. Everything fits into our cooler. It won't take a minute to pack it up."

Louisa was right. Within little more than a minute, we six were deeply embroiled in using our particular skills and observations—à la Inspector Barnaby—with an aim to what my aunt had described as "solving that poor boy's murder."

"What we have here is kind of a 'locked room' situation," Betsy suggested. "And the locked room, as I see it, is the vault in the closed-up bank—the vault where Walter Wyman picked up the items destined for the museum."

"Even though nothing was stolen from the vault?" my aunt asked.

"*Apparently* nothing was stolen," Pete corrected.

"But Walter Wyman either did something or saw something that got him killed," I said.

"With his own gun," Betsy put in.

"Possibly his own gun," Pete corrected.

"That would bring up the girl in the hoodie who was riding with him in the armored truck," Aunt Ibby said. "I think she shot him."

"All we know so far is that she, or he, has frizzy blond hair and sunglasses and didn't leave any fingerprints anywhere," Pete confirmed.

"No prints on the gun, either, I understand." Michael looked at Pete for verification.

"None," Pete agreed. "Either the killer took time to wipe down the interior of the truck, or else she—or he—wore gloves."

The reference to the blond hair brought me to my recent telephone call. "We've had some new information about the blonde—from Fiona Sullivan."

All eyes turned toward me. "So, was Fiona the girl in the truck?" Michael asked.

"I've been thinking she could have been," I admitted. "Now I'm not so sure." I recounted what Fiona had told me about the wig and the tiny shoe.

"Is Fiona trying to implicate her sister?" Michael wanted to know. "After all, Kitsue is the owner of record of the most valuable item in the Sullivans' collections."

"When I think of valuables—like jewelry or antiques or works of art," Louisa said, "I always think immediately of some kind of insurance fraud."

"That makes sense, doesn't it?" Louisa is our expert on insurance and money. "I hadn't thought about it, though, because"—I smiled at Pete—"nothing is missing."

"True," my aunt said. "But the detail about the missing shoe being found puzzles me. I mean, if Kitsue had the four-times-great-grandmother's shoe in her sock drawer, why would she concoct that story about packing it with the million-dollar cereal bowl?"

"Inspector Barnaby looked to the past to solve tonight's murder," Michael pointed out. "How long has Kitsue had that bowl in her possession?"

"I think she said that Grandmother Kitty gave it to her outright for her tenth birthday," I told him, "but she's been eating cereal from it for even longer than that."

"Do you suppose, Lee, that I could come to the museum and take a look at the Sullivan collection?" Michael asked. "I'm sure there are other things there of great value too. Maybe we're focusing on the 'shiny object' and ignoring something else in the room. Louisa's comment about insurance is interesting. Maybe the cereal bowl is the red herring in our mystery."

"I'm sure I can invite you into the museum," I said. "You're a licensed antiques appraiser. That means you're an expert I can interview for the documentary. Besides, you might very well see something there that non-experts have missed."

"Would tomorrow be convenient?" he asked.

"In the morning," I said. "In the afternoon, I have a date with a toy dealer about a drone."

"That sounds like fun," Michael said. "Tomorrow morning, then. I'll look forward to it. So many antiques in one place! I'm excited about it."

I wondered if I'd be out of line—if not completely off topic—if I asked Michael about the play Kitsue had mentioned. I had the impression it was a secret project, but maybe sharing it within our close-knit group might be permissible.

I didn't have to worry. Betsy, who is generally clued in to every important cultural or social function in Salem, asked the question for me. "Michael," she said, "is it true that you're working on a play? The grapevine is buzzing about it."

Slight, gentlemanly eye roll. "It's still in the 'talking about it' stages," he admitted. "Ask me about it next meeting."

Aunt Ibby, who, librarian-like, always attempts to keep things orderly and on topic, returned the conversation to the central question. Who killed Walter Wyman—and of growing interest—why? "The only indication we have that anyone at all besides the killer and the victim was present at or near the scene of the crime is the video of the hooded person—be that person male or female, blond or dark-haired, gloved or not," she declared. "Other than one blond sister's claim that the other sister has a blond wig that she doesn't attempt to hide, do we have anything concrete to follow here? Or shall we try another angle?"

"Another way to view what we know," Pete spoke hesitantly, "might be to look at the contacts of the Sullivan sisters. So far, we've found provable continuing connections among some of their high school classmates. Walter Wyman was one of them. So was the handyman, George Washington. The girls' grandmother Kitty tells us that Fiona and Walter once dated, yet Fiona didn't attend Walter's funeral, while Kitsue and George both did." He looked around the room. "Anything there?"

Betsy waved her hand again. "Do we know why Fiona and Walter broke up? If they used to be an item and she didn't go to the funeral, there might have been some bad blood between the two."

"Of course, maybe it's just the mystery author in me, cooking up a plot," Michael said, "but what if Fiona and Walter got back together again after all these years? And what if they'd become close enough so that he'd trust her enough to let her ride in the armored truck with him?"

I couldn't help finishing the thought. "That would put Fiona at the crime scene."

Cop voice from Pete. "Or would it put Kitsue in a blond wig pretending to be Fiona at the crime scene?"

We were right back where we'd started.

CHAPTER 29

After Michael, Betsy, and Louisa had left, and Aunt Ibby and O'Ryan were comfortably settled in front of their TV, Pete and I headed upstairs to our own room. "What do you think?" I asked him. "Did anything useful come from all that?"

"Maybe," he said. "It's interesting to have several views of the same facts, isn't it? It's like an informal brainstorming session. For instance, Betsy's idea about Fiona and Walter getting together again is one I'd not thought of. Louisa's insurance fraud thought is worth more investigation, and I especially like Michael's idea that we might be looking at the wrong 'shiny object.' What do you think?"

"I wonder about the gloves Hoodie Girl must have been wearing. She wouldn't have had time to wipe all the surfaces of the truck she'd touched. You couldn't see her hands at all in the video. But wouldn't Walter have been suspicious if whichever of the Sullivan sisters it may have been was wearing gloves in September?"

"You'd think so, wouldn't you? I've thought about that too," he said. "One of my mom's friends has arthritis in her fingers, and she wears tight black gloves for the pain sometimes, but that doesn't seem likely in this case."

"I went to elementary school with a boy who had some kind of itchy rash on his hands and he wore bandages sometimes," I remembered, "but that doesn't fit here either."

"Hey, it's possible that we have *both* Hoodie Girl and the shiny object wrong." He sounded glum. "Then we're all the way back to square one."

It was a discouraging thought. We were both pretty much silent making preparations for bedtime. Finally, showered, teeth brushed, pajamaed, and ready to climb under the covers, I brought up the subject again. "I'm anxious to see what Michael might come up with when he visits the museum tomorrow. Maybe he'll find something there among all the artifacts that we haven't noticed before."

"It could happen," Pete agreed. "Want to watch TV?"

"Sure. Let's see if Scott has scored another spot on the news."

He tapped the remote. Scott had scored another one—one I should have had. Apparently earlier in the evening, a Brink's truck had shown up at the museum. Scott had pictures—I knew they were Old Jim's because of the precise detail even in the fading daylight. Two uniformed armed guards carried metal-bound black chests into the building while Scott—using his "big network" voice—related that a large shipment of rare jewels, reputed to have been part of the maharaja's treasures, had been delivered to the site of the *Seafaring New England* museum exhibit, and they would be displayed in a specially constructed, circular, bulletproof glass case. He'd even used my pictures of Professor Bidani standing beside the topless glass tube.

I used what Aunt Ibby would term an "unladylike" expression. "Ugh. That should have been mine. This is one of those times I wish I was still a field reporter. I could have been right there when the jewels were being delivered."

"But just think, you'll be there in the morning when they're unpacked," Pete comforted me. "It's your documentary, and you don't have to let Scott in to photograph them if you don't want to."

"Michael will get to see them in the morning too," I said, trying to see the positive side of all this. "I can get his opinion on camera. I'll call Francine in the morning to be sure she gets there first thing. I've been collecting notes about the treasures those maharajas had. Maybe Mr. Doan will let us use the segment as a promo for the documentary and run it before Scott gets a crack at it."

"Good thinking," Pete said. "So, after you and Scott go to do that toy-store drone thing in the afternoon, you can let him in to see the jewels, and *your* story will already be in the can, right?"

"Darn right," I agreed. "That seems fair."

I felt much better about my part of the past day's events—from the morning meeting with Mr. Doan, the lunch with Scott, the encounter with George Washington and the diaper-wrapped gun, through the Angels' and Michael's contributions at the *Midsomer Murders* meeting, and the news about the maharajas' jewels being delivered. I had a light-bulb-over-the-head moment. "Pete," I said, excited. "I know where Buffy Doan can hold her Halloween party—in the upstairs part of the museum. There's an outside entrance, a good dance floor, plenty of room for buffet tables, and even a stage for the band!"

"That should help him decide to go along with your promo for the documentary idea," Pete said, and I felt sure he was right. It had been a not-too-bad kind of day after all.

I woke up before the alarm went off again. If this kept on, I thought, I'd be the early riser in the family—the one making the coffee. But no, the space beside me in the big bed was already empty, and I knew that downstairs, there'd be the aroma of freshly brewed decaf, the sounds of country music, and a good-smelling, showered, and shaved handsome guy ready to greet me with a morning hug and kiss.

Life is good.

We had a breakfast of coffee and a couple of those leftover petit fours. I called Francine—and good newshound that she is, she'd seen Scott's teaser and had already figured out that I'd need her at the museum early. We agreed to meet at eight, Francine with her best cameras and full sound equipment and me with short skirt, heels, and green jacket—WICH-TV's field-reporting A-team for sure. I texted Michael about the eight o'clock meet, then Pete and I shared a backyard have-a-good-day kiss and climbed into our respective cars.

Mr. Thomas gave our press cards a frowning,

extra-thorough examination. He'd been issued a security wand, too, and he gave us a perfunctory scanning before admitting us. I told him that Dr. Martell would be joining us, and boldly asked that no more press be admitted while we were filming. I had no idea whether I had any right to ask it, but it was worth a shot in case Scott tried to get in. From the doorway, I saw Sant Bidani beside his glass tower. There was a tall, narrow ladder inside the structure, and the two black chests I'd seen on Scott's report, still closed, were just outside the glass door. So were two large men in dark-blue security uniforms, contrasting with their white gloves. I noticed that Professor Bidani wore white gloves too.

"They must have to climb up the ladder to load the jewels onto the Lucite shelves on the spiral pole," Francine whispered. "Wow. What a display that's going to be."

"Let's get as close as those big guys will let us," I said. "I'll do an intro now, then we'll pick it up as soon as they start to open the chests."

Francine set up her camera, checked the lighting, and did a quick sound count while I stood a respectful distance away from the tower, knowing we could zoom in on anything we wanted to. I began the introduction. "Hello. I'm Lee Barrett, speaking to you from the site of the new Salem International Museum, where, in a matter of days, we'll welcome the debut event. It's called *Seafaring New England,* where visitors will be treated to a stunning display of items brought to America by long-ago ships who sailed from New England to faraway exotic ports around the world. Today we're privileged to be on hand to watch as Professor Sant Bidani supervises the assembly of a display to rival the crown jewels of England. From two large trunks, you'll see the jeweled treasures that once belonged to the great rulers, the maharajas of India, transferred to clear trays, which will slowly revolve within that glass tower to catch the glitter and sparkle of each diamond, emerald, and ruby, every golden crown, necklace, ring, dagger, and more." We paused, eyes wide, camera poised, waiting for the opening of the trunks.

I heard Francine whisper, "Here we go," as one of the guards, using a large silver key, stooped to unlock the first chest. I'd somehow expected to see something like the Disney World pirate chests—overflowing with gems—but it wasn't like that. I should have known better. Inside there were gray, velvety-looking bags of varied sizes. The first guard handed one of the bags to Sant Bidani, who carried it into the tube and started up the ladder to the top tray, while the second guard approached the door with another gray bag. Then I caught the glitter I'd been hoping for. Bidani carefully emptied the bag onto the tray. This bag contained a variety of amazing jewelry. The tray was a bit over my head, but I could plainly distinguish rings and multilayered necklaces and bracelets. There was a crown of gold almost entirely covered with emeralds, a sharp steel dagger with an enormous diamond in the hilt, and a huge jeweled circle that reminded me of a Super Bowl ring.

The parade of gray bags, each one revealing more and more spectacular items, continued. The gloved guards alternated handing the bags to Bidani. The second trunk was opened, and he continued climbing up and down the ladder, pausing now and then to move an item from one level to another, arranging each glittering piece to his satisfaction. The process took over an hour. I knew our film would need heavy editing, but I didn't want to miss a bit of it. I kept up a narration, telling about how in the eighteenth century, Delhi was among the richest capitals in the world, and how the jewels of the maharajas symbolized power from the divine. We wound up with a final shot of the completed spiral within the glass tower, as Sant Bidani removed the ladder and activated the revolving trays full of fabulous treasure. *So there, Scott Palmer*, I thought. *Top this!*

I stepped away from the dazzling display and realized that Michael Martell had joined us, Kitsue Sullivan at his side. Their expressions reflected the same kind of awe that I'm sure mine did. Francine had already sent the film electronically, and she was in a hurry to get back to the station to get involved with the editing process. She'd rounded up camera, light, tripod, and sound equipment with a speed that rivaled the Angels' amazing packing of the previous evening's repast, including china and glassware. "I'll see you back at work," she said. "Got to get this all set up in a hurry if we're going to make the news with it."

"I'll be there at noon," I reminded her. "Got a date with Scott to look at drones this afternoon." I approached Kitsue and Michael. "Shall we take a look at Kitsue's alcove now?" I suggested.

Kitsue smiled. "The treasures of the maharajas is a tough act to follow," she said.

CHAPTER 30

We'd barely stepped into the alcove when Michael began to move silently, excitedly, from case to case, display to display. He stopped occasionally, jeweler's loupe to his eye, to examine something more closely. Finally, in front of the pink-lighted cabinet containing the cereal bowl, he spoke. "Do you have the key to this case, Kitsue?"

"Of course." She pulled a large ring with a jangle of keys attached from her smock pocket. "You'd like to take a closer look at something?"

"I would," he said. "Did you place all these objects into their cases and frames by yourself?"

"No." She shook her head, shiny hair swirling around her shoulders, then settling perfectly back into place. "Priscilla, the display lady, did most of the work here. I just gave final approval."

"Uh-huh." He pulled a photo from his pocket. Looking over his shoulder, I saw it was Fiona's program photo of the bowl. "Would you take a look at the photo and then look closely at the bowl. Do the faces of the horsemen look the same to you?"

"I know the horsemen well. I named them all." She counted on her fingers. "Athos, Porthos, and Aramis."

"That's the Three Musketeers," Michael corrected.

"I know," she said. "I was just a little kid. Those were the only horsemen I knew about. It's the same three soldiers on both sides of the bowl. So, as far as I'm concerned, that's their names!"

"Works for me. But please look closely." He handed her the loupe. "Move right up close to the glass." We waited while she did as Michael had asked.

"Oh, my Lord," Kitsue wailed. "That's not my bowl! I know those faces as well as I know my own. Those faces look soft, pudgy. My horsemen were handsome, sharp-featured, straight noses, Aramis even has a dimple. That's not my bowl," she wailed again. Her right hand shaking, she put a key in the lock, trying to open the cabinet door.

Michael quietly reached for the key. "Here. I'll get it." He slid the door open. "Can you reach the bowl?" Kitsue didn't answer, but reached up, removing the bowl, holding it carefully with both hands.

She closed her eyes. "I'm afraid to look. But I know it's true. This isn't my bowl. It doesn't even feel right." She held it away from her body, toward Michael.

"Didn't you notice that when you unpacked the bowl?" he asked softly.

"I didn't unpack it myself," she said. "I was busy

hanging the cloud collar, but I saw Priscilla unpack it and put it in the case."

"May I?" Very gently, he took it from her hands. "No, it doesn't feel right. It's made from some sort of plastic. Didn't your display lady—Priscilla—didn't she notice that it is too light?" He touched the bowl lightly to his cheek. "It's not cold. Real jade is cold to the touch."

"Priscilla does displays of everything—store windows, magazine layouts. She doesn't claim to be an expert on antiques." The brown eyes flew open. "How—when could this have happened?"

Michael returned the bowl to the shelf. "If it arrived here in the original packing, I'd guess it happened either while it was at the closed bank or in Walter Wyman's truck."

"It did. We even examined the packaging when we were looking for the shoe."

"That's why no one found the shoe in the bowl," I suggested.

"No." Kitsue whirled around and faced a glass-topped case behind her. "The shoe has been found. The pair is right here in the case with all the others." She covered her face with both hands. "I was ashamed to tell anyone. Fiona found the missing one. It was in my own bureau drawer. In my own room. I don't remember putting it there, but I must have." She dropped her hands to her sides. "What's wrong with me? Am I crazy? And who has stolen my beautiful bowl?"

I put my arms around her. "Don't cry, Kitsue," I said. "No, you're not crazy. There's a logical explanation for all this. Something very strange is going on here, and we're going to figure it out. I promise." I wasn't making up kind words to calm her. I believed completely in what I'd said. I looked past the now-sobbing Kitsue toward Michael, who stood looking helpless as men often do in the presence of feminine tears.

Had Fiona told her, as she'd told me, about the recently styled blond wig? I hesitated for a moment, then asked, "Did Fiona have any other information about how the shoe might have been in your room? About why anyone would put it there? After all," I reasoned, "it wasn't actually hidden. You would have found it yourself the next time you opened that bureau drawer."

Michael spoke up. "You've certainly been under a lot of pressure here at the museum, Kitsue," he said. "You've done an amazing job here in your alcove, making the remarkable history of the Sullivan family a visible experience for the world to see. Such focused attention on this project, I should think, might lead to some mental stress—some memory confusion. I personally have experienced something similar when I was first released from the penitentiary. I was so focused on trying to find my way in the very-changed outside world that I once even put my cell phone in the refrigerator and a package of frozen green beans on my hall table." He smiled. "And I'm not crazy either."

"Thank you, Michael." She wiped her eyes with the back of her hand, and Michael handed her a white handkerchief. "But there's even more. Do you think I could have taken an old wig out of the closet where we keep Halloween costumes and washed and styled it? Could I have done all that and not remembered doing it?"

"Well," I said, "it is almost Halloween in Salem, and you've been deeply involved with restoring old costumes for the museum—like the cloud collars and the lotus shoes. Is it possible that you were thinking of costuming for the play you and Michael are planning that the wig fits into those plans somewhere?"

"I'd thought about a gray wig for aging Li Jing, in the play," she admitted, "but certainly not that old fake hair thing." She attempted a smile, and apparently catching a glimpse of herself reflected in the glass cabinet, brought both hands to her eyes. "I should never cry in public," she said. "My eyes are a mess." She hurried across the room to a small wooden desk, opened a drawer, pulled out a pair of sunglasses, and put them on. "There," she said. "That's better. Now, the important thing is to find my bowl—the *real* one." I managed to contain a gasp. Kitsue's sunglasses had red rims—like the ones we'd seen on Hoodie Girl.

"I'll call Pete right now," I told her. "We need to report the theft of your jade bowl. All those other things can wait for explanations." I called Pete, told him about the fake bowl, and hoped Kitsue would still be wearing those sunglasses when he arrived. I alerted Mr. Thomas that the police were on the way and hoped there'd be no sirens and flashing lights. That wasn't the kind of image that would benefit either the museum or my documentary. How could I soft-pedal the news that a million-dollar antique artifact had disappeared when the place hadn't even yet been opened to the public? Besides all that, I was now trying to wrap my own mind around the fact that Kitsue not only had the blond wig and the missing shoe, but also the sunglasses. All that was missing now was the hoodie.

I was relieved that Francine had left. At least

none of the action in the alcove since Michael's discovery of the phony jade bowl was on film. But I'd be willing to bet that Scott Palmer would be on hand with a mobile unit crew to record the action from here on in—and that police descending on the museum would likely ace out my maharajas' jewel extravaganza on the nightly news top stories.

I left the alcove and looked toward the now-jewel-filled glass tower. The guards were still there, but Professor Bidani had left. I watched from the front window as two cruisers with lights but no sirens, and the WICH-TV second-string mobile unit with Old Jim at the wheel, pulled up. Field reporter Scott Palmer was already out of the aging VW and onto the curb, mic clipped in place, ready to roll, before Pete and Detective Sergeant Joyce Rouse had even reached the front door of the museum.

Mr. Thomas didn't bother to check IDs this time, and Pete and Joyce were inside the alcove in seconds. Fast, efficient, cop-voiced interviews from both cops. Kitsue was still wearing the sunglasses. Pete's slightly raised eyebrow told me that he'd noticed. She answered questions softly, her voice breaking a bit when she described how the fake bowl differed from the missing original. Michael, speaking as an antiques appraiser, explained how he'd determined that the bowl wasn't the original—wasn't even jade at all. "Visually, it's a pretty good fake," he told them. "The average museum visitor probably wouldn't have noticed anything wrong with it. Even Ms. Sullivan"—he nodded toward Kitsue—"has been looking at it for days and didn't notice anything out of place until she used a magnifying glass."

"You said the weight was wrong." Pete addressed Kitsue. "Didn't you notice that when you put the bowl in the display case?"

"I didn't touch it," she said. "My display woman, Priscilla Decker, took it out of the box and arranged it on the shelf."

"Didn't she notice that it was too light? Didn't feel like jade?" Joyce Rouse asked.

"She isn't an antiques expert. She specializes in display. She wouldn't have known what it should feel like." Kitsue gazed at the bowl in the still-open cabinet. "It looks pretty. With that rosy light on it, it even fooled me."

"Do you have anything to add, Lee?" Pete asked me.

"The missing bowl isn't the only unusual thing that's happened to Kitsue lately," I said. "She may want to talk to you about her four-times-great-grandmother's little shoes."

"Is that right, Ms. Sullivan?" Polite cop voice. He already knew about the shoes, of course, but it might be helpful if he heard about them directly from her. Michael had heard the story before too.

Kitsue pushed the glasses up onto the top of her head and began to talk—not excitedly, not sadly—but in a bored-sounding monotone. Pete jotted a couple of notes in the notebook he always caries, and Joyce Rouse recorded the whole thing on her tablet.

"Where is Fiona Sullivan now?" Joyce asked. "Does she work with you here in the museum?'

"Once in a while she helps out," Kitsue said. "She'd like to do more, but she has so many other things to do."

"You say that she's the one who found those shoes?" Pete asked. He knew all about that too.

"And the wig," Kitsue added. "Do you want to know about the wig too?"

"Sure. Tell me about it," he said. So, she did.

"I don't think we'll have to use the yellow tape for this, Rouse," Pete said. "The theft must have occurred before the bowl was placed in the locked case."

"I agree," she said.

That was a blessing, I thought. That "do not cross" yellow crime-scene tape would not have looked good in my documentary.

CHAPTER 31

Thanks to Mr. Thomas and the two burly security guards, the WICH-TV crew was not admitted to the museum. I knew, though, from my own field reporter experience that there are ways to get the story anyway—at least some of it. The police radio scanner would have told them there'd been a theft. A little information-digging among certain talkative sources could even have told them exactly what was missing. Peeking through the window from behind a *Coming Soon* sign about the *Seafaring New England* show, I saw Scott proceeding with his stand-up in front of the police cars, saw him approach both Pete and Joyce for comments. I assumed that each of them had responded with a polite "no comment." I watched as Old Jim focused the camera on a shot of the building, and when the camera moved in my direction, I got out

of the way. I knew I'd hear all about it soon enough
when I met Scott for our afternoon Toy Trawler
date.

"Are you going to be alright, Kitsue?" I asked.
"Do you need a ride home?"

"I've called Fiona," she said. "She's on her way
here. I'll be okay. I'm just hoping the police will
find my bowl—not because it's so valuable, but because I love it so much. I'd never, ever, even think
of selling it."

I believed her. "I'm sure they will," I told her.
"Do you want Michael or me to wait for Fiona with
you?"

Tentative smile. "No. I'll be fine. Mr. Thomas
and those big guys are here. I'll be fine," she
repeated. So, Michael and I left, got into our respective cars, and drove away from the soon-to-be-
opened Salem International Museum—where
over a century of Salem history was about to be
clearly, carefully, thoughtfully explained—while
some recent Salem history remained totally unex-
plainable.

Michael left before I did. He had a creative writing class to teach as Fenton Bishop at the Tabby. I
tried to mentally shift gears as I drove the short
distance from the museum to WICH-TV. I was anxious to see what Francine had done with our
morning's work on the maharajas' treasure segment. At the same time, I was preparing my sales
pitch to Mr. Doan, hopefully convincing him to
use it right away as a promo for the documentary—preferably on Buck Covington's highly rated
news show.

I pulled into my regular parking space beside

the seawall. Francine's truck was in her usual space. So was the VW, telling me that Scott and Old Jim were already at work editing the field report. I let myself into the building via the studio side door. The cool, black-walled studio was silent with only the glow of a few small lights marking the various sets. It was so peaceful there that for a fleeting moment I just wanted to sit down somewhere in that soft, quiet darkness and turn off my tumbling thoughts.

As much as I'd sincerely tried to comfort Kitsue, to tell her that she wasn't crazy, that the police would find her bowl, I wasn't sure about any of that. I didn't want to think she could be a killer—but what about the blond wig, the red-rimmed glasses, the lotus shoe, and the murder weapon wrapped in the pink and white diaper? Kitsue was connected to all of them. Was she pretending that she'd forgotten all that? And was her almost-twin sister trying to help her by pointing out her recent forgetfulness—if that's what it was? Or was Fiona attempting to shift attention from herself? What if she'd found the bowl along with the other things in Kitsue's room before the items went to the bank vault? Everyone knew Fiona was in need of money to finance the inventions she was positive would make her rich. How much would a serious collector pay for the jade bowl? Maybe Fiona had enough money already to pay some kind of sculptor to make the fake one.

"Stop it!" I told myself. "You are not Nancy Drew. The police will handle it all. They'll find the bowl and find the killer, and my documentary will be a big hit." I pushed open the metal door and climbed the stairs to the second floor, trying hard to force the bad thoughts away. Rhonda's smiling face helped a lot.

"Hey, Lee. Good news. Doan loves the little promo you guys made. He's even ordering special graphics for the title and credits and all. Everyone in the whole listening area will be breaking down the doors to see those jewels. I can hardly wait myself."

"They are spectacular, and so are a lot of the other things you'll see in there. Salem was a pretty amazing place to live back in those days."

"Well, sure, if you didn't mind not having cars or television sets or hot running water or indoor toilets or deodorant or—"

"Got it," I interrupted. "And you're right. But it's fun learning about it. Not just the fabulous stuff they brought in back in those old ships—but about the people. Like Li Jing Sullivan and William Griffen and Jacob Crowninshield and . . . oh, never mind. You'll see it all soon enough." I glanced at the whiteboard. "Palmer and Barrett— client call at Toy Trawler."

"A client call, huh? Are we supposed to be selling Captain Billy something new?" I asked.

"Doan noticed there are a lot of ship models in your museum," she said. "He says for you to figure out how to tie in captain Billy's toy models with the antique ones."

"That's not a bad idea," I agreed. "Sure. We can do that. Is Scott in his office?"

"Yep. Waiting for you to go to lunch. Who's buying?"

"He is," I assured her, and headed down the ramp toward the newsroom and my office. It wasn't noontime yet, and I knew I needed to spend a little time attending to my somewhat-neglected program director duties. *Shopping Salem* was planning a Halloween costume fashion show and wanted me to connect them with Chris at Christopher's Castle for the costumes. Easy-peasy. No one likes free publicity better than Chris does. Ranger Rob had booked a local vet to talk to the little buckaroos about taking care of their pets and just needed my okay. Done. Nothing further needed my immediate attention, so when Scott knocked on my office window, I acknowledged him with a fake smile, picked up my phone, and tapped in his number.

"You about ready to leave?" he asked. "I figure the Friendly Tavern will be okay for lunch, right?'

"Suits me," I said. "It's a little early, but we can beat the twelve o'clock rush."

"Okay. I'll meet you at the elevator in five minutes. Are we both going to wear these green jackets?" He looked down at his at the same time I looked at mine.

There'd be no twinning with Scott, that was for sure. "I'll change," I said. "I have a sweater in my locker." I popped open the lock, shrugged out of the jacket, and hung it carefully on a padded hanger, then pulled out a soft gray cashmere cardigan. I was about to close the locker door when the thought occurred to me. How many people had access to it? How hard would it be for someone—anyone—to plant something incriminating in it? If someone were to hide, say, a gun, or a pair of sunglasses or even a small bowl on the top shelf, under my Red Sox baseball hat, how long would it be before I even noticed it?

I stood there, staring into the locker. Surely Mr. Doan had a key. The janitor must have one, and the occasional cleaning service crew must too. How about any previous tenants of this particular office? I was sure no one had ever bothered to change the locks on anything here. Once again, I wondered about the long and growing string of incriminating articles pointing to Kitsue Sullivan. A *rat-a-tat* knock at my office door announced an impatient Scott. I put on the sweater, slammed the locker door shut, twisted the key, and joined him on the way to Old Clunky.

We'd barely started walking across Derby Street to the restaurant when he began to grill me about the happenings at the museum. "I know you know all about what happened in the museum this morning. Is it true that somebody made off with that million-dollar Chinese bowl? I couldn't get a word out of your husband and the cute lady cop."

"I know," I said. "Case under investigation."

"I didn't even get that much out of them." He sounded glum. "Can't you give me anything? Any fingerprints? Any suspects?"

"It was the bowl," I told him, knowing the news would surely be released later in the day. "They think the theft occurred some time ago—maybe at the bank vault or in the armored truck."

"Suspects?" he asked again.

"No suspects yet," I fibbed, knowing there were several possibilities. Scott ordered a burger and fries, and I decided on a salad—considering my sugar-laden breakfast—which, I realized, might account for my present chaotic thought patterns.

Scott did one of his long looks—one that lost

some of the dramatic effect because he had mayonnaise on his upper lip. "What do you think of the fancy jewel display the Indian guy set up? Do you think all the stuff in the glass tower is real?" He licked the mayo away.

"Oh yes," I said. "They've upped the security since it arrived. It will be watched day and night, I'm sure."

"I should think so, after losing the lady's jade bowl."

"That's not the same thing," I insisted, and went for a change of subject. "Have you studied up on drones at all? I meant to, but I just haven't found the time to do it."

"I did—mostly just the basic information I found online. Old Jim knows a lot about drones," he said. "He even belongs to a drone club. They go over to Gallows Hill sometimes and fly them around, practicing landings, taking pictures, and all that. We should do that when we get ours."

"*If* we get ours," I corrected. He paid the check, I left the tip, and we were off for the Toy Trawler. "Let's go in your Jeep," he suggested. It was probably a means of his saving on gas money, but I didn't mind. I love driving it, and I get to open it up a little on Route One on the way to the toy store. Captain Billy himself looks every bit the fisherman part. I think of him as a cross between Spencer Tracy in *The Old Man and the Sea,* and Johnny Depp in *Pirates of the Caribbean.* I parked in the "No Wake Zone" and we walked together up the gangplank to the fo'c'sle, where the captain met us with a drone in each hand.

"Here you go, kids," He handed Scott the larger

one, a black-bodied, four-legged thing that to me, resembled some kind of alien cartoon bug. Mine was a pinkish-gray, smaller version of his. "Follow me out to my drone zone, and you can try them out." I handled mine gingerly, turning it upside down and examining the control unit. The drone zone was the backyard of the Toy Trawler, with a cleared lawn space and a couple of small trees. "Okay," the captain said. "Each of your drones has a high-definition camera with video, voice control, and altitude hold. I didn't give you the kind with magnets because a kid got one stuck on the water tower over yonder. Dang thing's still up there." He proceeded to give us some simple-to-understand operating instructions, probably not unlike the ones he'd given to Ranger Rob's little buckaroos, and within half an hour, we were each zooming our drones around the yard, giving them instructions, taking pictures and videos without bumping them into each other, hanging them up in trees, or slamming into the water tower.

"This is fun," I told Scott. "Do you think Doan will buy them for us?"

"Mine has the price sticker on it," he said. "It's only sixty-five bucks. I'm going to buy it."

"I'm going to shop around," I told him. "Maybe I'll get one later."

"Maybe I'll let you borrow mine," he said. "Let's stop at the common and try it out." We each thanked Captain Billy—me with a suggestion about his model-ship kits to tie in with the museum vessels—while he tried to interest us in some cool Halloween skulls. "I'm going to show these to the kids on Ranger Rob's show," he said. "These are made with resin, but the kids can make them easily with plaster of paris in these squishy molds. Sure you don't want a couple for Pete's nephews, Lee? They can paint them or put glitter in them. Lots of fun."

"I'll ask him," I promised, "but now I can hardly wait to play with Scott's new toy." I'd often seen people flying drones on the Salem Common before, and our visit with the captain hadn't taken as long as I'd thought it might.

Scott made his purchase, we left the Toy Trawler, and I drove back toward the common. With my press pass on the windshield, I found a parking space behind the old Phillips School, and we hurried onto the green. I sat on one of the long park benches and watched while Scott maneuvered his drone. My phone buzzed. Pete was calling.

"Listen, babe, this isn't good news, but I know you'll want to hear it from me first."

"What's wrong?" My thoughts flew to my aunt, maybe alone in our house. "Is Aunt Ibby all right?"

"Yes. She's fine. It's about Kitsue. We're going to have to bring her down to the station. It doesn't look too good for her right now."

"What happened?" I felt my heart speed up.

"Remember I told you I was going to send someone over to her grandmother Kitty's house to tie up a few loose ends?" He didn't wait for an answer. "Rouse walked in, and there was a dark-blue wool hoodie jacket, hanging on a coatrack right inside the front door. She asked the old woman about it and was told that Kitsue had brought it from the dry cleaners a couple of days ago. Kitty said she might as well hang it there because winter was coming soon. Rouse asked if she could look at it, and Lee, the damn thing has Walter Wyman's name tag in it."

"It's Walter's jacket?" It made no sense.

"It has his name in it, and Rouse checked the cleaners. They'd cleaned up a bloodstain. Kitsue dropped it off the day after the murder. Sorry, babe. Gotta go now."

CHAPTER 32

Scott reeled in his drone and hurried over to my bench. "We have to go," he said. "Got a call. Looks like more stuff going on at your museum. Howie's busy. Francine's going to meet me there. Come on."

We ran together to the Jeep. I was just as anxious as he was to get the museum. I didn't tell him what Pete had told me, and anyway, he was on his phone with one of his contacts. "Looks like they're ready to make an arrest in that armored truck killing," he said as I drove as fast as the law allowed back toward Salem.

Francine was already on-site when we got there. So were the police, blue-and-white lights flashing. I saw Pete's cruiser. "Have they brought anyone out yet?" Scott called as he jumped from the Jeep, reaching for the stick mic Francine handed to him.

"Not yet," she said. "They've only been in there a few minutes. Hi, Lee. Do you want a mic too?"

Of course, I wanted one, but this wasn't my assignment. "No thanks," I told her. "I'll see if they'll let me in." This was surely nothing I wanted to record for my documentary, but I felt strongly that I should be inside. Somebody should be there for Kitsue. Did she have a lawyer? Was Fiona with her, or at least on the way?

Mr. Thomas was still at the front door, but so was a uniformed Salem officer. I knocked and held my press card up to the door. Mr. Thomas nodded "okay," but the officer shook his head "no." I saw the WBZ-TV sound truck pull up to the curb. WESX-radio was already there, too, with their top woman reporter mic'ed up and on the air. *It must be the real thing,* I thought. *Poor Kitsue.* I knew I should get out of the way of the police, but I stood there in the doorway and knocked again. This time Pete saw me—exchanged a few words with the officer, and the door swung open.

It was surreal. The measured tones of a sea shanty boomed from hidden speakers, while Sant Bidani's trays of glittering jewels revolved slowly, almost in time to the music. A spotlight illuminated the sails of the good ship *Naiad,* and light shone from the doorways of every alcove in the room. I'd arrived at a dress rehearsal of the opening of *Seafaring New England* that no one had bothered to tell me about. It all looked and sounded wonderful. At the arched entrance of the Sullivan alcove, though, a crowd of blue uniforms surrounded the small brunette woman, hands secured behind her back while Pete read to her from a small, worn card. I couldn't hear the words he spoke, but I knew they began with "You have the right to remain silent."

The scene was too heartbreaking. I had to look away. I focused on the *Naiad*, searching for the tiny ill-fated sailor. I squinted. Where was William Griffen? *I should be able to see him from here.*

Thankfully, someone turned off the blaring music. The lights appeared to dim, and I forced my attention back to what was happening in the arched doorway right in front of me. A woman I knew and liked, but who was suspected of murder, was being taken into custody by my police-detective husband, who was simply doing his job. Maybe they both needed my support in this moment. I took a deep breath, stood up straight, and walked toward them. I spoke first to Kitsue. "Do you have a lawyer?"

"I . . . I'm not sure. I think we do. Lee, will you call Fiona?"

Pete spoke softly, kindly, not in cop voice at all. "The court will appoint one for you, Ms. Sullivan," he said, "and you can call your sister as soon as we get to the station." He looked at me with both love and sadness in his eyes. "Thanks, Lee." I knew they were about to head out the door into a wall of cameras and shouted questions and accusations. Pete was accustomed to it, but how would Kitsue handle it? Handcuffed, slim shoulders slumped, her head down, she moved ahead of Pete toward the red *Exit* sign. She looked thoroughly broken. I hoped they'd get her quickly into one of the waiting police cars and away from the growing chaos in front of the museum. I didn't want to watch. Turning away from the window, I moved closer to the *Naiad*, still searching for the sailor in the main topsail yard, realizing that greeting the little guy every day had become part of my museum routine.

William wasn't there. I searched the deck below the mast. Not there, either. Then I found him, facedown on the painted green-and-blue billowing waves below the ship. It was, for me, a disturbing discovery. Someone needed to be notified. I looked around. The people from the various alcoves had gathered around the windows and doorway, still watching whatever was happening outside. Only the several security people remained at their posts. I approached the closest one to me—one of the guards of the maharajas' treasures.

"Excuse me," I said. "Do you happen to know who's in charge of the *Naiad* display?"

"Oh-oh." He looked toward the giant ship. "Is the sailor out of his perch again?"

"Again?"

"Yeah." He walked to the display, with me following. "Yep. There he is. Same as yesterday." His voice lowered. "There's a rumor going around that this thing is haunted. I've got the display company's number. I'll give them another call."

"Haunted?" I managed to squeak out another one-word question.

"That's what they say. Keep it quiet, will you? We've got enough bad publicity going on around here as it is." He jerked a thumb toward the window. "You're the lady doing the video about the museum, right?"

"Right." *He must think I speak only in monosyllables.* Still staring at poor, prone William Griffen, I managed a full sentence and stuck out my hand. "I'm Lee Barrett. I'm preparing a historical documentary for WICH-TV." I handed him one of my new cards.

He shook my hand and told me his name. "So, Ms. Barrett"—he gave a half-smile—"do *you* believe in ghosts?"

For me, that's not a definite "yes or no" question. I've had enough experiences in my life to make me wonder, so with a smile of my own, I tap-danced around it. "Hey, this is Salem. Some people think the whole city is haunted. I hope William will stay put this time."

I'd more or less told Kitsue that I'd call her sister, so leaving the *Naiad* display and the treasure guard, I stepped back into the Sullivan alcove and called her. She answered with a professional-sounding "Fiona Sullivan. May I ask who's calling?"

"It's Lee Barrett," I said. "I guess you've already heard from Kitsue."

"I'm on my way to Salem now. What have they charged her with? She's so confused she didn't even seem to know."

"I don't know, either," I said. "I expect she'll be arraigned soon. She didn't seem to know if you folks have a lawyer. Do you?'"

"I have an intellectual property attorney for my inventions, of course," she said, "and Grandmother Kitty has a regular family law guy. I've already called Grandmother Suzanne in case Kitsue needs money to hire a criminal attorney."

"Criminal," I repeated. "That sounds so cold in relation to Kitsue, doesn't it?"

"I suppose it does, but if she killed Walter . . . ?" She left the thought hanging there.

"Will you go directly to the police station?" I asked. "Or will you come here? Somebody needs to attend to your alcove now that Kitsue is—um—away."

"Yeah. Kitsue and I talked about that. I can always be there nights. I never sleep anyway, and I'll try to hire that display lady, Priscilla, for the day shift," she promised. "She seems to be there all the time, doesn't she?"

"Now that you mention it, I've seen her here often," I told her. "She did most of the display work, and she seems to be genuinely fond of your sister."

"Sure. She gets paid by the hour, you know, and she doesn't work for free." Short pause. "I don't suppose you have any spare time?"

"Sorry, no," I said, surprised by the bold request. "As soon as things get squared away in here, I'll call my videographer back so we can continue with our documentary work."

"Do you know what it was that told them she did it?" she asked.

"I don't know for sure," I told her, "but I think it could have been Walter's hoodie jacket."

"She had that?"

"It was in the front hall of your grandmother Kitty's house. Didn't you notice it hanging there?" I asked, wondering how she could have missed it.

"The front hall? I don't always go in that way. There's a back door, too, you know." She sounded defensive.

"Uh-huh. Well, anyway, whatever it was, they've taken your sister in for some good reason," I said. "Please let me know what happens. I really do care."

She was gone, without saying good-bye.

I returned to the main area. Sant Bidani had joined the guards beside the tower, where the trays had stopped revolving. I supposed he'd heard about the haunted sailing ship by now, and I walked over to join them, to see what he thought was going on—surely, he didn't believe in ghosts. As I moved closer, I heard Sant's raised voice. Odd. The always-soft-spoken man was clearly agitated. "I need to get the ladder and unlock the door. Something is very wrong on the top tray!" he almost shouted.

"What's going on here, Sant?" I asked.

He immediately dropped his voice. "Oh, Lee. I'm sorry if I startled you, but I can tell something's missing from the top tray. Maybe the center pole is revolving too fast, or perhaps the items have shifted. I hope that's all it is. I need to check it myself."

By then, one of the guards had retrieved the slim ladder, and the other man held the door open. Bidani's hands shook as he adjusted the ladder into the narrow space and began to climb the rungs, carefully, one by one, revolving the pole by hand and halting to examine the contents of each tray. He reached the top tray, reached forward, then drew his hand back. "It's gone." The words sounded like a moan. "It's gone," he said again and backed down the ladder. "How can that be? Impossible, but it's gone."

He stepped out of the tube. I touched his arm. "Sant?" I whispered.

"It was a dagger." He spoke haltingly. "Seventeenth century. It was made for a Mughal ruler. The blade is double-edged carbon steel. A large diamond surrounded by rubies and emeralds is in the center of the solid gold hilt. It's valued at over a hundred thousand dollars."

"It was in a locked case in a locked building, guarded day and night," I muttered to myself. Then, aloud, I repeated what he'd said. "Impossible."

The police were called once again—this time for a crime unrelated to the death of Walter Wyman or the disappearance of the jade bowl— yet the cruisers, lights flashing, parked in a row in front of the same building. I stood aside as the same uniformed cops trouped into the museum, prepared to take statements from the same witnesses. Pete wasn't among them this time. I imagined he was still busy with Kitsue. I glanced again at the *Naiad*, where William lay on the painted sea, and wondered if the place was indeed haunted, or possibly cursed.

CHAPTER 33

It was nearly time for me to leave. As far as WICH-TV was concerned, I was just as much "on the clock" as was Priscilla. I knew I needed to get home to my aunt, too, and felt guilty for leaving her to fend for herself for so many hours, even though I knew that Betsy and Louisa would be there in minutes if she needed them. I rationalized, too, that I couldn't possibly be of help to Sant Bidani other than to commiserate with him on the loss of the maharaja's dagger. Francine would undoubtedly be back to the museum with Scott just as soon as this news was leaked. It was too bad we'd missed that dress rehearsal, but I sure didn't want to record any of the current mess. I said a fast "see you tomorrow," to Mr. Thomas and made my way through the gathering crowd on the sidewalk outside, finally escaping to the comfort and safety of my Jeep. I stopped at the Colonel's to pick up a bucket of chicken and biscuits and all the other fixings for supper, then headed to the comfort and safety of home.

Aunt Ibby was well, happy, comfortable, excited, and glad to see me. "What in the world is going on at your museum? Sit right down here and tell me everything."

"Are you hungry? Can I get you something to eat? I feel so guilty, leaving you here alone for so long."

"Nonsense. I ordered a pizza. There's some left for you in the refrigerator. Now, tell me what's going on!"

There was a lot to tell. I started with the sad arrest of Kitsue, and about Walter Wyman's hoodie jacket hanging in Grandmother Kitty's front hall, then moved on to the more recent, apparent theft of the maharaja's jeweled dagger.

"I can hardly wait to fill the Angels in on all this—and Michael will have plenty of ideas about it, I'm sure." Her eyes held the old sparkle. "Maybe I should call an emergency meeting."

"Oh, I almost forgot," I said. "It seems we have a haunted ship in the museum too." I related the tale the guard had told me.

"It's happened more than once?" She leaned forward so far in the wheelchair I was afraid she'd fall out of it. "The sailor fell into the sea, just like the old legend says he did?"

"So they say."

"An emergency meeting is definitely in order. Hand me my phone please, would you?"

I did as she asked, then went to the kitchen, thought about having a chicken leg, but helped myself to a slice of cold pizza to tide me over until

Pete got home—then I returned to see what my aunt was up to. She was still on the phone. She covered it with one hand and whispered to me. "Betsy wants to know what Pete thinks about all the happenings at the museum. Does he really think Kitsue is guilty of killing that boy? And what does he have to say about the haunted boat?"

"We haven't had a chance to talk about any of it," I told her. "I don't think he's even heard about the haunting. We'll talk when he gets home—and with the day he's had, I don't know when that might be. I got fried chicken for dinner. Want some?"

"No. The pizza was plenty for me. Betsy can't come to a meeting tonight. She's going to a *Hocus Pocus* costume party, and she's already in full makeup. Louisa is out of town, so that leaves only Michael. You don't mind if he comes over, do you? We'll just have coffee."

"I don't mind. I'd like to see if he has any ideas about how that dagger got out of the tube. Have you called him yet?"

"Yes. He'll be here around eight."

"I don't know whether Pete will want to join you or not, but I'd like to sit in for a while," I said. "Had Michael heard anything about Kitsue's trouble? I know he's planning to write a play especially for her."

"I just told him she's being questioned about Walter's death, and I told him about the dagger. That's all," she said. "Michael told me about how he'd figured out that the jade bowl in Kitsue's display was a fake."

"Yes. That was before all the rest of the drama started. Just looking at that bowl on the glass shelf with the fancy lighting, I don't think anyone but an expert with a magnifying glass would ever guess that it wasn't the real thing. Pete thinks the swap must have happened at the bank vault or in Walter's truck."

"Those hoodies have big pockets on the front, don't they?" she asked. "Big enough, I should think, to hide the jade bowl."

"It was wrapped up in some Bubble Wrap with a brown paper wrapper," I said. "I've seen the wrappings, and yes. I'll bet that the whole package could be hidden in one of those big pockets. So the switch would have happened in the truck."

"And Walter Wyman saw it happen." She wore her wise-old-owl look. "So, he's dead."

"Why would Kitsue steal her own bowl?" I asked. "That makes no sense to me."

"It doesn't," she agreed. "And Pete must know that it doesn't."

"He only follows the facts," I said, trying to look at things the way Pete had to. "The facts tell him that Kitsue had that hoodie and that the bowl is insured for at least a million dollars. Remember what Louisa said about insurance fraud? Kitsue could have both her bowl, and a million dollars too. Then she'd be able to follow her own dreams and to take care of Grandmother Kitty at the same time. It could be tempting."

Aunt Ibby reluctantly agreed. "That does sound logical. But I can't imagine Kitsue holding that gun and firing it at Walter. It just doesn't ring true to me."

"Then who else could Hoodie Girl be?" I wanted to know. "And more importantly, how did she get Walter to take her for a ride?"

I heard the sunroom door open and hurried to greet my homecoming husband. He looked tired, but his after-work hug and kiss were as enthusiastic and loving as ever. "Oh, babe, what a terrible day you've had," I said, hugging him extra-hard. "You must be exhausted."

"I just need a nice, long, hot shower and maybe a nice cold beer," he said. "It's good to be home. Is Ibby okay?"

"She is, but full of questions."

"After the shower and beer—and maybe some food. I want to hear about your day, too—and maybe ask some questions of my own." He headed up the stairs. I put the food into the warming oven, chilled his favorite beer glass in the freezer, and went back to my aunt. I'd had another disturbing thought about Hoodic Girl.

I pulled a chair closer to her wheelchair. "I don't believe Kitsue is guilty, even if the facts line up," I said. "I think it could be Fiona, though. *She's* the one who says she found those pieces of so-called evidence against her sister—the blond wig and the missing lotus shoe."

"What about the hoodie jacket?" Aunt Ibby asked. "And why would she go to all the trouble of switching the bowls? It was in the house where she lived. She could have swiped it anytime."

"I don't know about the hoodie yet, but Fiona is desperate for money. She talks about it—or the lack of it—all the time. She wants to finance all those inventions of hers. I'm sure there's a collector somewhere who'll pay her a lot of money for the original bowl." The more I spoke about it, the more convinced I became. "Chief Whaley says there are only three reasons for murder—money, love, or revenge. I'm betting this one was for money."

"Oh, dear. I've been hoping that neither of the Sullivan sisters were involved at all," she said. "There are surely other possibilities."

"After Pete has his shower and some dinner, I'm going to tell him what I think anyway," I promised. "I'd like to hear what Michael thinks about it too."

"So would I. This is going to be an interesting meeting." Her expression brightened. "Then after we solve this one, we can figure out who took Professor Bidani's dagger."

CHAPTER 34

By eight o'clock, Pete had showered, changed into a T-shirt and shorts, and enjoyed chicken, biscuits, mashed potatoes, coleslaw, and a cold light beer. He was so relaxed and happy that I didn't want to bother him with my recent theory about Fiona. Maybe later. Maybe never. The more I thought about it, the less sure I was about it, anyway. I brewed a pot of coffee, unwrapped a package of Little Debbie Swiss Rolls, and together, carrying our kitchen chairs with us, we joined Aunt Ibby in her room. Minutes later, Michael arrived, apologizing for being a few minutes late. "George showed up and finished installing my new cat door," he said. "Now all I need is a cat." He'd brought along a few blank notebooks and some sharpened Tabitha Trumbull Academy of the Arts pencils. "I thought it might be important for us to make notes this time," Michael said. "Sometimes when we get together—even without Betsy and Louisa here—we hop around from one point to another, and I'm afraid we miss some important thoughts. Mr. Pennington kindly donated the school supplies."

"A good idea," I said. "Even with all the modern technology we have, Pete always carries a notebook when he's working."

"I do," Pete agreed. "It helps me remember small details that once in a while turn out to be important."

"I'll remember to thank Rupert," my aunt said. "Now, to work. First, let's write down what we know for sure about Walter Wyman's death." The silence in the room was broken only by the soft scratching of pencils on paper. Pete was the first to finish, putting down his pencil. I'd filled half a page and had just reached the part about the attendance at his funeral. Aunt Ibby paused, her pencil still, eyes closed in thought, while Michael wrote rapidly, turned a page, and kept on writing.

When we'd all put down our pencils, Aunt Ibby called for comments. "Pete, would you go first? Your professional observations might keep us grounded."

Pete's comments, as I knew they would be, consisted of cold facts. Walter Wyman had died of a bullet wound, fired at close range, from his own gun. He gave a description of the gun and the date, the location and time of discovery of the body. He didn't mention the contents of the armored truck, Hoodie Girl, or the name of the vacant bank—just what he knew *for sure* about Walter Wyman's death, as my aunt had asked.

I looked at my own notes. Were they all things I knew *for sure*? I crossed out my observation about the funeral guests. I decided to keep what I'd written about Hoodie Girl, though. I hoped Michael would read next. Seeing Walter's death through the eyes of a mystery writer like Fenton Bishop, who was also a convicted murderer like Michael Martell, would be interesting. But were his copious notes about things he knew for sure? I doubted it.

My aunt called on me next, and I stumbled through my telling of Walter's death as I saw it. She read from her own notes next, written in her lovely librarian's round, neat, backhand cursive. She'd included the points that both Pete and I had made, but also added the names of people who we'd learned were somehow connected to Walter at the time of his death, including his high school classmates.

Michael read directly from his notes, and as I'd suspected, they read like the opening of one of his Antique Alley mysteries—even the mention of the purloined antique Chinese bowl fit the theme. The only thing missing was an antiques store cat. One sentence from his reading stood out to me so vividly that I wrote it down in my notebook. "Walter's killer," he wrote, "is someone he knew and trusted, someone who is by now so consumed with guilt over murdering him that he or she will be compelled to confess to committing this terrible crime."

Aunt Ibby declared a break, and Pete and I adjourned to the kitchen to carry in the coffee and chocolate-cream treats. As I arranged the treats on a tray, I whispered to Pete, "What do you think about what Michael said about the killer being compelled to confess? Is he reliving his own regrets, or is it possible that could happen?"

"Yes, it's possible. I've seen it a couple of times," he said. "It's usually what they call a crime of passion, where they hadn't planned to do it. Like how Michael killed his wife."

We rejoined the others, sipped coffee and ate the caloric cakes, and waited for my aunt to voice the next question or establish the next topic for discussion—in the same orderly way all the Angels' meetings were programmed. She patted her lips with her napkin and asked a question. "We've established certain things we know, or think we know, about the crime. Theories, anybody? The who, what, how, and why of this sad event?"

I was pretty sure Pete wouldn't—couldn't in good conscience—answer this one. Michael looked down at his open notebook but didn't speak. I *had* a theory, and my aunt had already heard it. Did she ask this to prompt me to repeat my fears about Fiona in front of the group? After all, she'd told me earlier that she'd like to hear what Pete and Michael thought about it. She gave an almost-imperceptible nod in my direction. *What's the worst that can happen?*

So, I told them what I thought. I talked about the wigs and the lotus shoe and Fiona's need for money to finance her inventions. When nobody looked bored, or told me I was nuts, I warmed up to the subject. "The girl in the armored truck was blond and wore sunglasses just like Kitsue's. Fiona has admitted that she'd always helped herself to anything of her sister's that she wanted to borrow. Hoodie Girl's hair looks like Fiona's, and Kitsue's sunglasses were in an unlocked desk drawer in the alcove." I was on a roll. "Fiona helped wrap the packages that were going to the museum. What if she saw the original that her sister had wrapped and then wrapped a fake in the exact kind of Bubble Wrap and brown paper they used for all the smaller items—only she had no way of knowing about the lotus shoe."

Aunt Ibby interrupted excitedly. "But she had the original stashed away somewhere unopened—so she opened it and got the shoe and pretended Kitsue had put it in her own bureau drawer!" She set her coffee cup down hard enough to spill coffee into the saucer. "What do you say, Michael? Pete? Does that work?"

Pete looked at me before he spoke. "Bearing in mind that it's a theory—there's certainly something to think about there. The evidence we have pointing to Kitsue is serious. Could Fiona have arranged any of it? It's worth considering."

"I like the theory," Michael said. "It's a fresh way of looking at the mystery. Are some of the so-called facts the police are using against Kitsue simply red herrings, put in their path by Fiona, giving her enough time to sell the stolen bowl and escape to who knows where?"

"That won't work, Michael," Aunt Ibby pointed out. "If she needs the money to finance her inventions, patent them in her own name, she can't remain anonymous. She has to pin the crime on somebody else."

"Like on her own sister? What kind of monster would do that?" I realized that my own theory had pointed to Fiona as exactly that kind of monster.

"That's where my idea that Walter's killer will

confess comes in," Michael put in. "What terrible guilt a killer must feel, watching his own flesh and blood pay for his crime with years of imprisonment. I guess that kind of murder still calls for twenty years or so, doesn't it, Pete?"

"It could," Pete agreed.

"If Fiona is our killer, then," Michael continued, "she's going to confess. I can almost guarantee it."

"This isn't fiction, though," Pete reminded him. "It's real facts. Real people. Real lives."

"Even so," my aunt reminded us, "*if* this was a book, the killer would make a fatal mistake. Can any of you see a mistake that Fiona—if she *is* the guilty one—has made?"

"I can't," I admitted, "and it looks as though Kitsue has made a whole string of them."

"A pile of evidence," Pete said. "Some is circumstantial, but the chief is liking it."

"I don't see the mistake yet," Michael said. "But she will make one, if she hasn't already."

"And then she'll confess to killing Walter?" I asked him.

"Of course, she will. That's the way it works." He closed his notebook as though it was the end of a story.

"A good meeting," my aunt declared. "Save your notes, everybody, and we'll go over all this at our next *Midsomer Murders* date. Let's see what the others think about it."

Pete and I stood and began clearing away the snack tray and cups and saucers. Michael headed for the sunroom. "I'll just go out the back way, if that's okay. Do you two want to come with me and take a look at the new cat door you gave me?"

We accepted the invitation, dropped off the dishes in the kitchen, and followed Michael into the backyard. His backdoor light was on and so was ours, so the area was well illuminated. We'd just crossed over the boundary line between our shared properties when we heard the unmistakable sound of a cat door opening and closing. We all ran toward the sound. It was impossible for me to miss the long-tailed, hind end of a cat going, uninvited, into Michael Martell's house.

At first, nobody spoke. Michael poked his key into the lock. "Well, kids," he said. "Want to come in and meet my new cat?"

"If only to make sure it's not a wandering possum or raccoon," Pete said.

"It's a cat, all right." I was positive about it. "A white cat."

CHAPTER 35

We tiptoed into the house—first Michael, then Pete, then me. If Michael had stopped short, we would have piled up on one another, like a scene from *The Three Stooges* or maybe *Scooby-Doo*. Michael flipped on the lights as we moved cautiously from the sunroom into the living room. The cat briefly looked up at us from the center of the gorgeous Danish sofa, her white fur nicely contrasting with the boldly striped fabric, then leisurely resumed washing her face.

"It's Frankie," I gasped. "I know this cat."

Frankie had, for several years, been an occasional visitor to my old apartment in Aunt Ibby's house. It was usually cold or rainy or snowing when she'd appear outside the kitchen window, crying to come inside. O'Ryan liked her, and so did Aunt Ibby and Pete and I. In fact, Frankie had saved me from a very bad situation once. She'd never stayed around for long. "I named her Frankie," I explained, "because of a Benjamin Franklin quote. He said, 'When all candles be out, all cats be gray.' He was talking about bedding older women, not cats, but the name stuck." I extended a hand toward the cat. "Hi, Frankie." I was rewarded with a lick on the hand and a short purr.

Michael ventured a pat on her head. He got a lick too. "Should I let her stay?" he asked.

"She's really a nice cat," Pete vouched for her. "She seems to have selected you. But, remember, she has a reputation as a wanderer."

"I like her," Michael declared. "She can stay." He crouched down beside the sofa and faced Frankie. "You can stay here as long as you like." Another lick, this time on his nose. "I have a can of tuna I could feed her," he said. "Tomorrow I'll shop for some proper food. And a cat bed. And some toys. And a litter box."

"Don't worry about the litter box tonight," I assured him. "She's quite fastidious about that sort of thing. She'll use the cat door and go outside if she needs to."

Pete and I left for home, surprised and pleased by the appearance of the cat. It had been our experience that Frankie usually seemed to show up at times when she could be of some kind of service to her selected humans, but of course, that could just be chalked up to coincidence. Maybe.

Aunt Ibby had managed to maneuver herself from wheelchair to bathroom and was in flannel nightie in bed with a book and O'Ryan. She was delighted to hear about Frankie's return, then she said good night and reminded Pete that she'd be needing those crutches before long.

Once in our own bedroom, Pete and I talked some more about the Sullivan sisters. "Your theory about Fiona is worth looking into, babe," he said. "I'll bring it up with the chief tomorrow. Did I ever tell you you'd make a good cop?"

"Once or twice, but I think I'm better at being a cop's wife." I shut off the light, snuggled up to my cop husband, and proceeded to prove my point.

I was up early in the morning, hoping to catch Captain Billy when he arrived at the station to appear on Ranger Rob's show. I wanted to thank him again for the time he'd spent teaching Scott and me about the drones and to suggest an appearance on *Shopping Salem* to promote the idea of drones as Christmas gifts. Pete was getting an early start, too, preparing for Kitsue's arraignment. "Her grandmother Suzanne in New York has seen to it that she has the best attorneys working for her. She'll be released on bail for sure," he told me. I was glad about that. Sometimes, when we both have an early start, we follow one another through the nearest Dunkin's drive-through. First one in pays for both. I was first, bought coffee and doughnuts for both of us, blew him a kiss in the rearview mirror, and headed for Derby Street.

Captain Billy's car was already there, easily recognizable because it's painted like a toy tugboat. I parked, took a nice deep breath of salty Salem Harbor air, and entered through the studio door. Ranger Rob's intro circus-carousel music was already playing when I hurried past the closed sets toward the largest soundstage. The day's cute little buckaroos were already seated, clearly fascinated as Katie the Clown put Paco the Wonder Dog through his paces. Captain Billy sat behind an orange-and-black Halloween-decorated table where an assortment of the decorated skulls I'd seen at his shop were arranged. I took a seat in the empty viewer's booth and watched on the provided monitor. Captain Billy had a great way with kids. He told a couple of silly knock-knock jokes, then picked up one of the skulls. This one was painted with a colorful design of flowers. "How would you like to make a great-looking skull like this one?" he asked and was answered with cheers and hand-clapping.

"Great," he said. "Now I'll show you how to do it. Anybody here know what plaster of paris is?" A few hands went up. "It's a white powder." He held up a clear glass cup full of the stuff. "When I mix this with water and pour it into a mold, it will get really hard." He tapped the painted skull on the table, then put it down and picked up a white object that resembled the skull, but with angled corners. He squeezed it, demonstrating that it was soft. "This is a silicone mold," he said. "Silicone is wonderful stuff. Scientists can do all kinds of things with it. Somebody took a hard skull model and put silicone all around it. Then when they took the hard model skull out, the silicone remembered exactly what the skull looked like, and then they could make as many as they wanted by pouring plaster into this mold. We could make skull candles with it, or even plastic skulls, or chocolate skulls, but this is a good way for kids to do it. When the show is over, I'm going to give every one of you your own silicone mold and plaster of paris to take home!" More cheers. "Here we

go." He mixed water and plaster, and explaining
each step, he poured the the mix into the mold.
"It will take an hour or more for this to get hard
enough to paint, so I brought one that's ready to
take out of the mold. Watch this!" He lifted a full
mold from under his table and easily popped the
finished skull from it. The kids "ooohed" and
"ahhhed" appropriately. So did I. I got up and left
the viewer's booth, then walked back across the
dark studio and out to the parking lot. Even with
Captain Billy's simplistic explanation of silicone
mold-making, I'd learned all I needed to know
about how to make a fake skull—or a fake Chinese
bowl. You just needed silicone.

I didn't even bother with a phone call or a text.
I drove straight to the Salem Police Station, sure
that Pete, and maybe even Chief Whaley, would
take my Fiona-as-guilty theory seriously—at least
enough to question her in some detail. Pete had
said he was going to bring it up to the chief, and
maybe this new silicone mold information would
cement—or plaster—the case against her. I parked
in the space closest to Pete's office window, hoping
he'd see me there, and walked around to the front
door.

He'd seen me, and he was already in the lobby
when I entered. "Is anything wrong? Is Ibby alright?"

"She's fine," I said, "but I know something else
about Fiona. I wanted to tell you and the chief."
He waited while I produced my ID—even though
the officer at the desk knew who I was—then he
led me to his office, where I told him what I'd
learned from a kids' TV show.

"Come on," he said. "I want the chief to hear about this. We've already talked about what you said last night." He buzzed the chief on his intercom, then led me down a corridor to the door marked *Chief of Police*.

"I'm nervous," I whispered.

"You'll be fine," he said. "Pretend you're doing a field report on the late show." So, that's exactly what I did.

I didn't take the seat Chief Whaley offered me across from his desk, but I stood opposite him as though I had a stick mic in my hand and a camera in my face. I took it from the top, telling him about Fiona's inventions, particularly her talent with silicone, her need for cash, her lifelong borrowing of clothes, and how the sisters liked to switch identities. I reminded him of the picture of the yet-unidentified girl in the hoodie riding with Walter Wyman. I described the sudden recent reappearances of the missing shoe and the blond wig and the red-rimmed sunglasses, all connected to Fiona. I told him about how she'd mended Sant Bidani's piece of Lucite, then finished with how I believed she'd produced the fake Chinese bowl.

He looked at me for a long time, not saying anything. It wasn't the creepy, long look Scott Palmer uses, but a thoughtful one. "I see," he said finally, then looked at Pete. "Mondello, why don't you look into this? Bring the other Sullivan woman here, and we'll see what she has to say for herself. If she's set up her sister to take a fall for murder, I want to know the facts before this goes any further."

With the chief's backing and with Pete working

the case, things picked up speed. I knew my cop husband wasn't going to be able to share any details about Fiona with me, but by the time Francine and I got to the museum later that same morning, rumors had already begun to fly. Even though most of the displays in the alcoves had been completed by then, I delayed the filming because I wanted to hear about what the police had learned. An officer had come by to talk with Sant, had asked to see the mended piece of Lucite, and had taken it away in an evidence bag. The forensics team already had the wrappings Priscilla had removed from the fake bowl—thanks to me—but Priscilla and George had each been asked about the chain of custody. Mr. Thomas had been asked if he kept a record of dates and times on who entered and left the building. He did. Each ID he'd demanded on entry had been time-stamped and photographed. I hadn't known that.

Priscilla had a high opinion of Fiona, and she shared how helpful she'd been in setting up the Sullivan alcove. "She's so good with tools," she said. "She even installed the beautiful antique chandelier over the lotus shoe case."

Naturally, all those who'd been questioned and those who had not, had plenty to say about the police nosing around again. Even the guards from the private security company guarding the maharajas' jewels were questioned about anything they might have observed, although it was made clear to them that this case had nothing to do with the missing dagger.

I could tell that George wanted to talk about the morning's excitement, so I approached him and told him about the cat who'd already used the door he'd installed. He laughed about that, then proceeded to tell me about what he'd told the police—and about what he'd heard about what others had told them. A handyman is one of those "invisible" people in any business. He's somebody who goes about his work, blending into the background, almost like furniture or store fixtures or paintings of ancestors. "They asked me if I knew Fiona," he told me. "I said sure. Known her all my life. We went to school together."

I asked if he'd heard anything new about Kitsue. "I heard she's got a good lawyer. Her grandmother from New York is paying. That's good. That girl wouldn't harm a flea. Everybody knows it. They didn't ask me about her at all. Just about Fi. They didn't even ask about the haunted boat. Should have, though."

"What do you mean?"

"Because Fiona Sullivan is interested in it. She was over there last night with her fancy tool bag, measuring it with her fancy tape measure."

"Did you tell the police that?"

He gave a short laugh. "No, ma'am. You don't tell cops anything unless they ask for it. They didn't ask me, and they didn't ask the guys who guard the jewel tower, either. I don't think anybody else even saw her."

"That's interesting, George," I said. "It seems as if the police are here every day lately. I noticed that the little sailor was missing from the boat right away. Did you?"

"Nope. I'm not that interested in the boats. I like looking at the jewels, though."

"I'm sure everybody will," I told him. "I guess I'd better get to work. Opening day is coming soon, and I want to cover all the alcoves." I joined Francine, who was making an angle shot of the ship's figurehead over the doorway of another old Salem family's exhibit. "That'll look good on some of the promo pieces," I said.

"I think so. Actually, I was hanging around kind of listening to the people in the alcove talking about the latest visit from the law."

"Me too," I admitted. "Did you learn anything interesting?"

"Just a lot of gossipy stuff about Fiona Sullivan."

"Gossipy?"

"It sounded that way to me. They're local people, all wondering about the sudden interest from the cops, and nobody had anything particularly nice to say about her."

"Like what?" I asked.

"Oh, that she's a social climber. A cheap restaurant tipper. She's conceited. She was a bully in school. That kind of thing," Francine reported.

"Surprising," I said. "I've found her a little distant—not as friendly as Kitsue, but nothing particularly negative. What about you?"

"Are you kidding? She knows perfectly well who I am, but I don't think she's ever even spoken to me." She frowned. "Real stuck-up."

"I wonder why."

"Simple. I'm not useful to her. Actually, she might see me as competition for her photo work." She aimed the camera at the entrance to the bookshop, where a portrait of Nathaniel Hawthorne stood on an easel. "You can make money for her. She's a people-user."

This was a new dimension of Fiona to me. *A people-user?* If Fiona was Hoodie Girl, had she used Walter Wyman for a free ride to the locked vault? And then killed him? Had she used Michael Martell for introductions into Salem's social scene? And what was she using Sant Bidani for?

CHAPTER 36

Francine and I used our time at the museum well and efficiently. Most of the alcove displays were finished, and those that weren't, were in good enough shape to photograph. We moved from doorway to doorway, getting cameos of each room as I gave brief descriptions of what visitors would see and learn about each one. We covered the Salem-oriented displays as well as the ones highlighting other New England locales. "You know something, Lee?" Francine said when we'd finished the shoot. "This documentary might be the best thing we've ever done together."

"And that's saying something," I agreed. It was true. We're a darn good team. I realized I'd be sad when the documentary was finished—which would be in a few days. I'd be back to being full-time program director, enjoying the work, but always off camera. "I'll miss you," I told her. "Even though we work in the same building, and we see each other all the time, it's not the same as field-work."

"Hey, if this one is as good as I think it is," she said, "maybe it'll lead to something bigger. Better. Want to take a final shot of the upstairs room? We haven't been up there for a while."

"Sure. I think Buffy Doan is going to rent it for her Halloween party," I said. "It's big enough, and there's room for a live band on the stage."

"A perfect place for it," Francine agreed. "All kind of spooky and dark and with those creepy mannequins in the windows."

"I hope they've put clothes on them by now." I got a key to the upstairs door from Mr. Thomas, and single-file, we climbed the narrow staircase. It was cooler up there than it had been in the main room, and there was a faint musty smell. The light-ing panel was just inside the door, and I clicked on all the switches. The bright white paint on the walls was a big improvement, and the blue velvet curtains on the stage looked quite elegant. The previously dismembered mannequins were indeed properly clothed in period costumes, and there was a blown-up vintage photograph of Salem Harbor where tall-masted ships, some at dockside and some at anchor, gave a sense of real history to the scene. A sea-green carpet tied the whole panorama together. "This looks wonderful. I had no idea so much work was going on up here." I clipped my mic to my jacket collar and took a posi-tion beside the long show window, preparing to tell the WICH-TV audience how much they'd enjoy partying or dancing or eating or watching a movie or a play in Salem's newest entertainment facility.

When we'd finished my slow walk around the upstairs room, with my running ad-lib commentary about the attractive—if a little bit spooky—venue, Francine put down her camera, and we each took a seat in the back row of the chairs set up in front of the stage.

"A job well done," she said.

"Damn straight," I agreed, then leaned back, relaxing in the unexpectedly comfortable chair.

We went downstairs, and Francine headed back to the station to get started on the editing. I returned the key to Mr. Thomas. "The upstairs room looks fabulous," I told him. "I had no idea they'd done so much. Who did the work? Maybe I could interview them for the documentary."

"I haven't seen it myself," he said. "I don't like going up there. It was mostly a pickup night crew. Just a paint job. I heard it took three coats to cover up those walls. The only fancy part was dressing those clothes dummies and gluing up an old picture on the wall. Those Sullivan girls worked together on that. Kitsue did the dummy dressing, and the other one hired the guy who blew up the picture. It only took them one night. It looks good, huh?"

"It sure does. Do you check in the night workers too?"

"No. They each have a special number for the keypad on the old elevator," he said. "They come in from outside and leave the same way. The door at the top of the stairs is deadbolted from this side so we don't have to worry about them getting down here. I check it before I leave every night. Anyway, Bidani's armed guards would easily take care of that problem." He laughed. "Those guys are enjoying their work. Sometimes they bring in pizza, turn down the lights, and play those old sea songs all night."

So, Kitsue and Fiona had been in the attic room together recently, Kitsue, I supposed, for her expertise in period fashions, and Fiona, because of a contact with someone who did those giant enlargements of photos. Fiona, I figured, must have made a hefty commission on that deal—and I had to admit, it did look amazing.

My work finished for the day at the museum, and with still several hours left on the clock, I said good-bye to Priscilla, Mr. Thomas, and Sant Bidani, and steered the Jeep back to WICH-TV. I had to smile when I reached the parking lot, where Scott stood on the seawall, flying his new drone over the harbor. I parked, walked over, and stood behind Scott. "Enjoying your new toy, I see?"

"Loving it, Moon. You should get one. I'm learning some new tricks. Listen to it. I got some noise-reducing propeller shrouds, so it's not so noisy."

He was right. It wasn't quite as *clackety-clack* as it had sounded on the common. "Yes," I agreed. It is quieter."

"I'm thinking I might go for some bigger, slow-spinning props to make it even quieter," he said. "That way I can sneak it up on people—watch them and listen to them."

"Why would you want to do that?" I asked, but I only got a smirk in return. I wished him a good day and proceeded to the front door of the station, then hopscotched my way across the lobby tiles and into Old Clunky.

Rhonda was waiting for me with good news. "Doan loves the new footage of the upstairs room, and Buffy has already booked it for her party. He wants to know if you can do the late news tonight with that beautiful segment about the maharajas' jewels you guys did the other day."

That was just what I'd wanted, and I was glad we'd shot it before the dagger had disappeared. "I'd love to," I said. "Is he here?"

"Yep. He said to send you in as soon as you arrived."

"I'm on my way." I gave the obligatory tap on Doan's door and was welcomed in.

"Glad to see you, Ms. Barrett," he said. "Will you be free to do a few minutes on the late news tonight to talk a little about the maharajas jewel exhibit? The segment you did is quite spectacular."

"I'd like to do that, Mr. Doan. It's going to be a great draw for the public. It's even more beautiful when you see it in person."

"I've been impressed with your work on this project, Ms. Barrett. I'd forgotten how effective you are on camera." He cleared his throat. "I've been thinking, and Mrs. Doan agrees with me, that perhaps we've been hiding your light under a bushel lately, so to speak. That perhaps we should try to find a regular on-camera spot for you."

This was unexpected. I stammered some kind of "thank you" then just stood there, waiting for him to tell me more. What kind of regular spot? Was I going to get my old field reporter job back? Was Howie moving on to greater things? Or was I about to get a *fourth* hat?

"Nothing is firm, of course. We're just thinking about it, but I thought I'd let you know that we like what you're doing. Carry on!" He gave me a kind of smiling, dismissive wave. I said "thank you" again and backed out of the office, both pleased and confused.

"I'll be doing that spot on the news tonight," I told Rhonda. "I guess I'd better whip up some notes about the maharajas' jewels so I'll sound like I know what I'm talking about."

"You always sound like you know what you're talking about," she said.

I told her "thank you," too, thinking about the many things I didn't actually know squat about that I'd shared anyway at the meeting in Aunt Ibby's room. I know I had a smile on my face as I rode down on Old Clunky. "A regular on-camera spot for you"—that's what the man had said—and, "We like what you're doing." But he'd also said, "We're just thinking about it." What was I supposed to make of all that? I thought about River's dream book boots—the ones that meant a powerful movement—boldness in your position. On-camera work sounded like powerful movement to me. I decided not to get too excited. Maybe nothing would come of it. I texted Pete that I'd be doing a spot on the late news and sent him a smiley emoji.

I was still smiling when the elevator clunked to the lobby level, and the door slid open. I know I was because my own smiling face looked back at me from the polished brass on Old Clunky's door—just before the flashing lights and swirling colors pulled me into another vision. The first sensation was dizziness. I put my right hand against the wall to steady myself, to keep from actually falling. I'd never had a vision give me vertigo before. My stomach churned, and I whirled helplessly. "Don't look down," I told myself, trying in vain to close my eyes. I looked down anyway, onto a trayful of glittering jewels, then spun away, hovering for a moment over a billowing sail. I watched helplessly as tiny toy metal William Griffen fell into a painted ocean.

The vision popped away quickly, as they always do, leaving me standing alone in the WICH-TV lobby, my hand against the wall, feeling queasy, unsettled. Whatever this one meant, it had been an extremely unpleasant experience.

I forced myself to move slowly, carefully, across the black-and-white tiles to the door, then out onto the marble steps. Still light-headed, I gulped down fresh ocean-side air. I rounded the corner to the parking lot. My Jeep, beside the seawall, looked as though it was a mile away. I moved toward it, feeling more normal with every step. Walking faster, I realized that Scott was still there on the seawall too.

"Hey, Moon." Scott looked at me closely. "You okay? You look a little green around the gills." I had to laugh at the old-time fisherman's analogy. I'd heard Aunt Ibby say the same thing many times.

"Just a rough elevator landing," I lied. "Maybe Old Clunky needs a tune-up."

"I know what you mean," he sympathized. "I'd rather use the stairs. Better for my thigh muscles anyway."

I had no wish to discuss Scott's thighs. I pointed up toward the nearly invisible drone overhead.

"Did you get any good pictures? Overhear any good conversations?"

"I flew her over Pickering Wharf and watched the shoppers. I couldn't hear what they were saying, though." He sighed. "I still need a lot of practice flights, but I'll get it to work the way I want it to eventually."

Boom. I knew where the vision had taken me. I'd been in a drone, flying inside the main room of the Salem International Museum. There was no mistaking Sant Bidani's glass tube full of jewels and the giant model of the *Naiad*. I'd been on somebody's practice flight.

I said good-bye to Scott and got into the Jeep with a lot to think about. I turned on the radio and sat quietly for a while, wanting to make sure all the vertigo had passed before I started driving. With Tom Petty's "Free Fallin'" for background music, I ran the conversation with Bruce Doan through my mind and again dismissed it as a "maybe." He and Buffy had really liked my work on the museum top floor, though. *Boom!* If somebody wanted to fly a drone above the first-floor displays, wouldn't being on the second floor be the best way to do it?

I was back to Fiona again. We knew she had a drone and used it to take photographs. Like Scott's drone, it could be modified and improved to do many other things. The thoughts began to tumble faster. How could a drone make a poor little metal sailor fall from the mast? Simple. A magnet. Even a kid's drone with a magnet could stick to a water tower. Okay. Was there something metal in Sant's jewel tray? There sure was. A diamond-studded dagger.

I needed help to sort this out—real help, not

the dream-book, tarot-card kind. I needed to run this new thing past my professional, just-the-facts cop husband. I texted him again. **Can U spare a minute to talk?**

Ariel's bench in ten? he answered.

I sent the smiley again, turned the engine off, then walked back to the bench named for the dead witch.

CHAPTER 37

Thankfully, Scott had left the seawall, so I didn't have to explain the sudden bench-sitting, and even better, Pete took less than ten minutes to get there. He parked behind the bench and stepped over the back of it to sit beside me. "What's going on, babe?"

I started with the vision, knowing he didn't like to talk about them, knowing, too, that this was an important one. I described what I'd seen in the elevator door and what I thought—no, what I *knew*—it meant. Someone, probably Fiona Sullivan, had flown a drone with a magnet in it over the maharajas' jewels, stolen the dagger, and in the process had dislodged a toy sailor. All I had was knowledge. Pete needed facts.

"Whew. That's something to think about, isn't it?" Serious cop voice. "I mean, it's possible, even plausible. Fiona has access to all the museum, including the second floor. So does Kitsue. So do you."

"They were together up there recently," I told him. "They created a display with mannequins and a giant photo."

"The usual facts, like fingerprints on a drone, or pictures of one of them flying it would be useful. Those don't seem to apply in this case."

"I guess not. The night security guys turn off the lights and play loud music at night," I recalled. "They might not hear a drone."

"What days did the guards tell you the little guy fell out of the boat?"

"It would have been both Wednesday and Thursday, I suppose."

"That, my love, is interesting. There's one lone night-vision camera in our original security setup." Excited cop voice. "I can bring it up on my phone. Let's see if it captured anything on Thursday."

He held the phone so that I could see Thursday's grainy screens pass by, one at a time. Since I'd just done a thorough walk-through of the museum, I knew exactly where each one was. I recognized some of the people and thought I even saw a back view of myself standing under the figurehead. "Okay. Here we go," Pete said. "This is the night-vision camera. It's motion-activated. Let's hope it's pointed in the right direction."

The scene was a sort of greenish black-and-white—and there, plain as day, was the drone moving slowly, deliberately, soundlessly over the round glass jewel display. It dipped down—almost gracefully—and grasped something. The diamond in the dagger's hilt flashed brightly even in the darkness. The bug-shaped thing rose from the tube, seemed to hover far above the ship model, then moved up higher, seeming to touch the ceiling.

I realized I'd been holding my breath. The next screen was black.

"Damn," Pete said.

"What happened?" I asked.

"I don't know," he said. "There's no picture coming from the second floor, and there should be. How many people have keys to the second-floor door?"

"Mr. Thomas has one, and I guess the other security people, and there's a keypad outside that lets people go up there by elevator. There's an old staircase on the outside, too, but it's always padlocked. It wouldn't be safe to let the public use it. Insurance risk. At night, the inside door is deadbolted from the top of the stairs in the main room."

"I'll check the Wednesday film as soon as I get back to the station, but I'm thinking it'll be a dry run of what we just saw," Pete said. "I want the chief to see this. At least we know for sure the dagger theft was an inside job."

"Pete, don't you see?" I pleaded. "Fiona is guilty. She has a drone. She needs money. She's stolen her sister's jade bowl, and now she's taken Sant's dagger. You can't let them blame Kitsue for what her sister did."

"It's a theory, babe. A guess. I can't arrest somebody without any proof. We have tangible evidence against Kitsue. She doesn't deny that she had the shoe and the blond wig. She had possession of Walter Wyman's hoodie. She had the cleaner remove bloodstains from it—told him she'd had a nosebleed. Both the dry cleaner and her own grandmother identified her."

"Irish twins," I told him. "The dry cleaner doesn't know either of them, and they used to fool the grandmother with the wigs all the time when they were kids."

"I'll keep looking into the Fiona idea, babe. I mean it. I'm taking it seriously. I need more. I need facts."

Bruce Doan thinks I'm hiding my light under a bushel. Maybe I am. Maybe I can turn on my light and find some facts about Fiona Sullivan. "Want to drive me to the station tonight?" I asked. "When I do my thing about the maharajas' jewels on the late news?"

"Absolutely," he said. "I'm so proud of you."

"Mr. Doan told me he's thinking of finding me something on camera again."

"Do you want to do it?'

"I don't know yet." It was true. "I'll see what he comes up with, if anything. I think I'll stop at the museum on the way home and see if Sant Bidani is still there. I could use some more information about those maharajas."

"See you at home," he said. "I'll show these security shots to the chief."

"See you at home," I echoed and walked to my Jeep. I was telling the truth about needing more information about the maharajas' jewels to share with the late-news audience. I also wanted to know if there was anything else in the treasure trove a magnet might pick up. I knew there was plenty of gold and silver in the mix, but those weren't magnetic at all. It would have to be something iron or nickel or steel. Like a dagger. If there was, maybe Sant and I could bait a trap and give Pete some *real* evidence.

I held my ID card up to the door, and Victor Thomas admitted me to the museum. "All's clear, Ms. Barrett," he said. "Not a policeman or a ghost hunter in the place."

"Ghost hunter? Have we attracted those already? We've only been haunted for less than a week." We both laughed.

"Yep. Some folks from a ghost magazine came by with gadgets to record ghost voices and special ultraviolet cameras, the whole shebang," he said.

"Did they find anything?"

"They think they heard the voice of that sailor who got struck by lightning, and they swept up some sawdust they found on the floor and said it was from his ghost ship passing by." He crossed his heart. "I swear, that's what they told me."

"It will sell some magazines, I guess," I said, "and it might bring some visitors to Salem. It's all good. Is Professor Bidani around?"

"Yes. He's worrying around here somewhere," Mr. Thomas said. "Poor soul. He feels bad about the little knife getting stolen when he was in charge of it. It's insured, of course, but he says that's not the same thing."

"I understand," I said. "I'll look around for him. I'm doing a little talk about the jewels on the WICH-TV late news tonight, and I want to get my facts straight."

"Back on TV again? Good for you."

"Thanks." I saw Sant Bidani standing alone in the archway of the Mystic, Connecticut, alcove at the back of the main room, then walked toward him, waving a greeting. I'd thought of dreaming up some sort of story about the use of lesser metals in the treasures, but I decided we didn't have time to tippy-toe around the subject. I'd just flat-out tell him my suspicions about Fiona, and he could come aboard with my plan—or not.

CHAPTER 38

"Professor Bidani—" I began.

"Sant," he interrupted with a grin.

"Sant," I said, "I need to talk to you about something important."

The grin faded. "Is it about the theft of the dagger?"

"Yes, it's about that and more." I looked around the huge round room. "Can we sit over there next to the *Naiad* display? I don't want anyone to overhear what I have to say."

"Of course." He followed me to the broad cushioned area surrounding the ship. He sat beside me and remained silent while I spilled the whole thing—from Fiona's early interest in helping him with the display up to the night-vision camera's revelation of the magnetic drone picking up the dagger. "I believe Fiona is responsible for the theft of your dagger, and I think she's behind the murder of Walter Wyman too. I want you to help me trap her. That is, I need you to bait the trap."

I could tell he was angry. His jaw clenched, and his hands turned to fists. "What can I do?" he growled. "How do we trap her?"

"I want to get her to steal something else from the tower using the drone. It will have to be something with magnetic properties, though. Carbon steel or iron or nickel. Is there anything else in the treasures that will work?"

He paused for a moment, thinking. "Almost everything in there is gold," he said, "but yes. It's not one of the most important pieces. Mid-twentieth century. It's a large nickel-plated, jeweled belt buckle that's believed to have belonged to Maharaja Yadavindra Singh."

"Is it worth very much money?" I asked. "Fiona's motive is always money."

"Not a lot. A few thousand. Nice jewels in it—mostly emeralds."

"A few thousand will do nicely, I'm sure." I said. "Now you'll have to tell her somehow that you're rearranging the top tray—because of the missing dagger. Let her know about the belt buckle."

"I can do it easily. Actually, it's quite a flashy piece. Quite contemporary. I'd love to wear it myself."

"Good. Tell her that. It'll convince her that it will be easy to sell." I began to get excited. "We're going to nail her, Sant! I'm sure of it."

"How has she managed to get the drone in here?" he wondered. "Past all the security?"

"I don't know yet, but the police have night-vision surveillance films from Wednesday and Thursday. Apparently, there was enough power in the magnet that when she flew it high above this ship"—I pointed at the *Naiad*—"it lifted the sailor off his mast."

"Where did it go after she picked up my dagger with it?" Jaw clenched again. "Do you know that?"

"There could be a trapdoor somewhere up in the ceiling, I think. That's where the surveillance film ended. The police will figure it out."

He gazed upward. "I knew she was smart. I admired her for that. But I didn't know she was devious." There was sadness in his voice. I understood.

"It looks as though we'll be solving the mystery of the haunted ship too," I reminded him.

"True," he said. "I was beginning to like that story. It gives the exhibit another dimension."

"I think the story will last for a while. The ghost hunters think they've contacted William's spirit," I told him. "They think he left them some splinters from his ship."

"Glad to hear it," he said. "Anything else I can help with?"

"Yes, you can. I'm doing a segment on tonight's late-news show about your tower of jewels. Tell me a little more about the belt-buckle maharaja. I'll look him up. Anything to add to his official bio? I'll pump it up in case Fiona is watching."

"Good idea," Sant said. "He was a champion cricket player, and he served in World War Two."

"That'll work," I said. "Let me know when you've set things up with Fiona."

On the way home to Winter Street, I felt good. I felt justified in what I'd done. If Pete needed facts to back up my "theory" about Fiona, it wouldn't be long before they landed right in his lap. I'd just passed the Witch Museum when that darn little still, small voice in my head began to whisper to me. *If you think Fiona is a murderer, smarty-pants, why are you putting your friend Sant in her path? Hmmmm? What about yourself? Don't you think she'll figure out that* you *have something to do with all this? Hmmmm?* By the time I was inside the house, I'd decided to call Sant—to call off the whole crazy idea.

Too late. He called me first. "It's done, Lee. She came in minutes after you left. The belt buckle is already in the top tray. She doesn't suspect a thing. She's still here, just wandering around, looking at the displays. I'll bet tonight is the night!"

What could I say? I told him to be careful, then I called Pete and confessed what we'd done. He was not happy. "Lee, if you're right about Fiona, and she's capable of murder, this was a reckless thing to do." His voice softened. "But it might work. I'm on my way home."

O'Ryan met me at the sunroom door and immediately began what I called his "follow me" mode. He runs away from me, then when I catch up to him, he runs again until we reach wherever it is he wants me to be. This time it was the bedroom, where he'd already dragged the long cardboard tube containing the museum floor plans into the middle of the room. "Why?" I asked him—but he'd already scampered away and down the stairs—just in time to greet Pete in the kitchen.

"Okay, babe, we have to move fast on this." Serious cop voice. "We had a guy who does image enhancement take a look at the night-vision footage. He says the entryway of the drone is in the ceiling at the back of the main room. It's approximately above where the elephant is."

I frowned. "There are no holes in the ceiling anywhere," I pointed out. "It would have been noticed."

"It's a high ceiling, and the image guy says he can see a faint oblong up there." He pointed up to an imaginary ceiling. "A skillful carpenter with high-tech tools could do it. Ring any bells?"

"Fiona," I said. "She knows how to make a neat hole in a ceiling. She installed the chandelier in the alcove."

"Now we just have to go over there and pinpoint the hole somehow—without attracting a lot of attention and scaring her away," he worried. "I wonder if she's still in there now."

"She was there when I spoke to Sant a few minutes ago."

"Mmmrrow," O'Ryan interrupted, and did another "follow me" maneuver. "We can do it from here," I yelled. "Wait a minute." I followed the cat upstairs, retrieved the long tube, and dashed back down. I pulled the papers from the tube and spread them out on the kitchen table. "See? Let's put the upstairs plan over the downstairs layout and see how they line up." It only took a minute to figure it out. The hole in the upstairs floor was inside the display case—the one with the costumed figures, the lovely old photo, and the carpet that Fiona Sullivan had personally donated and installed.

Things moved pretty fast after that. Our kitchen became "command central" with Pete on his phone. Unmarked cars were stationed near both entrances to the museum, the front door and the rear elevator, to watch for Fiona either leaving or entering the building. As the operation progressed, Pete kept me up to speed in short sentences.

"Priscilla left."

"Sant left."

"Fiona just left, and one of the plainclothes cops is following her."

"Thomas came out. No one left in there except the jewel guards."

I knew Pete had a SWAT team on standby. At ten o'clock, Fiona Sullivan approached the rear elevator and tapped in a code and Pete left home for the police station. At ten thirty I drove myself to Derby Street. I couldn't believe I was going to miss the action because I finally had landed the coveted segment on the late news. As Aunt Ibby had always told me, "Be careful what you wish for. You might get it."

The spot went as well as could be expected, considering that my mind was more on what might be hovering above the jewel tower, rather than what was in it. Francine's video of the maharajas' treasure was gorgeous, and I didn't doubt that once the museum opened, people would be lined up to see it. I'd barely finished my spiel when the "Breaking News" alert came up with a bulletin. "There is significant police activity on the west end of Essex Street—avoid the area. Detour in effect—report to follow." I thanked Buck for the interview and left the station in a hurry. I cut across Washington Street, where I might be able to see what was going on at the museum. Something was going on for sure. There were blue-and-white lights flashing all around the place, and a traffic cop directed vehicles away from the area, north toward Bridge Street. I joined the line of detoured cars and took a left onto Winter. I'd learn more from my TV at home than I was going to at this distance.

O'Ryan seemed excited to see me, and even more excited when I clicked on the kitchen TV. I peeked in on Aunt Ibby. Sound asleep. I pulled her door closed, turned the sound down, and sat on one of the Lucite chairs while the cat sat on another. Scott *and* Howie were both there on a split screen, Scott standing across the street from the museum, Howard Templeton on the narrow street overlooking the back of the place where the elevator entrance was located. Scott was on camera first. "Salem police have surrounded the building housing the soon-to-open Salem International Museum," he said. "Sources tell us they have halted a burglary in progress inside the museum. There's no word yet about any arrests being made." Hushed, big-network voice. "Howie, what's happening where you are?"

"They've moved in some spotlights," Buffy's nephew reported, "all focused on the back elevator door. There are several police cars here, and some officers with external vests marked with the special weapons and tactical team initials—a SWAT team—have entered the building via a stairway. Everything is quiet back here at the moment. Back to you, Scott." They bounced back and forth for a while like that, neither of them coming up with anything new.

"O'Ryan, we're not going to get the full story

until Pete gets home," I told the cat, "unless they make an arrest on camera." Scott was soon back on-screen, with Old Jim's zoom lens focused on the museum front door. Someone was being hustled out of the building, surrounded by uniforms. It was hard to tell if it was a man or a woman, but I was sure it had to be Fiona Sullivan. None of the cops responded to Scott's shouted questions. "Stay tuned for further developments," Scott commanded as the police cars began to leave, lights still flashing. "WICH-TV will continue to follow this unfolding story for you. We return now to your regular-scheduled programming." River North's theme music began, and I knew that at least one of the mobile crews would be packing up and heading fast to the police station. The other one would stand by at the museum.

Scott and Old Jim got there just in time to film the blond woman, her head down, hands secured behind her back, escorted by four policemen, two of them still wearing SWAT vests, hustling her through the front doors of the Salem Police Station.

I was right when I'd told O'Ryan that we wouldn't learn much until Pete came home. Scott and Howie chattered back and forth for another half hour or so without revealing anything new. "There probably would have been more action on River's show," I said to the cat, "and her viewers will be emailing the station like crazy complaining about *Tarot Time* being preempted by the news department."

"Mrrupt," O'Ryan agreed, then strolled over to his bird-watching chair, lay down, and closed his eyes. "Stay awake, big boy," I advised. "Pete will be home soon, and we'll get the rest of the story."

When Kit Kat showed almost 2 a.m, I was dozing, my head down on the table. I heard the sunroom door open. "Pete?" I called and hurried to meet him.

"Long day, sweetheart," he said, kissing my forehead. "Want to hear about it?"

CHAPTER 39

"First of all," he said, "you were right."

"About the hole in the ceiling being under the carpet?" I asked.

"Yep. When the team grabbed her, she'd just lifted up the trapdoor she'd built. Damned ingenious thing." He motioned with his hands. "It's wider at the top than at the bottom, so it can't fall through the hole. She even had a little recessed handle on it. The bottom of it is painted the same white as the downstairs ceiling, and it fits so perfectly the edges are almost invisible."

"So, she could just drop the drone down the hole and maneuver it over to the glass tower," I said.

"Exactly right. It looked like the drone scraped the edges of the hole a little bit and dislodged some sawdust."

"That would be part of the ghost ship *Naiad*," I said.

"Huh?"

"Nothing. Go on."

"Okay. The music was playing down below, the lights were all out, the guards were probably talking among themselves. She'd kept the upper room dark so the men downstairs wouldn't hear or see anything out of the ordinary."

"Did she put up a struggle?"

"Not a bit. She just said she wanted a lawyer. I suppose the rich New York grandma will be on the hook for that."

"Grandmother Suzanne," I thought of Kitsue, now out on bail, who'd been named for both grandmothers. "Is Fiona still denying knowing anything about Walter Wyman's murder?"

"That hasn't come up yet." He half-smiled. "One crime at a time. We've got her dead to rights on several charges on this one. We'll have to find out what she's done with the dagger. She's probably in touch with an international fence who finds customers for this kind of high-end hot merchandise. I'm betting she used the same one to get rid of Kitsue's jade bowl. Then we've got her on both crimes."

"Do you think you can find him? The fence?"

"With a little help from the FBI, I'm pretty sure we can," he said. "They keep track of those people. You'd be surprised how much of a market there is for stolen art and jewels and other pricey hot goods."

"At this point, my love"—I sighed—"I wouldn't be surprised by anything."

I was wrong about that. The surprises kept coming, and Pete kept me up-to-date on the case as much as he could. A search of Fiona's room at Grandmother Kitty's house yielded a brunette wig—not the scruffy one they'd played with as kids, but an expensive, real-hair number, well-styed to look exactly like Kitsue's hair. "We questioned the dry cleaner again," Pete told me, "and he says he can't *positively* identify Kitsue as the person who dropped off the bloody jacket."

Grandmother Suzanne's lawyers made short work of the case against Kitsue. The day after Fiona's arrest, Kitsue's name was cleared, and the same attorneys proceeded to get to work for their new Sullivan client. There'd been no sign of the stolen dagger or the jade bowl, though, although she'd been charged with breaking and entering, destruction of city property, and attempted burglary.

"We need a lot more facts to prove that she ever had possession of either one," Pete said. "Thanks to the wealthy grandma, Fiona's out on bail, under house arrest, wearing an ankle bracelet."

Kitsue returned to work on her display immediately, although with the grand opening days away, it was virtually complete. She dusted and polished, arranged and rearranged the shoes and photos and letters. I felt that she needed to keep busy—to keep her mind off her sister's problems with the law. They were, after all, still living in the same house. It made me sad to think of how the sisterly bond I'd admired—even envied—must be terribly damaged, if not destroyed, by now. Francine and I had finished our documentary all but the final editing. It was scheduled to run midweek, and I'd gone back to full-time program directing with the hope of an occasional field-reporting call. There had been no more mention from Bruce Doan about that possible "on-camera" job.

Scott Palmer kept busy too. As days passed, media interest in Walter Wyman's killing faded, and curiosity about the happenings at the museum demanded more coverage—including attention to the "haunted" ship model. Scott, bulldog-like, refused to let go of the armored truck driver's murder, and he'd convinced Doan to let him do a series of re-interviews with people he'd talked to before. I was glad he was doing it even if I couldn't. I was working on a *Shopping Salem* special featuring stuffed animals when he knocked on the glass separating our spaces. He gave the "call me" signal.

"What's up?" I asked him. He'd been keeping me up-to-date on his progress, which had been disappointing so far. "I might have something," he said. "I need a woman's point of view."

"Glad to help."

"I talked to Walter's mother today." Even the statement was cringeworthy. He'd put the poor bereaved woman though merciless questioning before. I couldn't believe he'd go after her again this soon after losing her son.

"Oh?" was all I could manage.

"Yeah. Remember she told me he had a girl-friend? That he was seeing a girl?" I didn't remember that, and I told him so. "It was back when she showed me his yearbook," he explained, "and I never pursued it. Well, now I am."

"I don't think Pete knew about that either," I said. "Did you ever even mention it on the air? Or to anyone?'

"No, I didn't. We'd found all the other class-mates by then, and I was off on a different track."

"We all were," I agreed. "What did she tell you?"

"Nothing yet. That's why I wanted to talk to you first. You always said I was too rough with her be-fore. I don't want to upset her. She's happy that I'm working on finding the killer. She said I could call her back this afternoon."

"What do you want me to do?'

"Can you stand by on speakerphone? Listen to us, and give me a hand signal if you think I'm being too—um—too aggressive?" I got the Scott Palmer trademark long stare.

"Okay," I said. "I'll be around all day, except I'm having lunch with my husband. What time are you going to call her?"

"Doan says I have to be sure Howie is available, so I won't be the only one here to do a field report. He's up in Maine visiting his mother. As soon as he checks in, I'll let you know," he promised.

Pete picked me up at noon beside Ariel's bench with a pair of crutches sticking up in the backseat of the Crown Vic. "I picked them up from Marie this morning," he said. "Just in time for tonight's *Midsomer Murders* meeting."

"She'll be thrilled. Listen, did you know any-thing about Walter's girlfriend?"

"I didn't know he had one," Pete said. "Who is she?"

"I don't know," I said, and told him about Scott's planned phone call.

"That could be important." Cop voice and fur-rowed brow. "I'll send Rouse over to talk to Mrs. Wyman."

"Can you wait 'til after Scott does his interview?"

I asked. "He's the one who discovered she exists." I knew how disappointed I'd be if the police moved in and stepped on a story I'd been working on for weeks.

"I suppose so. It's waited this long," he said reluctantly. "But I need to listen in too. Call me as soon as you know when it's going to happen."

"It'll be sometime this afternoon, after Howie checks in." We ran across the street for a quick lunch at the Friendly Tavern, instead of going downtown for something fancier. I didn't want to miss that call. As soon as we'd finished our burgers, I hurried back to my office and told Scott about Pete needing to listen in. He didn't disagree.

I was in Rhonda's office when Howie wandered in at two o'clock, looking rested and ready to work. I called Pete right away, then dashed back to my glass cubicle so I'd be there when Scott prepared to make his call to Mrs. Wyman. In about ten minutes, Pete arrived. Scott had decided the call would be made from my quiet office instead of from the noisy newsroom, so we three were all gathered around Scott's phone on my desk when Mrs. Wyman answered.

"I'm a little nervous," she said. "Can you hear me alright?"

"Yes, ma'am," Scott said, in his most respectful tone. "Thank you so much for talking to me. I know this is painful for you." He looked to me for approval. I gave him a thumbs-up.

"I appreciate it that you're interested in Walter." Her voice broke. "I'd begun to think that nobody cared anymore. Once my poor boy was buried, nobody cared."

"I certainly care, Mrs. Wyman. I want to get to the bottom of this. We need to find out why Walter was killed, don't we?" He looked at me again. I nodded my okay. He continued. "The day that you kindly showed me Walter's yearbook, you mentioned that he was seeing a girl. Do you know her name?"

"Lord, no. I never even saw her, but I knew he was seeing someone. I'm sure I wouldn't have approved of her, though."

"Why not?" I gave him a two-handed "calm down" signal, and he softened his tone. "I mean, I'm sure you have good reason to say that."

"He was sneaking her into his room, that's why." Walter's mother was clearly agitated, and her voice showed it. "I raised him better than that, but every time I changed the sheets on his bed, I could smell perfume. I knew she'd been there."

"You must have been terribly upset." Scott sounded entirely sympathetic. He was definitely getting the hang of this. "Did you ask him about it?"

"I didn't. I guess I didn't want to admit it, not even to myself." She sniffled a little bit. "But a mother knows these things. A mother knows. I can't bring myself to go back into his room, even now," she said. "I closed the door on it all. Maybe someday I'll be able to go in, clean it up. Good heavens. She even left her toothbrush there, out in plain sight in his bathroom."

I saw Pete scribble in his notebook. Scott caught the motion too. "How do you know it's hers and not his?"

"Walter was very fastidious about his teeth." She sounded defensive. "He's *always* used an electric toothbrush—ever since he was a youngster. He didn't even own a regular one."

Scott knew what to ask next. "Is her toothbrush still there? In Walter's room?"

"It certainly is."

Pete didn't need to hear anything more. He stood—very quietly—gave Scott a salute and left the office. I knew the police had searched Walter's basement room after the body was discovered and hadn't come up with anything out of the ordinary. I'd studied enough in my online criminology course to know that a toothbrush can provide a reliable DNA sample. We'd know soon enough who Walter's girlfriend was—and quite probably who Hoodie Girl was.

Things moved fast after that. Pete got a search warrant for Walter's room, but he didn't need it to get the toothbrush. Mrs. Wyman was "more than happy to get that cursed thing out of my house." As I'd suspected all along, the DNA was Fiona's. She admitted to having a "relationship" with Walter. On the strength of that admission, the wrappings from the fake bowl—which I had wisely saved—were checked for fingerprints on the sticky tape. Among the prints from George and Priscilla and Mr. Thomas and even the Angels and me—all of us who'd handled the wrappings after the fake bowl had been unwrapped—there were a couple of clear prints belonging to Fiona. She had to have handled it *before* it had arrived at the museum. She had to have been the person who'd wrapped it in the first place—the person who'd substituted it for the real jade bowl.

For a long time, Fiona continued to deny being

in the truck with Walter, but her protests began to weaken as the evidence—the facts—against her piled up. It could have been due to the constant questioning from authorities that finally made her tell the truth, but I think it was because house arrest meant that she had to stay in the house she shared with her grandmother—and the innocent sister she'd effectively thrown under the bus to take the blame for murder.

Pete let me read the transcript of her confession. It was chilling to realize that I'd known and worked with and liked and sometimes even envied this person. It was hard reading.

First question: How had she convinced Walter Wyman to let her ride in the armored truck, knowing that it was against company rules? That it could cause him to lose his job? She'd actually laughed at the question. "I'd been sleeping with him on and off for a couple of weeks. He'd do anything I told him to."

"You knew he'd been hired to move the Sullivan collection to the museum?"

"Of course. Why else would I sleep with a loser like Walter? That's what gave me the idea to make a fake bowl and get the real one." They asked her how she'd made the bowl, and she said just about the same thing Captain Billy had told the kids. She'd used the real bowl to make a silicone mold and then used one of her plastic formulas to produce the very realistic fake.

They wanted to know how she happened to have Walter's hoodie jacket. "Simple," she said. "I told him I was cold. The jacket was big enough so I could hide the fake bowl in it, and then hide the real bowl after I made the switch."

"And you slipped the fake bowl in among the ones that were going to the museum and took the real one?"

"Right. We'd decided that I'd get out of the truck and hide in the bushes while he made the delivery. Then he'd pick me up on the way out. We laughed about it."

The questioner asked her to explain exactly how she'd switched the bowls. She used an expletive. "I had to get into the back of the truck to do it, so I told him I'd hide back there so he wouldn't get into trouble. It would have worked perfectly if he hadn't seen me make the switch in his rearview mirror." She used another expletive—a stronger one. "He saw me do it. I didn't want to kill him. I sort of liked him, you know? But he saw me do it. I don't think he was even going to tell on me. He didn't say anything until after he'd delivered everything to the bank and walked back to the truck and I came out of the bushes. He opened the passenger door for me. Walter was always a gentleman. All he said then was, 'Why, Fiona? Why?' The gun was right there on the seat. I shot him. He fell on the leaves. I didn't even have to touch him. I was wearing boots, so I kicked a bunch of leaves over him. I took off the jacket, folded it, put it under my arm, package and all, ducked back into the bushes behind the closed-up mall, took the side streets, and walked all the way home. Nobody stopped me."

The questioner wanted to know why the gun was on the seat.

"It was his own fault." she said. "When I first got in, I told him I wanted to 'ride shotgun.' So he handed me his little gun. It was a joke. I didn't know I was going to have to use it. It was his own fault," she repeated. "I left it on the seat when I climbed into the back. So there it was."

"There were no fingerprints in the truck. Did you wear gloves?"

"I did," she admitted. "It wasn't because of the truck, really. I just didn't want my fingerprints on either of the packages. I had latex gloves on. I told Walter I needed them because I'd developed a rash from some of the chemicals that I'd been using for some of my experiments. He understood. He believed me. He was proud of my inventions. He was really kind of a sweet guy, you know?"

"When the picture of the woman in the hoodie jacket appeared, why did you try to make it appear that it was your sister, Kitsue Sullivan?"

She'd laughed again. "I wasn't going to admit that it was me, was I? I'd already swiped her cute red sunglasses because I liked them. The rest was easy. The wig, the stupid little shoe. I even had her believing she'd done it."

I put the transcript down, with Walter's last words ringing in my ears. "Why, Fiona? Why?"

I had all the answers. I felt sick to my stomach. I didn't want to know any more, or read any more, or think any more about Fiona Sullivan. Ever.

EPILOGUE

I've heard a lot more about Fiona Sullivan, whether I wanted to or not, and so has everyone in Salem and far beyond. With the help of the FBI, and cooperation from the shadowy fence she'd contacted, we learned that by holding out for top dollar, she hadn't yet sold either the jade bowl or the dagger. Each will be returned to the rightful owner as soon as Fiona's trials are over, reminding me of the Seven of Swords that showed up in River's reading: "A thief may return what he has stolen." Fiona is currently housed, pre-trial, in Framingham at Massachusetts' only prison for women—not a pleasant place to be. It looks as though all those inventions will have to be put on hold for a long time.

Aunt Ibby has progressed from wheelchair to crutches to walking boot, is enjoying her stairlift riding chair, and once again presides over the

Midsomer Murders meetings at her own house, where Michael Martell is being praised for his spot-on theory that Fiona "would be consumed by guilt and would admit to her crimes."

The *Seafaring New England* show at the Salem International Museum is off to a roaring good start and is projected to attract a million visitors during its run here. I like to think that the documentary Francine and I produced together had some small part in promoting it. Our video was not only shown several times on WICH-TV, but it was picked up by a few other cable stations around New England.

The Sullivan alcove has received well-deserved attention from the news media and has been featured in several magazines and newspapers—with particular focus on the love story of Edward and Li Jing. Michael Martell's play, *Tiny Shoes,* starring Kitsue Sullivan as Li Jing, is receiving excellent reviews. Kitsue has been recognized, too, for her expertise in putting the museum display together, and she now conducts a well-attended weekly class at the Tabby on "Collecting Your Family History." She's been able to give up the witch shop job, and she is still the caregiver for Grandmother Kitty, and still the faithful sister, she visits Fiona regularly.

Sant Bidani's "Treasures of the Maharajas" is probably the most popular and most photographed of all the outstanding displays at the show. Sant and the treasures will be present at the upcoming Mystic and Newport shows, he has signed a lease on a condo in Salem, and he has accepted a position at Harvard. We're delighted to welcome our Indian friend as a fellow New Englander!

Another display drawing a lot of attention at the museum is the giant model of the *Naiad*. William Griffen has remained at his post on the main topsail without further incident, but the ghosthunters continue to visit him regularly. I've heard that some shops are selling little vials of the swept-up sawdust, purporting to be from the ghost ship, although I'm sure the little bit of wood shavings from Fiona's drone flight couldn't have displaced that much!

Pete and I are enjoying our home. Construction of the attic wall between our space and Michael Martell's is complete, and we've planted a little vegetable garden in the yard. O'Ryan continues to commute between our house and Aunt Ibby's, and he enjoys being next door to his old friend Frankie. Yes, she's still at Michael's place and shows no signs of wandering off.

I'm back to my program-director duties at WICH-TV, along with the occasional—but more frequent than they used to be—field-reporter opportunities. I think sometimes about the boots in River's dream book meaning "boldness in my position." I'm still waiting for Mr. Doan to come up with that "regular on-camera job" for me he'd hinted at.

I think often, too, about the other part of River's dream book wisdom—the part about the leaves meaning fertility, growth, and openness—especially about the fertility part.

We're working on that.

ACKNOWLEDGMENTS

The first time I joined a writer's organization was way back in the early seventies. I had a pretty good background in writing advertising copy, but I was just tiptoeing into submitting nonfiction articles to magazines. The Suncoast Writer's Conference in St. Petersburg was my first conference, and there I attended a class on writing for "trade papers." Who knew there was a market for articles written especially for publications devoted to particular trades? Dana Cassell was the presenter, and she headed up an organization called "Florida Freelance Writers' Association." I joined immediately, partly so I could receive a monthly newsletter, but mostly because—too unsure of myself to use the term "writer" on business cards—I wanted to let the FFWA logo do it for me! Almost fifty years later, I'm still a member, and I still value the information in that newsletter—which has since grown to be Writers-Editors Network. As time passed, and I added fiction writing to my life, I've learned about the significant benefits derived from joining other writers' organizations. These groups, through their in-person and online meetings, their writer-to-writer contacts and their many shared interests, have become an important part of this self-imposed, solitary world in which we writers live.

So here's a happy shout-out to the Writers-Editors Network, WEN; the Bay Area Professional Writers Guild, BAPWG; Mystery Writers of America,

MWA; Sisters in Crime, SinC; Florida West Coast Writers, FWCW; Pinellas Writers Association, PWA; Novelists INC, NinC; Florida Gulf Coast Sisters in Crime, FLGCSinC; Florida Chapter Mystery Writers of America, FMWA.

I love and appreciate all of you!

RECIPES

Kottayam Churuttu
Sant Bidani's favorite dessert snack

Aunt Ibby says that Indian markets sell all the ingredients—she goes to a market in Malden, Massachusetts—and some are available in the local grocery stores. Some, like roasted coconut and rice powder, are available online.

Pastry Ingredients:
   1 cup maida (Aunt Ibby uses cake flour)
   ½ teaspoon vegetable oil
   Pinch of salt
   Water, as needed
   Fine rice flour—as required.

Put maida (cake flour), oil, and salt in a mixing bowl and mix well. To the mixture add enough water to knead the flour into soft and smooth dough. Form half-inch balls from dough and dip each ball into fine rice flour and roll into wafer-thin rounds. Lightly cook the rounds on a medium-hot griddle for just 30 seconds on each side. Stack the rounds on a plate and cover them with a damp cloth that will keep the dough soft and pliable.

Filling ingredients:
   Mix 1 cup roasted coconut with 1 cup
      rice powder
   1¼ cups sugar
   ¼ teaspoon powdered cardamom
   ½ teaspoon vanilla
   ¾ cup water
   1½ teaspoon lime juice

Mix sugar, water, and lime juice in a bowl. Heat, stirring constantly until you get a single thread consistency. (Aunt Ibby says that means a weblike thread when held 2 inches above the pot—or 230 to 235 degrees on a candy thermometer.) Remove it from the heat and set aside ½ cup of this syrup. To the remaining syrup, add vanilla and cardamom and the coconut/rice powder mixture a little at a time.

Now cut each round of pastry in half and form a cone with it. Stuff each cone with 1 to 1½ tbsps. of warm filling. Seal the edges together and place on a tray. Set aside for two hours until the syrup from the filling has moistened and seeped into the pastry. The churuttu is ready to eat.

Aunt Ibby's Lemon Bar Pie

Preheat oven to 350 degrees.

> 1 store-bought 8- or 9-inch graham
>   cracker (or gingersnap) piecrust
> 1 medium lemon (Aunt Ibby prefers
>   Meyer lemons)
> 1-½ cup sugar
> ⅓ cup unsalted butter
> 3 tablespoons flour
> 3 tablespoons heavy cream
> Pinch of salt
> 4 large fresh eggs
> Powdered sugar sifted for the topping

Cut the lemon into four wedges, then cut each one across and remove all the seeds. Put all the ingredients except the crust and the powdered sugar into a good blender and process just until smooth. Pour this creamed mixture into the crust. Bake at 350 degrees for 35 to 40 minutes. Place on wire rack. This pie sets as it cools. When it's cool, dust it with the powdered sugar just like lemon bars. Aunt Ibby says to serve this pie in thin slices. It is very rich. Best served on the same day.

Louisa's Casserole

1½ pounds ground beef
1 onion, diced
2 cloves garlic, minced
1 teaspoon chili powder
¼ teaspoon salt (or more to taste)
¼ teaspoon dried oregano
cayenne, to taste
1½ pounds russet potatoes, peeled and
    thinly sliced to less than 1/4-inch
    thickness
pepper, to taste
1 (16-ounce) can kidney beans, drained
    and rinsed
4 slices bacon, cooked and crumbled
2 (10.75-ounce) cans tomato soup,
    undiluted
1 cup cheddar cheese, grated
1 cup cornflakes, crushed and mixed
    with 1 tablespoon melted butter

Preheat oven to 350 degrees. Grease a 9x13-inch baking dish. In a large skillet over medium-high heat, cook the beef, onion, and garlic until the beef is no longer pink, 5 to 7 minutes. In the prepared baking dish, layer half the potato slices to cover the bottom. Some overlap is okay. Season the potatoes with salt and pepper to taste. Top the potatoes with half the beef mixture, half the beans, and half the bacon. Pour one can tomato soup over the bacon. Repeat the layers, starting with potatoes. Cover the baking dish with foil and bake for 1 hour. Remove the foil and sprinkle the top of the casserole with the cheddar-and-corn-flake mixture. Return casserole to the oven and bake uncovered until the cheese is melted, the topping is golden brown, and the potatoes are tender—about 10 to 15 minutes.